I0760935

Sand Dunes
&
Blood Moons

By Octavia J. Riley

Sand Dunes & Blood Moons (Coven Chronicles, book 4)

First edition October 2020

Book design by Poisoned Apple Publishing, L.L.C.
Editing by Poisoned Apple Publishing, L.L.C.

ISBN: 978-1-955222-96-9

Published by Poisoned Apple Publishing, L.L.C.
www.poisonedapplepublishing.com

Printed in the United States

Nia Rose & Octavia J. Riley

COVEN CHRONICLES

Spellbound & Hellhounds

Secrets of the Sanctuary

Spirits of the Black Forest

Sand Dunes & Blood Moons

Dedicated

To my mother who gifted me with boundless creativity.

DESERT TEMPLE

HEAVEN'S HAND

DRAGON'S MOUTH

HELL'S H

MOUNT TEMP

GAYGHA PESHTPENHVET I ESTVETSYT' AYNNIRUV

RED TIPPED MOUNTAINS

THE GOLDEN SEA

SILVER THREAD

TOLVAD

BANSHEE BOG

LORV

TEMPLE RUIN

JEWELED CA

AND
FOREST TEMPLE
TAIN
PLE
THE CURSED
MIRROR
SATVIRIYA
VEMEESE LAKE
THE BLACK
FOREST
HALF HEART
BAY
DE
THE GENTLE TITAN
O LAKE
S
THE DEVIL'S PITCHFORK
ANOPY
AERISTRIA

Chapter One

This was Supposed to be My Day Off

The heavy *woosh, woosh, woosh* of the weighted sickle chain as it swung in the air was loud in the quiet stillness of the Coven sparring room. Her opponent, lifeless but alive, remained as stiff as the stone it was made from under the malleable clay covering its rock core. The clay absorbed blows better so Coven members didn't break their hands landing punches, but Thea wasn't using her fists in this fight.

"Attack," she commanded, and the golem moved under the order. It brought its stone sword up into the air and charged forward with deafening, thunderous footfalls that vibrated the cement ground under her feet and clapped against the bare walls.

Thea steadied herself with a deep, calm breath. In the next moment, she hurled the chain forward. It wrapped around the sword like a constrictor crushing its prey and wrenched the weapon to the side just before it could make contact with her head. She sidestepped, light on her feet, and danced out of the golem's way and fell into a crouch. Using the rest of her strength, she leaped into the side of the large practice dummy and drove her sickle down into its neck with as much force as she could. She couldn't miss the loud snap of stone cracking as the sickle sliced through its target. She landed back on aching feet and barely managed to dodge the crumbling golem. It collapsed into nothing more than rubble.

She let go of a deep, shaky sigh as she placed her weapon back in the leather scabbard strapped to her back. She needed to do a light cool-down workout, hit the communal showers, and head back home. Well, Rafe's duplex… Namara may have been all fixed up and Cressida may no longer be her problem, but there were still ferals wreaking havoc on the city. Although, it had been a while since she'd gotten up close and personal with one.

Thea glared down at the pile of rubble and wished she was fighting real monsters instead of dummies. The council was still in shambles, and no one had handed down an assignment to her yet. After her two week "recovery," she was on restrictions to ensure a more strenuous mission didn't put her out of commission again. Thea had wondered if it was because the blue cloaks were suspicious of her, but she immediately threw that thought out. After what just happened with Isolde and Dmitri, Thea would have had her badge ripped away from her in no time had the blue cloaks suspected her of any foul play.

The door to the sparring room squeaked as it was pushed open, and apathetic clapping began echoing throughout the empty room. Thea found enough energy to turn around and bestow her unwanted spectator with a withering glare. It lessened significantly when she saw it was only Namara crashing her training session.

"You know," the kelpie started off, and Thea was already rolling her eyes, "most people *relax* and take it *easy* on their day off." She pulled a steaming mug, of what Thea assumed was just hot water, out of the crook of her arm and cupped her fingers around the porcelain. A little purple umbrella stuck out of it like it was some fruity cocktail.

"That's how you get complacent," Thea huffed, still winded, and brought her arm up to wipe her sweaty brow. "Besides, there are no days off in the Coven. Not right now, anyway."

"Says the only woman in the Coven with a day off."

Thea's scowl darkened, and she returned to glaring at the pile of rubble at her feet once more. She wanted to go ahead and summon another golem, but she had already been pushing herself with the last one.

Perspiration was rolling off of her in constant, fat beads of salty water. She felt like she'd just been the victim of one of Namara's hug-fests. Wearing only a faded blue corset—for the purpose of training her body to be ready to fight *whenever*—her lightweight, tan summer hosen, and lace-up brown boots, she wasn't suffocating in the thinner attire, but it still weighed heavy on her exhausted body.

"They won't assign me a mission yet."

"Really?" The kelpie raised her dark eyebrows in surprise. Water was dripping from her long, tangled black mass of hair and leaving a growing pool under her seafoam green feet. Her white gown was a stark contrast to the color of her skin and clung to her curves wetly. She changed the subject before the tension in the room worsened her owner's mood and nodded over to the crumpled pile of stone and the many others that were behind the Spellweaver. "How many does that make?"

Thea pulled the hairband from out of her hair and shook out her curls. Reluctantly, she mumbled, "Thirty-two," before wobbling over to the rest area that was pushed up against the wall and collapsing into one of the high-backed seats. She yanked on the strings of her corset and loosened the material, sucking in a large breath of air and slouching against the chair.

So much for a cool down, she thought to herself.

"Thirty-two!" Namara shrieked in admonishment. "You're not even fully healed yet! Your lungs need to recover more before you take on thirty-two blasted golems!" She quickly collected herself and sighed heavily as if exasperated with a small child. It, unfortunately, went in one of Thea's ears and right out the other.

"Okay, well, it's fair to say you're not complacent. Can we go now? I can smell you from over here." As if to emphasize that, the creature wrinkled her nose in disgust.

Thea snorted. "Says the creature that always smells like a swamp. Besides, no one asked you to come. Why are you even here?" She wasn't really surprised. Namara had been following her around like a lost puppy ever since she and Rafe had come hobbling back to his place after the whole sanctuary incident a few days ago. Of course, Namara would rather return to Hell before she admitted that to her master, but it'd been nice having someone actually care.

The kelpie merely lifted her steaming cup up as if it were obvious. "They have free hot water in the break room."

"That's because you get it out of that nasty coffee contraption."

Before Namara could answer with a sarcastic rebuttal, the doors to the sparring room opened again, squealing to announce that someone else had entered. Her cue to leave, as most Coven members liked training alone unless they were specifically sparring with another being, but she froze in her seat when she watched as none other than Second Chosen Winona Cavett waltzed in. Supple black leather adhered to the woman's body like a second skin, complete with real gold embellishments on the crimson corset that complemented her red cloak. Gold eyelets blinked on her knee-high boots, clasping the material together in the shape of bats. All of it flaunted her position and wealth in the Coven like nothing else would—especially now that Second Chosens had been made an official rank. Thea would have to watch her tongue. Winona wasn't Summoner status anymore.

The older woman's nose wrinkled similarly to the kelpie's, but she didn't comment. Her mercury eyes landed on the Spellweaver and her pet, and she stared down Thea critically. "A little fairy told me you were here."

Ell, probably, and only because she'd been forced to answer her superior. She'd been the only one to see Thea slip into the sparring room early that morning.

Thea rose from her seat and pushed back her sweaty, loose curls. "Can I help you, Winona?" She refrained from placing her hand on her dagger handle, even if her fingers itched to do so.

Winona's eyebrows disappeared into her salt and pepper bangs. "Too early for formalities?"

It *was* pretty early by normal standards, but Thea's eyes had refused to shut last night until, eventually, she had thrown herself out of bed and teleported to HQ. She'd busied herself in the libraries trying to tire her eyes out by reading reports, but after a few hours, she'd accepted sleep wasn't going to come and had chosen to start training. Right about now, the sun was most likely just bleaching the sky of its twilight hues.

"It's my day off," the Spellweaver replied smoothly, which was her way of saying *go away*. She heard Namara snort behind her and decided the noise sounded very horse-like.

The Second Chosen motioned to the sparring room. "And, yet, here you are."

"It's so she doesn't get complacent," Namara chimed in sweetly from the side. Thea frowned at her, and the kelpie returned the look with one of her own.

"Good," Winona chirped, gaining their attention. "If there was ever a time not to get complacent, it would be now. Thea, I'll need you to report in along with your Summoner partner. Please meet me in my office. I have something you both will want to hear."

With that, she left, pivoting and whipping her graying brunette plait behind her and tossing the squeaking doors open in a swirl of scarlet and ebony.

When the doors clicked shut, Thea was the first to speak. "I think I'm getting assigned something."

"You don't sound happy about it."

"Maybe because the last time we spoke I asked her why Torro was at the Dark Market, and she left in a big rush."

Namara stared owlishly at her owner. "You really think you can keep flirting with death just because you escape it all the time?"

"Relax. I've got as much dirt on her as she has on me."

She exhaled heavily. "Rafe's not going to like this."

"It'll be fine," Thea assured.

At least, she hoped it would.

Chapter Two

Time for Terrible Trials, Tribulations, and Tea

Thea was awkwardly sipping tea when the knock on Winona's office door announced Rafe and Mokana's arrival. It had been maybe half an hour since she'd left the sparring room, called Rafe on one of the communal crystal balls—she still didn't have a replacement yet; her coin pouch had gotten lost either in the Dark Market or the rainforest, and she had refused to let Rafe buy her a new one—took a shower, and changed into clean clothes. She felt infinitely better after the workout, but dread had settled into the pit of her stomach, and no amount of ginger tea was going to fix it.

The presence of Rafe walking past the threshold eased her discomfort slightly. He looked out of place in the more feminine office, and she wondered absently if his office looked anything similar to Winona's. He was a Summoner after all, but she'd never actually been in his office the whole time she'd known him. It was probably decorated the same, just maybe less womanly.

Matte sapphire was the color of choice for the walls, complete with a gold, shimmery ceiling. A small chandelier hung from the center of it. Potted plants took up most of the wall space, the smallest ones in the windowsill. In the middle of the room was a large desk, and two comfy armchairs were situated in front of it. Thea took up one of those chairs, but Namara had decided to stand behind her and toe at the overly large black feline, a cat-*sidhe,* that couldn't decide if it liked her or not.

"Good morning, Summoner MacBain," Winona greeted civilly and stood from her chair behind the desk. "Tea?"

"I doubt it will be good for long, Second Chosen Cavett, and no, thank you," he replied just as diplomatically, yet his eyes regarded her coolly. When they flicked over to meet Thea's gaze, she looked away. They were icy blue, a clear indication of his mood.

Well, Namara had called it.

While Rafe took the second chair, Mokana slunk up behind him to stand quietly near Namara. She was wearing a long, billowy outfit Thea couldn't quite pinpoint. Slung across one shoulder was a small yet dazzling purse. Broken pieces of glass in varying colors, sizes, and shapes were adhered to the front of the bag, reflecting light in a rainbow display on the wood floors. Thea eyed it curiously, and she noticed Namara eyeing it as well. That was certainly new. She was brought back to the matter at hand when Rafe cleared his throat and gestured for Winona to start.

"Let's get straight to it then." The female Summoner reached into the top drawer of her desk and pulled out a thick file. She dropped it on the desk in front of them and regarded them with a cool look all her own. She cleared her throat, and the silence that stretched afterward hung in the air like heavy tapestries. Then her gaze snapped to Thea. "You were assigned to investigate the influx of magic-based creatures entering a local sanctuary. I can only assume you found a lead because shortly after the assignment was given out, you both filed reports about demon sightings in a Vemeese village. This is also where the kelpie was reportedly injured and remained at the sanctuary for a week. Have I gotten it right so far?" She eyed both Coven members who had tensed up in their seats. This was common knowledge that anyone could find out if they bothered to look, but because it was Winona relaying the information, Thea knew she was going to find herself cooking in a hot cauldron very soon. Regardless, she forced herself to nod in answer.

Winona continued.

"However, soon after conversing with Leslie Templeton, you visited a portal keeper at the Grim Bean and warped to the Dark Market. You witnessed Councilman McTaggart there, and as *controlled* chaos ensued, you swiped an uncleansed tethering stone. This is where things get interesting. You, Thea, were then separated from Summoner MacBain, and, after a week in the Jeweled Canopy and a week recovering, you handed over the tethering stone to the sorceress in charge of the sanctuary. I do not know what happened past that, but the sorceress has since lost her magic. That would not happen unless the magic-eating disease confirmed in her records stole it all. If that were the case, she would be dead. The only other possible option is to transfer magic. Transferring magic is neutral magic, but the intent behind it will either turn it black or keep it neutral. However, such a spell has not been done in over three decades because it requires an immense grounding agent. The only thing powerful enough to do that would be the combined strength of the High Priest Council." Winona leaned further over her desk, locking eyes with both a shocked and dumbfounded Thea and Rafe. "I do not know what was used as the grounding agent, but the spell should have been enough to rock the viewing orb off its pedestal if not for the deflectors Ms. Katsaros had in place. Something must have gone awry, for only a tenth of that power leaked through, startlingly massive though it may have been, and this is why two Summoners showed up so quickly. Imagine what would have happened if the deflectors had not been there at all?" A brief pause. "You two are lucky because if not for those deflectors, every Coven member enlisted would have come raining down on that doorstep. *Especially* in light of the Dmitri and Isolde debacle and the ferals running all over the city." Another pause. "Did you think just because you saw Torro at the Dark Market that you had dirt on him? On me? That I wasn't going to find out what went down at Srbeveara?"

Thea couldn't find the words to counter the Second Chosen. Silence stretched. She could feel Namara grip the top of her chair, could sense Rafe's tension without looking his way. She knew she was in trouble—the most trouble she'd ever been in.

Eventually, her mouth bobbed open, and she croaked out pathetically, "How did—?"

"I have my sources," Winona cut her off. She raised a brow at the Spellweaver. "When you get to my position and you've seen the things I've seen, you don't need to read someone with a spell to tell if they have magic or not. Cressida is magicless now, and Ernimoens do not possess magic. Why, then, does Ms. Castel?" She didn't give Thea the chance to answer. "Because magic was transferred in an attempt to escape Medusa's Kiss. I'm not stupid."

Rafe shifted in his seat, breaking the statuesque grip on his body. "Why haven't you reported us?" his deep voice queried, bringing attention to himself.

Winona leveled him with a sharp look. "Oh, I have. Trust me, everything I just told you is written in this file." She drummed the tips of her fingers against the folder on the desk for emphasis. "The recordings on the communal crystal ball Spellweaver Bauer used are in here too. It's enough to have you both stripped of your positions and locked away for the rest of your lives."

Thea found her voice, though it was a little weak even to her own ears. "Why are you telling us this?"

"Because," the Second Chosen began and pulled out a second file from her desk, dropping it on top of the first one, "I have a proposition for you both. *This* file is a false document detailing the happenings of what went down at the sanctuary, conveniently leaving out your involvement past the initial investigation."

Oh? Thea sat up straighter in her seat, eyeing Winona skeptically. She dared a glance at Rafe. Bags were slight but present under his eyes. They never fully went away after the rainforest incident. His hair was slightly damp, and his face was freshly shaven. He looked tired but alert, and the frown twisting his lips told the world of his unhappiness at the situation. Still, when he caught Thea's stare, he gave a small nod.

"What do we need to do?" Goddess above, the last time she had asked that she had been dragged through the Dark Market and then fell through the rainforest only to become a ragdoll for one overgrown giant.

Winona leaned back in her chair. "The past few days, besides my own investigations of Srbeveara, I was researching the Draconians."

Thea's eyebrows shot up in surprise. "For a cure?" It would make sense, but not much was documented about them. There weren't any books about them in the Coven's library—she would know. All members started off as Record Keepers, or glorified receptionists, then moved on to being Cleansers, before finally making it to Hunter status. Some preferred the safer jobs and never went further than shelving books and copying reports. She may not remember every text in the library, but Draconians were something that had never popped up while she'd spent her time as a Record Keeper.

"Correct. I believe it is possible for a cure to exist," Winona concurred and relaxed her arms over her chest. "And before you ask me where I found that out," she said just as Thea opened her mouth, questions buzzing in her brain and making her antsy in her seat, "if you agree to my proposition, I'll tell you where to find the information yourself. However, I need you to be absolutely certain before you agree. The information I'm prepared to give you is highly classified."

Thea nibbled on her bottom lip as she wondered how information on the Draconians would be so highly valued.

"What's your proposition?" Rafe questioned cautiously. Mokana was quietly gathering his long hair together and parting it with her sharp claws. An intense look had settled on her face, bringing out the sharpness in her features and the anxiousness in her swirling blue-green gaze.

"I need both of you to cross the desert and find the Draconians. Find out if there is truth to the claim."

Thea sputtered, nearly dropping her teacup, and she hastily set it down on the desk. All the questions that had been burning up the forefront of her mind vanished. "Cross the desert? Are you insane? Not even researchers make expeditions out that way!"

Winona wasn't surprised by the outburst, but she did send Thea an unimpressed once-over that had the Spellweaver quickly settling down. "This is bigger than the Coven. This is finding a cure for what has been, up until now, an incurable disease. This is saving all those who have it and telling those who contract it in the future that they'll live. A lot of us know what it's like to lose someone to this disease." She muttered the last bit bitterly, and her silver eyes turned hoary as they glazed over.

Thea winced and slid back in her seat. The Second Chosen had lost a beloved niece to the disease years back. Everyone knew about it. It had been the only thing to break the hardened warrior.

"In any case," she continued passively, "I don't think I need to stress the importance of this mission any further. The details will be given to you later, and under no circumstances are you to repeat them to anyone. This will also be a lot easier for me since both of you will be out of my hair should the Council have any questions. Now, I know you won't be able to take either of your pets with you. It would be a death sentence to them both. However, to counteract this, I will allow you to suit up with any weapon in the

Coven's armory to prepare. Feral demons are dangerous and will try to kill anyone they come across—but they're stupid. They're wild and driven by instincts alone, but the Draconians have evaded humans since the beginning of time. They're intelligent, deadly, and two hundred times the size of a Hellhound. You'll need all the weaponry you can get your hands on."

"If the sand wyverns have always evaded humans, then how do you expect Thea and Rafe to find them?" Namara demanded. Her fingers were digging ruthlessly into the fabric of the chair in her silent rage, causing water to soak the fibers. If Winona noticed, she didn't comment.

"That's because whoever had gone looking for them wasn't familiar with the desert. Now, who do we know that is?" She left the question hanging in the air, and the obvious answer dangled right in front of Thea's face.

"Are you saying Blythe would leave Cressida while she's ill?" Mokana asked, gracing the rest of them with her voice for the first time.

"The information I received informed me that the Draconians may not only cure Medusa's Kiss but *all* ailments." She gave Thea and Rafe a meaningful look. "So, what I'm *saying* is that Ms. Castel would most likely suffer no qualms in traveling through the desert she grew up in to find a cure for the woman she loves. Now," her silver eyes narrowed into slits, "which file should I report?"

Did they really have any other choice? No, they didn't, but Winona wasn't threatening them over corrupt reasoning as Cressida had. She may hold personal feelings about finding a cure, but a cure would benefit every being capable of using magic. Besides that, Winona was offering information privy only to her. Still…

"What would the Celestial say if they knew Torro was at the Dark Market the same day Dmitri and Isolde acted against the

Council?" Thea pressed, and even though she felt Rafe stiffen beside her, she needed to know.

Winona merely shrugged. "What makes you think they aren't already aware?"

Thea reeled back in her seat. The High One could not possibly be corrupt—it was not in their constitution or nature. They were on a higher level in all things. The concept of greed for power or money was not one they lived by. If they were aware of Torro being at the Dark Market, then it couldn't be because he was doing it with ill intentions.

She weighed her options again and heaved a massive sigh. A weight had settled over her chest, and she could feel the stress build her heartbeat into a more staggering rhythm. Casting another look at Rafe, she met his level gaze, and she strongly disliked how his eyes reminded her of the ones she'd seen when they'd gone undercover through the Dark Market. Steel traps protecting the emotions within. He would travel the desert with her, regardless that this was all her fault. She didn't want to drag him into her messes anymore, but she couldn't do this without him.

Thea bit her lip anxiously before asking, "What do you think?" She already knew what his answer was, but she had to hear him say it.

"Well," he began and leaned back in his seat. His long black hair fell over the top of the chair, and Mokana began combing absently through the strands. Thea was beginning to notice it was a common tick of the rusalka's. "Traveling through the desert and possibly finding death is better than spending the rest of our lives in prison." He glanced over to Winona, who shrugged as if in agreement. When he looked back over to Thea, she knew from the glint in his eyes, blue-green once more, that he agreed.

With a small nod, Thea had her answer. "We'll do it."

Chapter Three

Whipped into Shape

Winona placed a crystal ball wrapped in soft, lavender velvet in the center of her desk. She then picked up the first folder filed with all the incriminating evidence against the Spellweaver and Summoner and lit it on fire, similarly to how she had set the notebook ablaze back at the sanctuary. Without the presence of magic, the file was swallowed up in regular yellow-orange flames.

"I understand you're not equipped with a crystal ball. This is the newest one off the market. If you come back and decide you don't like it, I have the receipt, and you can exchange it out for a different one."

Thea didn't miss the "if" Winona subtly dropped, but she had to ask why the Second Chosen was supplying her with a crystal ball in the first place. "Thank you, but…I don't see why you're giving me this."

"Don't go thanking me yet," Winona retorted and dug out her own crystal ball from her belt pouch. She showed it off to them both and said, "The type of crystal ball I'm supplying you with is the first of its kind where I can track your movements. I had to buy one for myself so I could connect to your magic's location. It's called MGPS—Magic Global Positioning System. Quite clever."

Thea picked the glass sphere off the desk and scrutinized it, but it looked like any other crystal ball to her. "I guess, though I don't like the fact you'll have the ability to track me after the mission."

"Come back alive, and I'll take it off," the woman quipped, earning a scoff from Thea. "Oh, and pay attention to this particular feature." She set her crystal ball down onto the desk and stood away from it before saying, very clearly, *"Hello, Kristal."*

Thea watched in amazement as the crystal ball lit up without being touched and chimed softly.

"Call Summoner MacBain," Winona ordered, and not even a moment later Rafe's orb was whirring in his pocket. His eyes widened as he went to grab his crystal ball. Sure enough, when Winona picked her own up, her face filled the glass in Rafe's hand.

"What sorcery is this?" Mokana inquired with eyes as large as the Summoner's, snatching the orb out of his hand and eyeing it quizzically.

"I've disabled some of the social applications as you won't be needing them. I am also equipping you with a third-party translator," Winona stated, ending the call and pocketing her orb. She picked up the velvet cloth off the desk and used it to dust the wood before she pocketed that, too.

"You mean an imp," Rafe frowned, taking back his own crystal ball and stowing it away. Mokana huffed but went back to making sloppy braids out of his hair.

"I have a couple that come to mind."

Thea winced. "Would one of them happen to be Leslie?"

Winona's grin was all teeth. "Call me after you've collected Mrs. Castel, and I'll have him dispatched to your location. You may find your mission scroll with Ell down at the front desk. The details of the mission will be at her own discretion. And remember, if so much as a word of those details be discovered by anyone, Zaraltrac will be the least of your worries. Now, I cleanse my hands of you."

They all shuffled out of the Second Chosen's office quickly and without commentary, and, as the door gently clicked shut, foreboding silence descended upon the group. The tension in the air could be cut with a blade as the weight of the world was suddenly resting on the two Coven members' shoulders once again.

"I can't believe that just happened," Namara finally said after a long moment. Her words were enough to bring Thea out of her stupor, but she could only nod in agreement. Words still wouldn't come to her, and rather than force some half-crafted apology, because there was no denying that this was the result of her actions, she turned away from the closed office door and made her way to the spiraling staircase. She could hear the others following behind her, could feel their eyes on her back. She remained quiet.

"We're lucky we're still tethered to them," Mokana spoke up, referring back to Namara's statement. "If they would have lost their positions, we would have lost our connection to them and be forced to live on our own. Say, if they don't make it back alive, want to room with me?" It was clear Mokana was trying to make light of the situation.

It was a bit too soon, though. "That's not going to happen, and you know it," Namara snapped, and her raspy whisper spat the words out like a hissing gorgon.

"Just drop it," Rafe chastised lowly, leaving the last step of the stairwell and a miffed rusalka behind. The group couldn't afford to have their conversation overheard. People and beings alike were rushing about in the Coven's lobby preparing for the upcoming promotion ceremony scheduled for that afternoon. While it was certainly quieter than it had been days ago, the expressions on the faces of those that passed by reaffirmed the level of stress everyone was currently under. Not only was there a promotion ceremony set to go on in a few hours, but the Second Chosens had been made an official rank, Dmitri and Isolde were still being contained, and two new blue cloaks had been sworn in. The amount of paperwork that would have to be done would be staggering. Not to mention the fact that the feral situation was still very much ongoing, and now hordes of untamed demons were crowding up the local prison.

Thea had been ignoring those passing by, too lost in her own haywire thoughts to the point her subconscious had taken control of her actions, so she startled when a warm hand slipped into hers. She looked down dumbly to see that Rafe had taken hold of her. He squeezed reassuringly, and she couldn't help the corner of her mouth twitch. The weight on her chest wasn't so heavy in that one moment. She wasn't alone. He didn't harbor any animosity toward her. They were okay.

She was okay.

She picked her chin up and continued toward Ell's desk that was just up ahead, and while part of her was excited to know of the new mission details, another, much more sober part of her, wanted to go home and get some proper sleep. She knew that wasn't going to happen, though. Not with a long list of to-dos before they even ventured out of the city.

The mental checklist was still being added to by the time they reached the service desk, but Thea was relieved to note that *someone* had at least gotten some proper sleep around here. Ell looked much more put together with her tamed hair clipped back out of her face as she tediously stamped a collection of drafts piled up on the counter. Pristine was pawing at a loose scroll that had rolled away from its stack, though the familiar was quicker to react to their approach than Ell was.

It was only when their shadows fell over the blonde that she looked up, and her olive eyes were brighter and were no longer weighed down by purple bags of exhaustion. They lit up in recognition, and she gave a startled squeak and jumped up from her desk. Somehow the chair toppled over in the process, startling

Pristine enough to hiss and glare at her soulmate. Every Coven member in the nearby vicinity paused at the commotion but quickly resumed what they were doing when they realized it was only Ell making a ruckus. It didn't stop the blonde's face from flaming up in embarrassment, though.

Thea felt the urge to facepalm and chuckle at the woman's antics. Instead, she greeted the woman with a gentle smile and leaned against the countertop. "Good morning, Ell." Considering she and Rafe weren't in shackles right now, the morning *was* looking rather good.

Bright red in the face, Ell quickly righted her chair. "Sorry," she whispered. "Oh, and good morning to you as well. I have something for you guys." She peered around the bunch as if making sure no one else was around before she grabbed the scroll that Pristine had been toying with. "But, first, I'm going to need one of you to throw up a privacy spell."

Thea and Rafe exchanged a look with one another, but it was Rafe that spoke up. "We don't have the ingredients for a privacy spell."

"Oh! In that case..." Ell dropped the scroll back on the desk and began rummaging through the drawers down at the bottom. Receptionists always had a few ingredients for common, or, in this case, private-seeking spells locked away in their drawers. Ell's was almost always full because...well, she never used them. "Ah! I've got some rune pieces and a...awe, man." Her head popped back up, hair an absolute mess somehow, and held up a broken Nightengale feather. "Will...Will this still work?"

Thea and Mokana started snickering at the saddest-looking feather they'd ever seen. Rafe sighed at their childishness but aimed a reassuring smile at the woman. "Yes, Ell, it will still work. I'll handle the spell."

By the time the magic words had been uttered and the spell cast, Thea and Mokana had managed to get a hold of themselves. Ell was still pouting at their reactions, but her lips soon thinned, and apprehension settled in her large green eyes. She handed the scroll over, wringing her hands nervously as she said, "I hope it helps."

A phoenix burning in its nest, the symbol that marked the era and pinned itself to every Coven member regardless of rank, was stamped in red wax to keep the parchment from unraveling. Rafe did the honors of popping the seal, but when he unrolled the piece of paper his brow wrinkled in confusion.

"It's blank." He flipped the scroll around, but the back was just as bare. Thea and the others shared in his confusion, though Ell was suddenly looking pretty proud of herself.

Her voice was soft despite the privacy bubble that encompassed the desk. "Because this mission involves researching top-secret materials, I went ahead and concealed the directions. Only yours and Thea's voice will reveal the words." She aimed an apologetic smile at Namara and Mokana. "Sorry, I'm still not good at practicing magic, and it took a long time just to get their voices linked with the spell."

Mokana shrugged and thumbed over to the Summoner. "I just go wherever he goes. Well," she paused for a moment and it was clear the upcoming mission was on her mind. "Most of the time, anyway."

"And it's not like I get told about anything anyway," Namara quipped with an annoyed glance at her owner.

"I told you earlier that I was sorry," Thea huffed with a scowl.

"I'm impressed, Ell," Rafe cut in over the banter, still looking over the piece of paper as if the words were going to jump out of him at any time. "I didn't think you had it in you."

Ell beamed, and her face bloomed in color once again, this time accompanied by a shine in her gem-like irises. "Do you mean it?"

"Yeah," Thea agreed, becoming the new recipient of the woman's radiant smile. "It's pretty amazing. I know when I first started messing with spells it took me a long time to get it right."

"Yes, it did," Rafe concurred under his breath, earning him a sharp elbow in the rib from the Spellweaver.

Ell muffled her giggle with the back of her hand. "Um, so, in order to see the instructions, you just say 'reveal,' and to hide them again you say 'conceal' so…will you try it out for me? Just to make sure I did it right?"

"Of course." Rafe flashed her a reassuring smile. He then muttered the key word, and—sure enough—elegant scrawling began bleeding black onto the page. Ell sagged in relief with a loud sigh, eliciting grins from the others.

"Thank the goddess above," she groaned. "I was afraid I messed up somehow. I didn't want to have to rewrite that all over again."

"It *is* a lot." Thea noticed the writing extended to the back of the scroll as well. She looked up and, seeing Ell's worried expression, hurried to say, "That's a good thing. We need as many details as we can get."

Ell blew out a sigh of relief, ruffling the messy blonde bangs on her forehead, and she clapped her hands together cheerily. "Oh, good. Well then, if that's all, I'll leave you to your new mission. Just make sure you read it all before you get there and—" Ell's eyes suddenly seemed to track something behind them before widening, and she gasped out, "Oh, Second Chosen Markian, wait! Drat! He can't hear me!" She grabbed the thick stack of papers she'd been stamping earlier and made to hurriedly leave and run after the Second Chosen, but stopped, turned around, looked back over at

Markian who was quickly walking away, then speedily turned back to Thea and Rafe. Thea thought for a moment the blonde was going to offer an apology and dash clumsily away, but the strained face Ell presented them with caused both Coven members to pause. "If I wasn't being pulled in ten different directions, I would give you guys more details, but I trust both of you to keep quiet about what's on this scroll. I don't want to think about what will happen to you otherwise." Then she was off. "Second Chosen Markian, wait up! I have the process improvement summary form from Councilman Amor!"

Thea let go of a long sigh and stretched her neck until the satisfying *pop* released the tension building there. Just what had they gotten themselves into? She was used to the threat of dying at the hands of black magic practitioners, shady citizens that wanted to get even, or, hellfire, feral demons at this point.

She was not used to subtle death threats from her colleagues.

"Honestly, you couldn't pay me enough to do her job," Namara spoke up after a moment.

"I heard she gets really good incentives, though, and a bonus every quarter," Rafe informed with a shrug, but he was still staring down at the scroll with a grim expression. He stated the key word to mask the directions and rolled up the parchment, handing it off to the rusalka to stuff in her new bag. He had recently restocked on powders, so his pouches were full.

"With the amount of work that woman does I wouldn't be surprised if she got paid as much as a Summoner," said Mokana with a small grin. Her blue-green eyes lit up with mischievousness as a new thought seemed to enter her head. "When we get to the armory, can I help you pick out your second weapon?"

Rafe sent her a scrutinizing look. "I'd trust you to pick me out some garden shears."

Namara giggled at the affronted look on her drier counterpart's face. The rusalka didn't bother replying. She turned on her bare heels and marched in the direction of the Coven's armory, cheeks puffed out in indignation.

"Trust me to pick out a weapon that's so amazing you wouldn't even know how to use it," she hurled over her shoulder.

Rafe cupped the side of his mouth with one hand so his voice would carry over the growing distance Mokana was putting between them. "That would be just as useless."

Thea slapped him playfully on the shoulder, though she snickered herself, and the three began following after their companion. Namara's footfalls were by far the loudest, wet and *slappy,* and drawing one or two disgusted looks from passersby, but Thea knew that, if anything, Namara reveled in the discomfort of the judgmental. She'd be lying if she said she also didn't get some sort of petty satisfaction out of it as it was one of her leading motivations for keeping her pet properly soaked.

The Coven's armory was down the large corridor that branched off to the right of the circular anteroom. One could see all the way down to its end from Ell's centered reception desk, so the four of them had a simple, straight path to follow. The white and gold marble on the floor stretched up over the walls until it hit the lower hall ceiling, glinting in the light of the grand sconces. Storage rooms were marked boldly, along with "authorized personnel only" in the form of several runes so that all beings could read the message.

Runes were often seen throughout the Coven and other Coven-funded buildings, like the sanctuary. Since one couldn't trust an imp farther than they could cast a spell on them, runes had become more and more popular as a translation for all. Since anyone could make runes, non-magic beings included, it boosted jobs among the populace and granted the runesmiths, those that imbued the runes with its specific properties, more work.

At the end of the hall was a large door, separated in its importance by the ornate molding surrounding its frame. A clipboard levitated in mid-air, and the shifting light from the sconces and high windows cast the magic wrapped around it aglow. Pearl pink and pale yellow twinkled as the clipboard bobbed in the air slowly. Mokana was standing beside it, impatiently tapping her clawed foot on the stone flooring.

Thea gripped the object, unclipped the quill attached to the top, and quickly signed her name on the blank piece of paper. She sidestepped away to allow Rafe to do the same, and as soon as he placed the pen back in its perch, the ink soaked into the paper and disappeared. A loud click echoed through the hall, and the door slowly opened.

The rusalka stepped inside first, tugging Namara along in her excitement. They stopped abruptly in the doorway in awe, and Mokana looked back over her shoulder to whisper fiercely, "This place is huge!"

Rafe brushed past the two creatures with a raised eyebrow directed at his pet. "Do you not remember coming here after I summoned you?"

Mokana dropped her reverent expression and made a face at her owner. "Do you not remember how confused I was? I had just been sucked out of Hell. All the trips I took to the surface landed me in some kind of forest, not in the middle of a ceremony."

"Fair enough."

"I was never brought here," Namara said to no one in particular as she surveyed the room.

Thea hummed in agreement. "I picked up my weapons before summoning you." It had been the best choice, considering she hadn't had to worry about keeping up with a creature spawned by Hell in a room full of nothing but weapons.

The armory was dimly lit by more wall sconces that added a soft, tawny light to the smooth gray walls, but the room only seemed more dismal because of it. The layout was designed in a long hallway with two small rooms branched off to the right and left in the middle. The stone ceilings were vaulted and accented with darkly stained wooden beams. The more primitive weapons were stored and mounted on the walls where Thea and the others were currently located. These weapons were not imbued with magic, but because they were not as effective in battle, the Coven offered a wand to any member who chose these weapons.

A variety of shortswords, longswords, broadswords, hook swords, sabers, and claymores were mounted on both walls. They were accompanied by an assortment of sharp daggers and throwing knives. Thea wasn't one for swords, though. They were too bulky and wielding one never felt quite right. She already had a dagger anyway, so she continued down the rather short hall until she entered the middle layout. A cement table was anchored to the floor, offering members the choice to set down anything on their person so they could get a good feel for the weapon they were choosing.

To the right of the table was a shallow room where more primitive weapons were mounted. A variety of crossbows, sickles—the weapon Thea had chosen, though she forewent the wand and instead picked up a dagger—spears, and the classic bow and arrow were on display. To the left of the table was another room mirrored in depth, only this room had wands in every make and style floating by the wall. Thea recognized a few like the ones made from thousand-year-old trees, hardened celestial blood, precious stones, and unicorn horns that had been harvested after the creature had shed them post mating season. Taking a unicorn's horn while still attached would only result in the wand being as crude at the base as the ones at the Dark Market.

Up ahead were the weapons that were the most sought after, as they all had magic properties. There were staffs that resembled Rafe's and some that looked like Cressida's, scythes that when used on an opponent would temporarily sever the magic from its owner, snake-like whips that could set one's entire body ablaze with intense pain just from a nick, freezing grenades, magically-enhanced gloves that spiked a user's normal strength tenfold, and automatic crossbows loaded with the user's magic supply rather than normal arrows.

Mokana bee-lined it for the magic weapons, sweeping past Thea in unbridled enthusiasm. Namara, not so keen on window shopping, perched herself in a crouch on top of the cement table. Her bottomless black eyes watched the rusalka pick up one of the whips by its long bone handle. The snake-like material uncoiled in Mokana's grasp and fell to the floor with a heavy *wump*.

Thea snorted. "I didn't know you were into stuff like that."

"Thea!" Namara quickly admonished from behind her while Mokana sent her a horrified look, much to the Spellweaver's amusement.

"I was actually planning on looking at one of those," she admitted and slid past the rusalka to unhook another rolled up whip. She also looked at the crossbow a mere moment before grabbing that as well. She set them down on the table next to her pet and stepped back, eyes bouncing from one weapon to the other in contemplation.

Mokana groaned from behind her. "Neither you nor Rafe are ever going to get a wand, so I want to look at them before we leave."

"Don't touch the ones made of pure materials," Thea warned, never looking away from the weapons laid out before her.

"I'm not suicidal like the few humans I know," Mokana retorted snippily. Thea easily ignored the creature.

The whip would be useful against any creature she came across, so it would be highly beneficial. However, it would be hard to use with one hand already occupied with her sickle. Her concentration would have to be split, and, in battle, that could be fatal. The crossbow would have to be enhanced by a runesmith, as her magic wasn't as powerful and in overabundance that needed proper channeling, but she could grip it with one hand and fire at will.

She heard rather than saw Namara shift closer to her when she went to pick up the whip to test its weight in her hand before setting it back down. "I didn't know *you* were into that," she grinned cheekily.

"You don't want to know what I'm into."

She took her eyes off the whip long enough to watch Namara glance over her shoulder and eye Rafe walking up to the table with a large, tri-bladed boomerang in his hand. The kelpie wrinkled her seafoam green nose and frowned. "You're right. I don't."

"What are you two talking about?" Rafe asked as he set down the weapon beside the other two.

"Nothing," Thea and Mokana said in unison.

He gave them a strange look but didn't press. Instead, he looked down at the two weapons Thea seemed stuck on. "Having trouble deciding?"

"I'm leaning more toward the arrow launcher. It'll complement my sickle better," she said with a shrug. Then, quietly, she looked up at him and asked, "What do you think?"

Rafe's eyes widened briefly. To ask another Coven member what they thought when it came to weapons choosing meant utmost trust was placed in the opinion of the person asked. The weapon they would carry with them would be used to save their life on numerous occasions, so it went without saying that asking someone what they thought was akin to putting their life in the person's hands. He straightened a bit and gestured toward the whip. "I think the automatic is your best bet, but pick up the whip and test out its weight while you hold the sickle," he instructed.

Thea nodded wordlessly and pulled out her weapon from the holster on her back and stood like she was prepared to slice something's head off before she picked up the whip. The weapon came alive in her hands, and she felt a tug in her soul when it connected to her magic. She made a face at the foreign feeling, like magnets snapping together, but shrugged it off. It was lighter in her hand when connected to her, almost feeling as light as air. Purple zaps of electricity snaked its way down the whip, and when she flicked her wrist, the snap that echoed off the armory walls hurt her ears. She received a startled hiss from Namara, and Mokana came bolting out of the wand room with a curious expression.

"Is that what you're choosing?" she inquired with a frown. All innuendos aside, it was clear the sound the whip made alone wasn't winning either creature over.

"I don't know yet," Thea answered thoughtfully. She couldn't rule it out on the simple fact it hurt her ears a bit. The sickle had blistered her hand for a straight month before she grew used to the abrasive bone texture.

The whip was much easier to maneuver than normal whips, she noticed. She didn't have to tax the strength in her arm or overexert the dexterity in her wrist to make the loud *crack*. She could slice with one hand and whip with the other easier than she thought she'd be able to.

"It's not bad," she mused but quickly set the weapon back on the table. "I want to try this one out." She picked up the arrow launcher and set it on her arm and quickly tightened the straps.

"Concentrate on just making one arrow at a time," Rafe stated. "You don't want to overdo it."

She refrained from answering that with a sarcastic rebuttal. She knew her magic wasn't up to par with his, so conjuring anything more than one arrow would leave her on the brink of passing out in her current condition. "I'll definitely have to take it into a runesmith," she said instead. A small rune would amplify her magic as well as better channel it to the weapon. She'd be able to fire more than one arrow, and they would all be stronger than the one she was about to create.

The crossbow was heavy and solid on her arm but not unbearably so. Her arms were more muscular than the average woman—the sickle was no feather—so the weight didn't bother her. It was actually a relief; she would always feel it when she carried it and know it was there on her person.

Steel met dark red wood with carvings etched into both made the weapon elegant and deadly. The limbs were made from a crystalline structure similar to ceramic and fanned out like sharp, demonic bat wings, all silver and reflecting in the low light. The cables and string found on regular crossbows were missing, as it wouldn't do to constantly have to re-cock every time she needed to fire an arrow. They would have to be supplied by the user's magic as well, and the magic would automatically cock the bow. The trigger was centered under the weapon within her finger's reach to better stabilize it on her arm and keep the stock on her shoulder more easily.

"It feels right," she commented after quickly admiring its beauty. "And it doesn't connect to my magic without my consent like the whip did."

"That might be because you have to concentrate your magic in order to form the arrows and strings," Rafe gauged. "That could change if you equip it with a rune."

She gave a curt nod and closed her eyes. She could feel when her magic connected with the weapon, but it felt more like her slipping on a glove rather than snapping magnets. Lilac cables slipped through the cams on the end of the limbs and pulled the bow tight. A light purple arrow materialized into the track, and when Thea pointed it at the entrance door at the far end of the armory, the arrow flew through the air and smacked the door with a loud thud. It vanished after it met its mark.

The corner of her mouth quirked up in satisfaction. "I believe that settles that."

Chapter Four

A Gift in All Forms

Wet footfalls echoed behind Thea as she stepped outside the armory. Namara followed closely after with the new crossbow in her sage-colored arms. Thea eyed the floating clipboard with distaste. "They could easily give somebeing a job just to stand here and hold a clipboard. Why do they have to use creepy magic like this?"

Rafe exited after his pet and closed the door with the hand not holding his new weapon. He'd have to get a holster for it before they left town. "Don't ever become a Summoner if this creeps you out," he said as he handed the boomerang to Mokana and grabbed the floating clipboard, signing out his weapon.

Thea rolled her eyes, taking the clipboard from him when he was done. "Never planned on it. I happen to like being a Spellweaver—when I'm not tackling feral demons, striking deals with crazy sorceresses, or trekking across the blasted desert."

"Can't say I signed up for that, either," he replied with a wistful sigh.

Thea paused in her signing and bit her lip. He was right, after all. He hadn't signed up to trek across the desert and encounter almost certain death. He'd had the threat of imprisonment loom over his head. Not for the first time today, guilt flooded her being, and she had a sneaking suspicion it wasn't going to go away anytime soon.

She released the clipboard and grabbed his hand, threading her fingers between his in a sign of assurance. She tugged him in the direction of the lobby. "Come on. Should we go home first or head straight for the runesmith? What did the scroll even say?"

"It's probably best we read it away from prying ears and eyes," he said, eyes wandering as they entered the anteroom to the many Coven members still lingering about.

Thea eyed the loitering beings and hummed in assent. They bypassed the arrival and departure gates and exited the building through the front doors which dwarfed Srbeveara's in size yet were surprisingly lighter in weight. The front of HQ was bathed in the light of the early morning, and with it came the warmth from the sun. Thea had to squint to see the sky.

The world could pass for peaceful in that moment. Newborn buttery rays filtered the morning in a soft glow, catching on frost-covered tree branches and glistening like crystals. Pallid blue washed the sky from the earlier soft pinks that had reached over the horizon at dawn. The gusts of wind, still bone-chilling, carried the promise of spring as they disrupted the dark puffs of smoke from stone chimneys broadcasting which businesses were open for the waking population.

She tucked her cloak tighter around her body as they moved away from the two towering, hooded statues guarding the front of Coven Headquarters. Menacing looking and as tall as the building itself, they sent shivers down her spine even on a warm day.

Rafe stopped right at the edge of the property line where the cobbled stone road began and asked Mokana to pull out the scroll. The roads were littered with large puddles of melted snow, but there were plenty of dry patches to stand in. The Cleansers had done a good job of ridding the city of most of the mushy nuisance. More and more shops were opening back up, too, despite the threat of feral demons, and, in turn, more and more people were on the street again. Only in the open and brightly lit spaces close to the Coven though. Further out, people were less brave.

"Well, what's it say?" Thea asked impatiently after a moment of silence from the large Summoner.

Rafe grunted, only half hearing her as he continued to read. Curious, she stood on the tips of her toes, but she couldn't see anything because *Goddess forbid* he hold it at arm's length. No, he had to have his face right up in the paper like he was trying to snort the instructions into his brain, and the Goddess might have cursed Thea with height taller than most women, but she'd went and double cursed her with a man taller than most men. It was ridiculous and, honestly, a little unfair.

Regardless of what she might have looked like in that moment, she shoved her head under his arm.

"Thea," he grumbled, not really annoyed but not exactly happy with having wild curls tickling his chin.

"You take too long to read," she grumbled back. She set her eyes to scan the impeccable handwriting, rejoicing in the fact that it wasn't as clumsy as the woman who wrote it. What she read had her slipping out from under his arm and casting him a wide-eyed look. "She's leading us to the sewers?" she whispered fiercely. Only three things could be found in the sewers of Tolvade—none of them pleasant—and that was sewage, trash, and giant rat-men called the Skrittish.

Mokana pulled her thin, chapped lips between her elongated canines and darted her anxious gaze between the two of them. "Aren't the Skrits down there?"

Rafe looked up from reading to frown at his pet. "Don't call them that. Apparently, it's a derogatory term." He pointed to the passage where Ell had written the warning boldly and underlined. Mokana slapped her hands to her mouth in disbelief. "You address them as the Skrittish or Skrite for singular. Also," he continued, "it says no demons allowed."

Namara snarled in anger, the sound wet at the back of her throat. "That's blatant discrimination. We're allowed everywhere else, so why are we not allowed down there?"

Thea snatched the scroll from Rafe's hands, skimming the page for the answer herself. "It says that 'because of the wards put in place, nothing from Hell may enter.' That means we'll be safe from possible ferals, so you don't need to worry about us. Can we go now?" She turned to Rafe with her question. She was tired of standing around. They knew where they needed to go. They could read the rest later.

He raised an eyebrow at her eagerness. "Shouldn't we get holsters for our weapons first? And you need to rune your crossbow."

Thea huffed. "Fine. It'll take all day for Smithson's to fit me in for an appointment, so the sooner we drop it off the better. *Conceal*," she uttered the last word with finality and handed the scroll back to Mokana for safekeeping.

"We could split up," he suggested as his pet placed the scroll back in her purse.

Thea's eyes lit up at the promise of shaving down time. "You go buy the holsters while I set up the appointment?"

He smirked. "I can see how impatient you are."

The corners of her mouth quirked. "Meet up outside of Tasgall's afterward?" The short redheaded witch was one of the first shop owners to open her doors to the public, so business was booming. It wouldn't look too out of place for a Coven member to be standing around waiting up on a colleague.

"See you there. And, Thea?" he called after her before she could start marching off. She turned back to him in time to catch him swooping down and planting a kiss on her cheek. He turned and left with a giggling Mokana before she could say anything.

Color bloomed on her face, hot with embarrassment, and she scowled at the gurgled snort her pet made. At least the man had had the decency not smack a kiss on her lips right out in the open where everyone could see.

"Let's go," she demanded in a clipped tone. She wasn't upset over the kiss, despite her abrasiveness. In fact, her stomach was doing flips at the moment as she replayed the small gesture of affection in her head over and over again. It was just…new territory. She'd never been shown such acts of *attention* before. Hellfire, she was just now getting over the slight awkwardness of hand holding! She didn't know how to respond. What was even more frustrating was that it was *Rafe* of all people. She knew the man better than most of his family, just not in this particular way.

"Why would the Skrittish have wards up against creatures from Hell?" Namara wondered aloud, following behind Thea who had started walking toward the tavern. One could see the two rivers that ran through Tolvade split from each other if they ventured around the strip of buildings Tasgall's was sandwiched between. The ground dropped off down into the water below, so no one ever really went around back. Thea was one of many who had never seen the back of Tasgall's. She did know, however, that where the rivers split she would find the entrance to the sewers.

"Makes me wonder if they knew feral demons would escape in the first place," Namara continued.

Thea pulled her hood up as another gust of bitter wind blew by. "Or maybe we've found someone more paranoid than Torro."

Namara's black eyes lit up in amusement. "Better not give them a reason to feed you to the incinerator."

"You seem surprisingly accepting that you aren't coming with," Thea said, looking nearly as amused as her pet, "considering you nearly ripped off Rafe's head a moment ago."

The kelpie flushed a dark green. "Did not," she muttered under her breath. "And, anyway, if the Skrittish have wards like Ell says, then you'll be fine. Besides, I trust Rafe."

Thea threw her hands up in the air and cast her pet a disbelieving look. "Does no one have faith in me?"

Namara only snickered.

Smithson's didn't have a bell to alert the shop owners that customers had arrived, but a tinkling noise did sound throughout the reception area, followed by a scattering of glitter-like magic that floated down and caught itself on the rays of light coming in from the large, stained glass windows. Black walnut wood was the theme throughout Smithson's from the floors, to the formal reception desk built into the dark walls, to the beams decorating the rounded, cove ceiling.

The walls were decorated in weapons just like the armory, only the ones here were too flashy for Thea's tastes. Decked out in jewels, fine metals, and ornate filigree, the armaments were more for aesthetics than battle. They were also much, much more expensive.

"Don't touch anything," Thea warned quietly to her pet as they walked inside. She looked over her shoulder and squinted at her pet before loudly clearing her throat.

Namara shrunk back from the shiny, gold-plated ax on the wall and hid her dripping wet hand behind her. "I wasn't going to," she hissed in return.

Thea snorted as she strolled over to one of the display tables. Shiny daggers attached to one another fanned out behind the table in an extravagant display. On the table itself were small knives such as gimlets, butterflies, and switchblades. She turned to find her pet creeping through the racks of shields. "They don't sell halters here, so I don't know why you're looking."

A low growl came from the creature. "I suddenly can't wait until you're gone," she replied scornfully.

Thea stuck out her tongue, to which Namara tossed the Spellweaver a look of disapproval.

"Can I help you ladies find anything?" a bubbly voice called to them.

Thea and Namara glanced toward the reception desk to find a short, beaming woman standing idly by a large stack of binders. The woman's glossy black hair fell down to her lower back in waves, and wispy bangs framed hazel-brown eyes. Her smile was wide and accompanied by dimples on either side. She was also heavily pregnant.

Thea's gaze remained on the woman's stomach for a second longer before she was stuttering out, "Uh, actually, I-I'm here to drop off a weapon for runeing."

The woman smiled and pulled out a binder from the stack beside her. As Thea walked closer to place the arrow launcher on the desk's ledge, she spied a nameplate adhered to the counter next to a silver little bell. It read in dainty, curling letters *Receptionist Bridget Neiler*.

"Do you know what rune you're wanting specifically?" Bridget went on to ask while flipping through some pages.

Thea tried racking her brain for all the runes she could remember outright, but most wouldn't aid her in battle or couldn't be paired with a weapon. She blew out a breath. "Not really. I need something with high attack power that channels the magic I already have."

The receptionist hummed as she nodded her head, flipping through several more pages before she went, "Ah!" and propped the binder up on the ledge for Thea to peer through. "The ones you're looking for would be on this page. They range from least to most expensive. We bill you when you come to pick the weapon up."

"Oh, thank you," Thea said with a smile. She eyed Namara peering over the ledge and subtly dragged the binder full of unlaminated papers away from the dripping wet kelpie.

"Boy or girl?" she heard Namara ask. The creature was hunched over so that only her head and hands clamped down on the desk were visible from the other side. Her all-black eyes were wide with unbridled curiosity as she peered down at the lady's stomach.

Bridget's smile got impossibly wider, and her hazel-brown eyes melted into a soft green color. She gently rubbed a hand over her belly and giggled. "A little boy. We've been trying for seven years now."

Thea glanced up with stunned eyes, and Namara's jaw had dropped. "Congratulations," they both uttered, though Thea's voice was by far more subdued than her excitable pet's.

Bridget only giggled again, and her cheeks were now glowing. "Thank you! We're so excited we haven't been able to pick out a name yet." Her gaze trailed over to Namara who, even with eyes as dark and as bottomless as hers, appeared to be in awe. "Would you like to feel him? He's not usually active right now, but when he feels someone's hand, he likes to give a little kick."

Namara shot straight up with an enthusiastic smile, and if she had a tail it would have been wagging hard enough to propel her over the desk. "Really? Uh..." She looked down at her hand and grimaced. The happy aura around her wilted, and she stepped back with a wry smile. "It's okay, I don't want to get your shirt wet."

Thea stopped skimming the details of the runes under her fingertips and cast her gaze over to the kelpie. Her lips thinned as remorse tugged at her from within. She, personally, had no interest in touching people's stomachs, pregnant or otherwise, but having the option of feeling the beginning of life just out of reach because of what you were… She teased Namara daily for the way water constantly fell from her being, but at that moment she felt truly bad for her companion.

"Oh, honey," Bridget said with a wave. "A little water never hurt anyone."

Namara shook her head. "The water would soak through and ruin your shirt in seconds."

The receptionist lips quirked up into a smirk, and she brought the hand caressing her stomach up to wiggle her fingers. "People in the Coven aren't the only ones who can perform magic, ya know. Let me go get my dust belt. The darn thing won't fit me anymore," she laughed as she disappeared in the next room.

Thea closed the binder after coming to a decision and placed it back down with the others, but she jerked her hand back with an aborted scream as something jumped up onto the desk. No bigger than a kitten, a ruby red, scaly lizard scurried onto the pile of binders and flared the tiny wings on its back. Sparks ignited in rapid succession from its mouth as a warning to steer clear.

Bridget rushed back out from the hall she'd disappeared behind, now hauling a heavy-looking belt in her grasp. "What the devil is going on—Ferdinand!" She dropped the belt onto the wooden desk and snatched up the little dragon. "I leave for one moment and you're already scaring the customers," she admonished, but contrary to her words, she started snuggling the beast. She turned apologetic eyes at Thea and Namara. "Sorry about that. He's gotten so protective ever since I've been pregnant. Now, you, go on and stop causing me trouble," she directed at Ferdinand, and gently tossed him to the floor, smiling as his wings caught the air and glided him safely to the ground below. She then started rooting around in her belt. "All right. Let me get this spell taken care of then I'll get your weapon and choice of rune documented, and you ladies can be on your way."

Bridget was quick and efficient with her dusts, and while the spell was activating, she jotted down Thea's information, the serial number on the arrow launcher, the choice of rune, and then stored away the weapon in no time at all. The receptionist's belly was now glowing a soft orange color, and Namara, while a bit hesitant, reached over and placed her hand over Bridget's stomach.

Thea watched her pet with a slow smile starting to form on her face. She'd never seen the creature so awed. There was a sparkle in those all-black eyes. She couldn't hold back the huff of laughter as Namara gasped, presumably after the baby decided enough touching was going on. She never truly faulted the kelpie for what she was, but she wished things could be like this for Namara all the time.

She wished, more than once now, that her friend didn't have to live life inconvenienced.

Chapter Five

Stop to Smell the… Sewers?

"What did you *do?*" Thea shrieked in horror as she bolted around Tolvade's main fountain and plowed into Rafe, grabbing his face in her hands and looking him over with wide eyes. The Summoner only grinned wildly back.

"Like the new haircut?" He asked casually and ran a calloused hand through his dark locks—locks that couldn't even be *considered* locks anymore with how short they were. Gone was the long hair Thea had always known, replaced with short black tuffs that stuck up when he raked a hand through them. He appeared more rouge-ish this way, and his features were much more pronounced and angular. He looked like a completely different man, but those eyes were no one else's, and they still made her heart stammer when he held her gaze. His grin transformed into a devilish smirk as words continued to elude her.

Banish a banshee, why did he chop off his hair?

"Because the desert is hot," he explained after Thea asked him this out loud. "One day there and you'll wish you'd done the same thing."

Thea ripped her hands from him and wrapped them over her head protectively as if the Summoner was wielding a pair of scissors.

"As if!" She turned and glared at Namara who had burst out laughing at her initial reaction and was now snickering with

Mokana off to the side. Her eyes traveled back to Rafe where they lingered a little too long on his head and shoulders, where hair should be.

Rafe rolled his eyes, smiling brightly as he laughed. "You are so dramatic when you want to be."

"What?" she squawked indignantly, only to be cut off as he wrapped an arm around her shoulders and pulled her close to him.

"Come on, we'll get you a haircut next," he teased next to her ear, still grinning impishly. Thea slapped incessantly at his hands until he let go of her, though his smirk remained even as she stormed off.

Thea and Namara had been on their way to Tasgall's when the kelpie's gasp and nudging fingers forced Thea to turn around and spot Mokana first. It had taken her longer to find Rafe, and when she did, she'd had to do a double-take. Now, that they were grouped up, it made sense for the tethered creatures to stay behind rather than following their owners up to the tavern. Mokana gave Rafe the scroll, which he shoved into his back pocket, and he handed Namara Thea's new crossbow holster for her to carry back to his place. His new weapon was secured to his pouch belt and sitting at his lower back under his staff holster.

They split up at the water fountain centered in the middle of the town square amidst the marketgoers. Frigid water spewed out from the structure, misting the air with an icy spray. The concrete statues of two human-esque beings with six arms were so eroded with time that the faces of the beings were indistinguishable, and the objects they were holding were nothing more than gray, algae-coated lumps. Thea was not surprised to look back over her shoulder and see the two demonesses splashing in the water as if it were a warm, sunny day. She lost sight of them as they rounded a corner, but she continued hearing their squeals of glee for a few more moments.

Adjacent to the street they were on loomed Runerite Academy. It would have been nostalgic seeing the sprawling courtyard lead up to wide, concrete steps that marked the entrance to the school had it not been for the cautionary tape surrounding the building. A small gazebo, designed to replicate the academy's baronial style and dark, slate-tiled roof, sat off-center in the middle of the courtyard. Every student had seemed to gravitate toward it during their time enrolled at Runerite.

"Remember when I walked into the middle of Meldi confessing her love for you at that gazebo?" she asked as they strolled past it. She caught Rafe's glare and snickered. He was as red in the face now as he was back then. Meldi had been just as embarrassed, and Thea remembered vividly how the witch had squeaked, chucked her love letter at Rafe, and bolted back into the academy. She ran a bakery now, imbuing all her pastries with good fortune or wisdom. The one time Thea had walked in was awkward enough to have her not come back. The strudels had helped her pass a test at least.

He groaned and massaged the bridge of his nose. "Why do you remind me of these things?"

They skirted around a couple more buildings and approached Tasgall's. Thea shrugged with a grin. "Payback for earlier. Anyway, Namara and I were wondering why the Skrittish would have wards up that guard against demons. She thought they might have predicted ferals escaping for a while now. I think they're overly paranoid. What do you think?"

Rafe hummed in thought. "Both could be true." He suddenly reached out and nudged her arm with his elbow, a newfound theory clear in his blue-green gaze. "Or, think about it, the Skrittish have been around since the birth of Raen. They were here when second and third-tier feral demons roamed the city two hundred years ago. Since they never leave the sewers, it would make sense they never took the wards down. They may think the demons never left, and if one feral gets down there, it could mess up our entire infrastructure."

That was a valid point. The Skrittish were the trash collectors of Tolvade, and, as alchemists, they converted the trash into reusable energy for the city as well as cleansed the air. If a feral demon messed up the power system, all the districts would experience a total blackout. So their reasoning for keeping creatures out seemed justifiable, and they themselves were probably nice and everything, but Thea couldn't get over the depictions of large teeth, beady eyes, and furry bodies the size of golems covered in sewage water. Her nose wrinkled at the thought.

"I'm just wondering how visiting them will help us with the Draconians," Thea wondered aloud, slipping on her facemask and bringing it up to her nose at the sudden bite from the wind.

"We'll find out when we get there," was all Rafe had to offer.

The cowbell of Tasgall's could be heard from the constant door opening the closer they got to the tavern, and Thea watched as all sorts of beings poured in and out of the establishment. A centaur stumbled out on his wobbly horse legs, laughing at something his human companion slurred beside him. Thea shook her head at the sight. Any minute a feral could come bounding around the corner and these two would be easy pickings.

"You know, I've never actually been past Tassie's," she mentioned as they passed the inebriated duo and the long row of shops affixed to one another. Tasgall's, and the other, smaller businesses that sandwiched the tavern, were backed up against a sheer cliff face overlooking where the rivers split.

Her admission caught Rafe by surprise if his widened eyes were anything to go by. "Really? You're about to be amazed then."

Already she could hear the rush of cascading water now that the market was closed down and the town was a little quieter.

"Why do you say that? It's just another part of the...*whoa*."

The Spellweaver stopped in her tracks once they made their way around the shops. She hadn't realized just how high up they truly were. At the bottom of the cliff, hundreds of nauseating feet below, an enormous wall jutted straight up from the ground. Hydra Dam, as large as a hydra itself, was a sight to behold. Water from Dragon's Mouth Gulf flowed over the dam and spilled into a deep, dark blue pool below. Thea recognized the two large, rushing bodies of water that branched off from the reservoir as the beginnings of the two rivers.

"Isn't the point of a dam to *stop* the flow of water?" she found herself asking even as she felt awed by the sight. It was beautiful, even in the winter. Mist uncurled from the bottom of the manmade waterfall and drifted up into the air. The water was a stunning sapphire color, reflecting the cold, cloudless sky above. Hills surrounded the dam on both sides, the land rising and falling as it raced toward the horizon where bigger, wider hills became the bases for even larger mountains.

"No, the dam just controls the water flow. Do you see that large rotating wheel over there?" He pointed to the base of the dam's wall where a colossal wooden wheel stuck out from the concrete by a horizontal beam, turning and scooping up water as well as catching some of the water that fell from the top of the dam with wooden trough buckets. The wheel then dumped the water it collected into a small creek that raced down the side of one of the hills, where it disappeared around a bend.

She followed the trail and felt her brow scrunch in confusion. "Yeah. Why does it deposit the water down that hill though? What's the point?"

Rafe chuckled, but the sound was dry and had Thea looking at the Summoner curiously. "That's the irrigation system for the farms in Adalith."

Thea's jaw dropped. "What! Those snobs don't even have to pay for their crops to be watered?"

Farmers were some of the richest people in Tolvade. Her father, no matter how much schmoozing he did at the galas, conventions, or posh parties he was invited to, could never be on the same level as the farmers in Adalith. The only people more important than the farmers were the High Priests and the Celestial.

Rafe shrugged and let out an annoyed sigh. "Their taxes pay for the wheel's upkeep if it makes you feel any better." Not really, and she could tell it didn't make him feel any better about it either. They probably didn't even miss the coins that left their pouches. "Come on, I'll show you the entrance to the sewers."

She felt her lips thin out and muttered, "Can't wait."

She took one last look at the dam and the hills around it. Beyond the mist that shrouded the tops of the faraway, snow-capped peaks, Thea wondered if the red dragons really did still exist up there. Before the era of the phoenix, it had been the dawn of the elves. The Elven Era had seen the rise of humans with magic and the fall of giant beasts that had roamed the land for centuries. Myths and legends tell that it was the elves that banished the dragons to faraway lands. If that was the case, though, what of the sand wyverns in the desert?

"Look, I know you're not excited, but you can't just stand there all day," Rafe called from halfway down the steps.

Thea shook herself and hurried after the departing Summoner. Stone steps built into the side of the steep decline carried them down to the river's level. The last few were wet with the spray of water, and glowing green moss clung to the rock stairs even in the blistering cold.

The rush of the falls was louder down where they were, nearly deafening this close up. She glanced over her shoulder and, even from across the way, she felt incredibly minuscule compared to the immenseness of the dam. Just the waterwheel alone was bigger than HQ, and the trough buckets looked more like oxcarts from where she was standing.

It was much colder down by the water as well, forcing Thea to bundle her wool cloak closer. They crossed a large wooden bridge that extended over to the other side of the river, connecting to a narrow piece of dry ground backed up to a rocky hill that jutted high in the sky.

"This is the entrance to the sewers?" she asked once they stepped off the bridge. An iron gate, rusted from continuous exposure to moisture, was embedded in a slim opening in the rock face.

"It's glamoured," Rafe announced after a quick inspection. "Though, it has so many layers I'm not able to see underneath it. Wards are pretty strong here, too."

Thea pulled off one of her gloves and reached out to run her finger down the frigid metal, pulling back with a grimace when she encountered slime. "Gross," she grumbled, wiping off the slick substance onto her leather pants and pulling back on the glove. "It feels real enough."

"We'll be able to pass through," he said, grunting as he pried open the rusted gate, "it just won't be a pleasant experience. Ladies first." He grinned, sweeping his arms out for her. She scowled at him. There wasn't a wall of snow for her to walk right into like the last time he pulled the gentlemanly act, but the thought of dark, dismal, and slimy places didn't exactly have her rushing forward.

"I really don't like you right now," she told him, pressing forward into the darkness. Her shoulders scraped along the wall, and her face twisted in disgust. The cost of cleaning a wool cloak was nothing to shake a wand at.

"Oh, come on, Thea," Rafe said from behind her, though she could hear the struggle to wiggle through the cavern come through in his voice. "Doesn't this remind you of—" a slick scrape accompanied by a grunt, "—that Borlimane run?"

A puff of air escaped her, visible in the cold, dim light. Not quite a laugh, not really a snort. "Do *not* bring up that mission ever again. I cannot believe I fell on my face in front of all those Summoners."

Rafe huffed behind her. Definitely a laugh. He had been one of those Summoners and, amidst battling a blood mage, had had the audacity to laugh at her for being tripped up by a runaway black witch who had decided darting through an active warzone was her best course of action. A fireball that had been meant for someone else had swiftly taken her out. Thea had hidden out in an outhouse in the *tamer* parts of the swamps for an hour trying to ambush the escapee, and it had indeed been just as slimy and claustrophobic as this tunnel.

"For what it's worth, Jarret let you claim the kill."

She clicked her tongue. "Which I didn't, since I couldn't conjure a fireball to save my life at the time."

"You say that like you can conjure one now."

Thea elbowed him somewhere and was satisfied by the rush of air that escaped the Summoner. Squinting ahead into the darkness, she announced in a hushed breath, "I see a door." It was an old door, made of metal, and as rusted around the hinges as the iron gate had been.

She gripped the handle and had to yank upwards in order to turn it, thankful for the gloves on her fingers. She could feel the cold sear through the thick material. The door gave a loud, groaning creak into the stilled silence, making Thea wince.

"Way to keep this operation a secret," Rafe mumbled behind her, close enough to send involuntary shivers down her back as his warm breath wafted over her frozen ears.

"Shut up," she hissed defensively, yanking away and plunging into the sewers. The smell hit her like a brick wall, and she nearly went stumbling back.

Dear Goddess above, that is putrid!

She just barely managed to hold back the gag threatening to force her nonexistent breakfast up. The sewers were what she expected them to look like. Large, rounded tunnels of red brick walls weaved this way and that, branching off into hundreds of different directions. A large canal of wastewater flowed beside her, the color of fresh gravestone dirt after a downpour. The "walkway," as she was apt to describe the dirty cement she was standing on, was wet and slippery. Gross puddles of standing water filled each dip in the uneven ground, glinting in the light of the flickering torches secured to the walls. It was warmer in the sewers. Moist and humid and thick, making the cloak over Thea's shoulders uncomfortable and heavy.

She clapped a hand over her nose and turned to Rafe. His face was half-hidden under the collar of his wool cloak in an attempt to escape the horrid odor. "Get the scroll out," she said in one short exhale, shoving her mouth deep into her elbow to take another breath.

He quickly complied, all but yanking out the rolled-up piece of paper from his back pocket. "Reveal," he grunted. Ell's words flowed onto the page for them to see once again. Again, Thea had to push up onto her tiptoes to read.

Follow the tunnel you initially entered and head north. Take the first tunnel that branches off to the left. Then take the next tunnel that branches off to the right. It is accessible by a bridge that connects to the other side. It will lead you to a dead end. Facing the brick wall, you both must say aloud—

"I know of your secrets, and I wish not to tell, for I abide by the three L's…?" Thea murmured aloud.

"That's everything written," Rafe said with his nose pinched between his fingers. If Thea wouldn't have to breathe back in the disgusting air, she would have laughed at him for how ridiculous he looked. "Conceal," he commanded, and the words bled together before disappearing once again.

Without another word, they both marched north with purposeful yet cautious strides. Their footsteps echoed and bounced off the brick walls, the sounds of splashing through murky puddles accompanying the sounds of wastewater steadily moving through the sewer canal. They took the first tunnel that branched off left and then crossed the cement bridge over the canal when the first tunnel that branched off right came into view. Sure enough, the tunnel was a dead end.

The brick was darker at the end of the tunnel, meaning it was older. It wasn't noticeable, and, upon a glance, no one would spot the difference. Thea had seen too many spelled walls in her day not to spot the distinction in the red tints of the clay.

Finding Rafe's gaze, together they chanted: *"I know of your secrets, and I wish not to tell, for I abide by the three L's."*

A sharp click alerted the two that whatever they had just said must have worked. Thea watched in fascination as the brick and stained mortar detached down the middle and slowly swung open like two grand gates to reveal...

A library?

Chapter Six

What Has Branches and Leaves but Has No Bark?

As wide and as long as one of the sewer tunnels, a library stretched out before them. As Thea and Rafe stepped forward, Thea could feel that the air was different here, and it wasn't just because it was noticeably devoid of the disgusting odor of the sewers. This place felt as if it were frozen in time, teleported from another dimension but got lost along the way and fell below Tolvade's floors. The long, grand hall was alight with unnatural brightness, for there were no windows. There wouldn't be underground. Yet, the library was washed in a golden glow and casting shadows as if it were sunset.

Large, square stone tiles, the likes of which Thea had never seen before, *clacked* under her heeled boots with every step she took. The color of the stone shifted in hue every time it caught the light, morphing from red to brown to gold to copper as the two Coven members walked further inside. It glittered as if a pixie had slow danced across the ground to a love song in the moonlight, leaving dust twinkling in its wake.

The bookshelves were beautifully carved from rich, dark wood, shining like they were oiled daily with the utmost care. They towered over Thea and Rafe, reaching the ceiling that was straight out of a storybook—simply because it was not a ceiling at all. A shimmering loch hung suspended in the air, reflecting back at them. Violets and magentas, mixed with trails of stardust, created a nebula of galaxies in the water while shadows moved under the stars. A vast, dark silhouette swayed within, causing ripples to spark the surface as its immense, fluid shape disappeared into the depths of the mere.

"What in the name of magic…" Thea trailed off in awe.

Rafe must not have seen the creature swimming above him, for his gruff voice was asking about something further down the hall. "I wonder if that's the incinerator for Tolvade's trash?"

Thea blinked, her mouth still unhinged from the surprise that had gripped her. She cast her gaze down the library, but her eyes kept wandering back up to the ceiling. Only when she was confident that whatever had been lurking there wasn't coming back did she move on.

Up ahead, in the middle of the grand hall, was a massive wooden cradle mount one would see for large globes. It stood twice as tall as Rafe, but nowhere close to touching the body of magical water hanging above them. Instead of a globe in the giant mount, a ball of pale flames hovered within. The white flames crackled like they normally would over logs, licking up the side of the mount but never burning it nor causing it to crumble.

The wall behind them clicked as it shut, gaining the two's attention. They were now locked in here.

"I don't even know where to begin," said Thea as she cautiously stepped forward, twirling slowly around as she took in everything.

She heard Rafe's boots scuff against the tile, and she turned to see him run a finger over the spines of a few texts. "If the books are alphabetized, we can start with the obvious sections first. D for desert, dragons, and Draconians and S for sand wyverns."

"And if they're not?"

Rafe sighed heavily. "Then I don't know. It doesn't look like there's anyone here."

There is always someone here, far-children.

Quiet and raspy, a whispering voice floated into Thea's head and caused the hairs on the back of her neck and down her arms to stand on end. From the wide-eyed expression Rafe wore, she knew he'd heard it too. They both looked up at the water hanging above their heads, but the large creature they'd seen swimming in the colorful depths wasn't surfacing or giving any indication that it had been what spoke.

Thea's eyes traveled back down to the Summoner, a silent request to hurry this mission along, but the words died prematurely on her tongue as a gasp escaped her, and her hand reflexively flew back to her sickle. Rafe didn't waste time questioning her reaction and whirled around with his own hand flying to his staff, but a furry, human-like hand halted their advancements.

Thea's grip tightened over the bone handle, but she didn't unsheathe her weapon in the face of the figure standing before her just yet. Its height easily topped that of a centaur, draped in long, nut-brown robes with intricate bronzed patterns along the sleeve borders. The hood covered its head and shadowed its features, but a hairy, whiskered snout was just visible enough to distinguish the creature as one of the infamous Skrittish.

Her grip loosened at the realization, and Rafe dropped his hand altogether. They most likely wouldn't have stood a chance against the Skrite, for this was one of Aeristria's ancient alchemists staring them both down. It knew more than Thea and Rafe would ever hope to know combined. Telepathy was certainly not something easily mastered by just anyone.

"You're a lot bigger than I thought," Thea said after the silence began to stretch uncomfortably, earning an incredulous look from the Summoner beside her.

Movement under the hood had Thea wondering if it was the creature's ears perking up. Again, the voice from before slid into the forefront of her mind. *You would not be the first human to have thought so. I assume you were sent here by a member?*

Thea and Rafe exchanged a look with each other.

A member? As in a member of the Coven?

"Second Chosen Winona told us we could find what we were looking for through Ell, and she's the one who led us here," Rafe spoke up, fetching the scroll from his cloak.

There is no need for proof, far-child. Thea watched in a state of apathy as Rafe puffed up at the term 'child.' *Both are trusted here. Before I show you where you wish to go, I must tell you the laws of the library.*

"The three L's?" she asked, again noting the twitching under the hood.

Yes, far-child. Remember them during your visit here. They are the following: listen to those who speak in tongues, learn from the pages long forgotten, and leave with nothing more than gained knowledge.

Rafe cleared his throat and gingerly rubbed the back of his neck, eyeing the creature with wary acceptance. "Understood."

Thea nodded in agreement and lowered her hand. Internally, she was wondering how this could be considered a library if nothing was ever allowed to leave. Out loud she asked, "Where can we find information on the Draconians?"

There is limited information covering the wyverns in the desert, and they are separated throughout the library. One section you may find is down this very hall. The Skrite pointed its clawed finger, aiming at a particular area behind her, and Thea followed its direction with her gaze and wondered what the creature was talking about. There was only one hall. *Past the cradle and down twelve steps on the right is where you will find information on the desert. I shall accompany you to another section covering all dragon types.*

Thea turned back to find Rafe already looking at her, thin-lipped and annoyed. "You're going to suggest we split up, aren't you?"

"It's like you know me."

Rafe rolled his eyes. "Don't break anything or fall into the fire. I'll go with…" he glanced over his shoulder at the Skrite watching them wordlessly, "…him."

Very well then. Should you require anything, far-child, you need only to call for help.

Before she could ask what a far-child was and why he kept calling them that, the Skrite turned and vanished into thin air. Thea blinked owlishly, eyes landing on Rafe who appeared equally as shocked. He brought a hand up and hovered it in the same space the alchemist disappeared, and Thea's eyebrows flew up in surprise when the Summoner's hand vanished as well.

He sighed in relief, apparently knowing what type of magic he was working with. "It's a glamoured passageway. It only looks like one long hallway, but there are camouflaged breaks in the shelves. Thank the goddess I'm not portal jumping."

Thea's jaw dropped when Rafe walked into the bookshelf and disappeared right along with the alchemist. She whirled around, looking at the library in a whole new light. There was no telling how big this place truly was if there were multiple passages like this branching off what appeared to be a single hall.

She placed her hand on the cool wood of the shelf and set off down the hall. Her hand dipped once, twice, three times before she got to the cradle holding the white flames, all two deep breaths apart. The soft crackle of the magic fire grew steadily louder, though the sound wasn't abrasive in the quiet library. Two more hidden passageways revealed themselves as she counted the twelve steps before she found herself in front of tomes wrapped in worn scarlets, dusty roses, and yellow stone colors. Some of the titles had words she couldn't pronounce.

Bet they're in Ernimoen. Blythe would have been useful here.

Not knowing where to begin, she plucked one of the thicker books off the shelf and flipped it open. A plume of dust wafted into the air and she coughed. The smell of old books was nice, but not when inhaled all at once.

"Ugh," she grumbled and waved the dust away.

Skimming through the pages told her nothing but the history of the desert civilizations in the Golden Sea. While fascinating, she was on a time crunch. The next book covered desert plants and their many uses—she filed all the poisonous ones away in her head. In the third book, she came across the familiar word *keresela* or "desert cat." The colored drawing associated with the word was that of a large, muscular feline with russet fur. Emerald green eyes had slits for pupils, and its ears had long black hairs that came off the tips.

Red hair, green eyes, and mean-looking. Very fitting, Blythe.

The fourth book wasn't what she was looking for either, but she inhaled sharply at the incantation written out on the brittle page.

Fluid of infinite shape and form
Doth by which we all are born
Reverse the untaught flow forevermore
Henceforth no longer shall thou endure

It was a containment, regeneration, and water spell all in one. Thea's eyes widened as they skimmed the purpose for the spell. Its intention was to keep a human alive in the desert by disallowing sweat while still keeping the body cool. However...

Would this work on Namara?

She read the incantation over and over again, singing the spell as if it were a song in her head to remember it better. She'd write it down first thing after leaving the library, but she didn't want to forget a single word until then. The ingredients weren't worth remembering, as there were only two: gold dust and the sweat from the person being spelled. Namara didn't sweat, but she did drip water constantly.

So engrossed was she in the spell that she didn't hear the softly padded paws making their way toward her.

"What are you reading?"

Thea *eeped* loudly and nearly dropped the book in her hands. She floundered for a second trying to catch it, pulled it close to her chest in protection, and turned to glare at—well, she didn't quite know what she was looking at.

It looked like a cat, but this was no Pristine. This cat was massive with giant paws the size of Thea's hands, with long, black, wiry hair covering its large body. Gray splotches in matted fur made the creature look as if it had just rolled around in ash. Round, human eyes the color of amber melting over moss glinted at her in what appeared to be amusement. Its abnormally circular head tipped to the side, and its huge, pointed ears, lost in the mass of sooty hair growing out of them, twitched.

"What are you?" Thea found herself asking.

The creature made a noise similar to a purr, but the noise sounded too delicate to have come from it. "What is hard to find but easy to lose, worth more than gold but costs less than copper?" The cat's voice was velvet and smoke, and when it made the same purr noise, it was just as bewildering as the first time she'd heard it.

Listen to those who speak in tongues, she remembered the cloaked figure saying.

"Um…I don't know." She shrugged sheepishly. "I'm sorry."

The creature's face crumpled. Its strange eyes looked so forlorn all of a sudden, glistening with unshed tears. "No one ever does," it murmured brokenly, and the sadness rolling off it was near tangible.

Thea's eyes widened. What did she do? What did she say? Was it because she couldn't answer riddles? "Uh, um…oh!" Rafe liked riddles. Rafe loved all kinds of brain teasers. "Hold on, I know someone who probably does."

Just like that, the sadness vanished from the creature so quickly Thea felt she'd just been duped. Regardless, she pulled out her crystal ball from her pocket. Hopefully, she could still form a connection in the library. They could have stepped through a pocket dimension for all she knew, or the wards keeping demons out might mess with her ability to make calls.

She didn't bother with the magic words that would call upon her partner but rather focused on him like she was used to. The orb came to life in her hands just like her older one, and within moments Rafe's face filled the glass.

"You insisted we split up, and yet you're the one already calling me back."

Thea bit the inside of her cheek to keep from grinning. "Any luck?" she asked instead, ignoring his quip.

The big man chuckled, and his bright smile was nearly infectious. "Of course, I *am* amazing, after all."

Thea nodded with a hum, managing to keep her straight face. "So humble, too."

"It's like you know me."

She snorted. "Do you remember the way back? I haven't found anything but a water spell I want to try on Namara and maybe even Mokana. Nothing for the journey, though."

"I was actually on my way back to you right now. I found…something else that you'll want to take a look at."

She arched an eyebrow. "Alright. Something else also found *me* that you'll want to take a look at." She eyed the cat creature quickly before catching Rafe's puzzled expression. She smiled reassuringly and cut the connection.

It was only a moment later that Rafe made a sudden appearance, but Thea anticipated his arrival. Only she imagined him with his long hair for some reason, so it was a shocking reminder to see him without it. He came through the same passageway he left, but as he turned and caught sight of—whatever this cat creature was—he stopped just as abruptly.

"It's not dangerous," she called down to him. "That I know of," was said more quietly and out of earshot of the Summoner now warily walking in her direction. The creature's grin widened, and the teeth inside its mouth were fat, wide, and flat. More human than feline.

"What is it?" he asked once he was close enough.

She shrugged. "I asked it that, but it only gave me this weird riddle. I figured you could be useful for once," she said with a smirk threatening to surface.

The tension in Rafe's back receded, and he barked out a laugh. "Keep talking and I won't show you the surprise I found." He stopped just shy of the creature's back, and the cat peered over its shoulder with its strange grin and odd eyes full of amusement once more. "So, what are you?"

It repeated its riddle, and Rafe's brows only scrunched for a moment before he guessed, "A friend?" Thea eyed him quizzically, but he merely shrugged.

The same peculiar noise caught their attention again, and Thea watched the giant cat slump onto the ground, strange eyes lit in approval.

"Very good, human. I am, indeed, a friend. You may call this friend Bajun. Would you like Bajun to tell you a story? Or, perhaps, recite a favorite poem?"

Thea had no need for storytime, nor did she even have a favorite poem, but Rafe seemed to be mulling things over in his head if the long, silent stare-down he was giving Bajun was any indication.

"Can you answer the questions I have about the section of books I found?"

Bajun's tail twitched in the air lazily. "Only if you prefer the answers in the form of riddles."

Rafe nodded. "I can deal with that. Let's go, T." He reached over to snatch up Thea's hand and tugged her along back the way he came. "We could probably get there by going through another one of these passages, but I'm not confident enough to try finding my way through this maze."

She tried concentrating on the conversation rather than the warmth coming from his hand and the stupid nickname he continued to use to address her. The one she secretly liked, because as silly as it was, it was more than anything else her family had ever given her. "I don't blame you. This place gets weirder the longer we stay here."

The soft crackling of the magical fire nestled in the wood cradle began to fade until only the sounds of their soles clicking over the color-shifting tiles could be heard. Thea kept glancing up at the large body of water hanging above them, wondering if the monster hiding in the depths would make its appearance again.

Bajun happily kept up beside them, fluffy tail high in the air while they slipped through passage after passage. She felt blind at that moment, thinking she was going to run into something that wasn't there and using touch over sight to help guide her. She could hardly trust her eyes here.

Finally, after several turns that had her mental compass spinning uselessly in her head, Rafe stopped pulling her along and let go of her hand when they entered yet another passage. Three books were stacked neatly on the ground a ways away, and he picked one of them up and handed it to her. "These three were the only ones that mentioned sand wyverns. All the other books in this section were about other dragons. Which, by the way, if we ever see the ocean I'm not getting anywhere near the water."

Thea flipped open the faded leather tome in her hand and gazed over the yellowing pages. "Why, scared of hydras?"

"Do you even realize how *close* they can get to shore?"

Thea frowned at the thought. Now, she may never step foot in the ocean either. She shook the thought from her head. "Are you sure these are the only books? You didn't miss any?"

"Well, this is the part I needed you to look at." His voice dropped, and the serious tone that bled into his words had her looking up from the book in her hands. She watched him take a few steps back and gesture to the shelves next to the section they were currently standing in front of.

Interest piqued, she placed the book back in its pile and neared the shelves. One book on the shelf caught her eye in particular, for it was badly burnt and nearly a pile of ash. She went to grab it, to test how well it stood up to human touch but stopped when the one beside it was singed as well. And the one next to it, as well as the ones above and below them. She stepped back, eyes widening as all the books were some variation of burnt. Some were more charred than others.

"Rafe," she whispered, turning to gauge his response. "Why would the Skrittish keep a large number of burnt books?"

His mouth was set in a grim line, eyes hard as he scrutinized the shelves. He looked older, more earnest. "I wouldn't know, but I do know that from the looks of the more legible ones, they are incredibly old."

"How old?" She picked up a leather journal and began skimming through its contents.

"It's hard to tell." His eyes swept over the books before falling on her.

She handed him the journal and stepped back enough to see just how many burnt books they were dealing with. The collection expanded all the way down the hall until she had to crane her neck in order to see the spines. "There's so many."

"There's also nothing of significance in them," he continued, placing the journal back on the shelf, though he seemed to second guess its placement. He made a face but didn't move it. "They all hold common knowledge. It's everything that we already know."

She shifted closer to the shelf and pulled a different book out, grimacing when some of the corner fell away. "Who's we?"

Rafe shrugged. "The Coven. The ones I read just look like duplicates of—"

Thea gasped sharply, and her eyes flew to his. He gave her a small nod of understanding. He didn't even need to finish his sentence.

"Do you really think…" She had to be sure.

He cast a determined look at the bookshelves. "It's got to be."

"What's got to be?"

Rafe cursed in surprise while Thea jumped at the sudden smoky voice that sounded like it was right beside her ear. She spun around and pinned Bajun with a glare, but the feline only grinned that disturbing smile of his.

"Don't do that," she hissed. She'd completely forgotten about the cat.

"Do what?"

"You know what."

"Okay, okay. You said you would answer my questions on these books, Bajun. Can you tell me why they're burnt?" Rafe asked, resting a hand on one of the books in question.

Bajun spun around in an excited circle before throwing his massive paws to the ground with a heavy *whump*. He straightened and puffed out his chest as he replied with, "A spirited jig it dances bright, banishing all but darkest night. Give it food and it will live; give it water and it will die."

Rafe sighed in aggravation. "A fire."

The creature's tail twitched in the air as he chirped loudly. "Yes! They were burned in a great fire."

"I already knew that!"

"Did they belong to the old Coven?" Thea asked in exasperation, getting straight to the point. She didn't want to be here talking in circles all day, and if these texts did belong to the old Coven, there might be remnants of spells to de-summon the ferals popping up all around Aeristria's core.

Overly long black whiskers twitched. "If you want me, you'll have to share me, but if you share me, I will be gone. What am I?"

"A secret," Thea and Rafe said in unison. When Rafe raised his eyebrows at her, Thea only shrugged. "Context didn't make that one very hard."

Bajun flopped down on his back and stretched, giant paws curling and uncurling in the air. "Correct. Yes, these books were collected from the old Coven and brought within the Secret Society."

Thea's brows furrowed. "Secret Society?"

The cat flipped over and stood, bowing with a stretch and wide yawn. "Oh my, I've said too much. How silly of me. It's nothing but boring stories anyway. Stories I could go on and on about, but it would bore me to tears."

Thea wanted to ask if this Bajun creature could really cry, but she feared he'd only sing-song her another riddle. Besides that, this so-called Secret Society was much more interesting. This library had to be their base, and if Ell sent them here then that meant she was part of this society. Did that make Winona part of the Secret Society too? The Second Chosen was too crafty to not know about it, especially since she entrusted Ell with the mission scroll in the first place. The fact that these books belonged to the old Coven, if Bajun could be trusted, was a veritable goldmine of information at their disposal. Everyone believed the old Coven's library had been lost in the great fire. Who had managed to salvage them, and why had they been placed here? Did Winona know about these books? If so, why wasn't she using the information to her advantage?

"Can you tell us if there's a de-summoning spell here? Does it even exist?" She asked, turning hopeful eyes to the creature.

Bajun cocked his head to the side, and the angle was positively unnatural with how far it bent. "As I said before, I have spoken far too much. I cannot tell you any more."

Thea held back a sigh. Just when they thought they had a lead. One spell cast, two spells rebounded.

"Well, if you can't tell us about that or about this Secret Society, can you tell us about the Draconians?" Rafe's question brought her back to the here and now, and she looked up to meet Bajun's odd gaze. The amber color intensified right before it shifted into cat-like green, but the round pupils still threw the Spellweaver.

"With the rich, I am blue, with the poor I am red, with the dead I am cold but with the living, I am hot instead, what am I?"

Rafe squinted at the creature and crossed his arms. "Blood, but what does that have to do with anything?"

"It is their blood you seek," Bajun purred, and his long, bushy tail twitched high in the air.

A thud from behind them had both Coven members turning around and finding one of the books Rafe had picked out strewn across the floor, opened to a page titled "Blood of the Beast." Thea went to retrieve it first and waved away the dust that floated up into the air. She turned back to the creature but he, too, had up and disappeared as quickly as he had come.

"Does no one do proper farewells around here?" She sighed out her irritation before wondering aloud, "Why does he think we need the sand wyverns' blood?"

"I have no idea, but half of that book is in Ernimoen. I already checked."

Thea groaned out loud and slid down the shelves to sit on the floor. "Are you serious?" Then, more quietly, "The Skrite told us we couldn't take anything out of here! And I doubt they want more people barging into their Secret Society, so bringing Blythe in here is probably out of the question."

Rafe shrugged one giant shoulder. "Can you call her and have her read the pages?"

Thea huffed. "I could try, but how long will that take? Is that even allowed?"

"Since when, in the past month, have rules stopped you?"

A beat of silence passed. Thea's lips thinned as she glared at her partner. "Fine. I'll call her." She pulled out the crystal ball from her pouch and scowled at the little sphere. She closed her eyes and thought of Blythe's name, face, and persona, but nothing happened. She opened one eye when she didn't feel the familiar whirring in her hand from the energy connecting, but all she saw was an image of a crystal ball with a red X over it. The words "cannot manifest" flickered under the bottom of the X.

"I can't call her," she said grimly, lips twisting into a scowl once more. "I guess the wards the Skrittish have in place are blocking magic from connecting to anyone outside the library."

Rafe sighed beside her. "Maybe Bajun will come back and find us another journal to read from."

"I doubt there'll be another journal with the same information in it." She ran her finger over the glass, dismissing the image, but before she could stow the crystal ball back in her pouch, another picture, smaller in comparison, caught her attention. "What is this?"

Rafe leaned over her shoulder. "What is *what?*"

"This," she said as she pointed, her finger grazing the surface of the orb. The image disappeared abruptly, and a distorted version of the floor became visible through the glass.

"Did you break it?" Rafe asked, reaching for the orb.

Thea scoffed and jerked it out from his reach. "Of course not." She angrily tapped at the glass, but the image only froze. "Great," she snapped. She probably really did break it.

Two out of two, Thea, great job.

Except, the image, blurred as it was, unfroze, but a little icon at the bottom of the sphere appeared. She touched it with the tip of her finger, and the same image appeared again. "What the…?" she wondered aloud, more to herself than to anyone else.

"What?" Rafe asked again, clearly confused.

She flipped to the first page of the book. "Hold on a moment. I'm on to something." She ignored Rafe's silent question and hovered the orb over the contents. She steadied her hand, and the image became clear enough that, if she spoke the language, she'd be able to read what it said. Carefully, she tapped the glass again, and it froze just like the last time. Her breath hitched when the little icon popped up, the image of the book's words clear as day. Rafe stood over her, watching her every action as she flipped page after page until she had taken still-shots of the entire journal.

"Assuming that's all the information we need, we can go," she said as she closed the book and placed it back on the shelf. She glanced over at the shelves containing the old Coven books and bit her lip. "On second thought…"

She held out her crystal ball and snapped a wide shot of all the books in their varying degrees of disrepair. Then she paced closer and captured several images of the more legible journals, tomes, and texts.

"Now we can go."

Rafe nodded beside her. "I remember the way back, I just have to count my steps." He placed his hand on the wood of the bookshelves and began walking down the hall. Thea shoved her orb back into her pouch and quickened her steps to catch up to him. She didn't dare break his concentration by speaking, though she figured he'd find it again effortlessly. The man could concentrate better than anyone she knew, but she guessed that was why he was such a good Summoner.

Thea got lost in the ceiling again, if one could call it that, as Rafe led them out of the library. The water rippled, casting the nebulas in different shades of mauves, golds, and sapphires while the stars sprinkled throughout shined brilliantly like zircon. The large shadow was back and moved elegantly through the depths, pausing just over her head as if studying her in curiosity.

Whatever it was, it was old. She could feel it. Knew it without knowing how she knew it. The library was much stranger than the sanctuary and the Dark Market combined, that was for sure.

She was so engrossed in the...being, whatever it was, that she nearly ran into Rafe's back once he came to a stop. She dropped her gaze and looked around, noting that they were back in the hall they'd entered through the sewers. The crackling of the magical fire suspended in its cradle welcomed their return with eager *pops* and *crackles*. Standing beside it, a Skrite was peering into the white flames while its whiskered snout moved as if it were chanting under its breath. Quiet clicking sounds coming from the alchemist mingled with the noise of the fire and floated up into the air like embers. Its mouth stopped moving abruptly, and, ever so slowly, it swiveled its head toward them even as its body remained facing the blazing sphere.

Chills erupted along Thea's spine as she felt the gaze of the creature settle on her. Words abandoned her as the Skrite's body finally turned in their direction. Grace accompanied its fluid movements when it proceeded up the hall.

Did you find the answers you were looking for? It whispered in her head as it neared them.

She swallowed. "Uh, yeah. We were wanting to head out now."

"Thank you for your hospitality," Rafe said from behind her.

The alchemist came to a stop a couple of feet from them, and once again Thea was reminded of the sheer height the Skrittish imposed on humans.

Should you find the need to return, remember the rules lest I not be here to remind you.

Thea didn't know why—it wasn't like she could tell where the creature was looking—but she felt like the words were directed solely at her. Maybe it was just her guilty conscience.

Leave with nothing more than gained knowledge, it had said.

Well, technically she hadn't taken anything.

Rafe placed a hand on her shoulder and started to pull her in the direction of the brick wall they'd entered through. "We'll remember them well," he vowed. His hand dropped down to Thea's, and he gently tugged her along.

She allowed him to haul her to their exit without fuss. Her mind was still clouded with all the information she had learned during their short visit. She'd found a spell for Namara, some general information on the desert, discovered the possibility of a Secret Society—but she wasn't sure just how reliable Bajun could be—an entire book on the Draconians, and what could potentially be the treasure trove that was the old Coven's athenaeum.

They were almost at the exit when she peered up again. The dark mass was motionless above them. "Wait," she said, and Rafe released her. His brow furrowed in silent question, but Thea was already looking back to the Skrite that hadn't moved from where it stood.

One of its ears twitched under its hood, so Thea could only guess she had its attention. She looked up again and pointed at the beast floating under the ceiling's surface. "What is that?"

The Skrite regarded the water above them for a long moment. Without the sounds of soles over tile, without their voices, without the questions strumming through her mind, quiet engulfed the library. Even the fire seemed so far away now. After seconds became a full minute, then two, Thea wondered if she had overstepped her boundaries and took a hesitant step back.

When the being's words entered her mind, they did so out of nowhere. The Spellweaver startled as the Skrite murmured, *Essentially, it is a collection of many lives lived. Eternal, it has no beginning. No end. A prevention of madness; a vault of secrets. It is many things, yet living is not among them. Not even I know what it has seen, what it holds within itself.*

With those final words, they were subsequently dismissed. The rough sound of brick scraping over brick notified them that it was time to leave. Thea stood stupefied as the being in the water disappeared once again in the depths of the lake. She jolted when she felt Rafe's hand clasp onto hers once again, and as he began pulling her out into the sewers, she didn't miss the way the Skrite was staring at her as they left.

It continued to watch her until the wall closed back up. For a split second, she thought she saw the shine of beady black eyes under its hood.

Chapter Seven

A Cursed Cure

Thea had been in this position before, but she found herself in it more often than not over the last month. Now, that Namara knew she wasn't coming on an incredibly dangerous mission, Thea was once again being held hostage in Rafe's huge garden tub in the only bathroom in the house. She was already pruning, but like Hellfire was Namara going to let her get out.

The bathroom was smaller than Cressida and Blythe's master suite, but it was roomier than her own. She visited her duplex every so often, however, because she was paired up with Rafe, the Coven had cut her rent into thirds for the time being. Now, she was surrounded by burnt orange walls with copper finishings and the smell of tree sap emanating from the green candle in the corner. She was convinced she'd spent more time in this bathroom than her own, even when she did live in her duplex.

She'd bought herself and Namara fitted outfits made of some sort of dark blue synthetic fabric for these specific occasions, and, though the costumes—called swimmers—were a bit revealing, they had both seen each other in more scandalous situations before. The kelpie was currently moping in the tub, seafoam green arms crossed over the edge as she rested her chin in a scowl that resembled more of a pout in Thea's opinion.

"Hey," Thea said as she splashed her pet. "We've been through this. It's no different from when you weren't able to come with me to the Dark Market or when I was at the sanctuary the last time."

Namara glared over her shoulder. "When I was out cold, you made a deal with a black sorceress, bartered with an imp for information, went to the Dark Market without approval, got lost in a—"

"Okay, okay," Thea relented with her hands raised in defense. Not her best example, she realized.

Silence descended upon them. Thea awkwardly moved her toes in the water while Namara sullenly stared off into space. Thea's lips thinned in annoyance, and she shoved her toes into the kelpie's ribs. The creature jumped and let loose a warbled yelp.

"Knock it off," Namara growled, swiping the air with her blunt claws.

"Are you really going to spend my last night here ignoring my existence?" Thea snapped back.

Namara gave a harsh sigh before she slipped her whole body under the water without another word. Bubbles forming on the surface of the water was her response.

"Seriously?" Thea grumbled, rolling her eyes skyward. "You're such a child."

She looked back down to find the kelpie poised under the water as black, bottomless eyes pinned the Spellweaver in her spot. The hairs on the back of Thea's neck stood on end, and her heart tripped up in her chest. She prided herself on her instincts, and though she cared for Namara more than she had ever cared for any of her family, her instincts were currently screaming *danger*.

"Nama—" She didn't get the rest of her name out before the demoness sprang from the water and launched herself at her owner. Wet, green arms grappled around her neck as Thea choked back a surprised gasp. The jostled water that threatened to slosh over the side of the tub soon began to calm into gentle waves, lapping gently at the porcelain. Namara refused to move. Her head was shoved into Thea's shoulder, blocking the Spellweaver from viewing her face, while her long inky strands drifted in the settling water.

Thea waited for the kelpie to speak, but after a long, tense moment of silence, she realized Namara wasn't going to. It was only when she placed her arms over the creature's back did she notice Namara was trembling. Alarmed, Thea tried to lean back to see her pet's face, but Namara's iron-grip around her neck made it impossible for the Spellweaver to move even a hair's breadth away.

"Namara, what—"

"I don't want you to go," whispered a small voice, muffled and fragile. "What if you get separated, or eaten, or dehydrated or…or…" She leaned back, onyx eyes neither red nor teary, but full of sorrow so deep Thea was at a loss for words. Kelpies didn't have the ability to cry, even in their human forms. It was her most ironic trait. Looking over her distraught pet, Thea knew she'd never be able to handle tears. She was completely out of her element as it was.

"I won't…" She trailed off, unable to make a promise she might not be able to keep. She couldn't promise she wouldn't die. She didn't know what was going to happen during this next mission. This was easily her most dangerous yet.

A tremor racked the kelpie's body, and Thea gingerly wrapped her arms around pale green shoulders and let Namara lay back on her chest. This was the only way she knew how to offer comfort.

She couldn't tell her about the spell. Not yet. She couldn't give Namara false hope. There would have to be a trial run, and testing out a spell for the first time in the desert was not something she was willing to do.

"I don't want to go either," she confessed at last, resting her chin on Namara's head. "I'll do everything I can to come back, though."

Namara was quiet for a long moment, and Thea let her pull her thoughts together without interrupting. She felt the kelpie sigh against her. "As long as you try… I'm sorry for acting this way. Especially on your last night here."

Thea shook her head. "You have nothing to apologize for."

Shortly after that, they climbed out of the tub and went their separate ways for the night. Thea rubbed the towel over her damp head as she walked into the guest bedroom she'd been occupying over the last couple weeks. The sun was already long gone, but she had been mindful enough to light some candles before her impromptu bath. They lit the room in a soft glow, enough for Thea to see into the drawers and pull out some pajamas.

After both towels were tossed in the hamper, she flopped her whole body onto the bed and sighed heavily. Tomorrow was going to be impossibly long. If she were smart, she'd fall asleep fast and get as much rest as she could. Eyeing the crystal ball beside her, cradled in a pewter dragon claw stand on the side table, curiosity got the better of her.

She reached over and grabbed the orb. Touching the little icon at the bottom, she brought up the images she'd taken in the library. She flicked her thumb over the surface and found the images moved faster that way, and she quickly found the first page.

He said half of it was written in Ernimoen, but maybe it's just being translated?

Reading tiny words by candlelight wasn't one of her better ideas, but she had to know. She may not get the chance to read much on their journey considering they'd most likely be traversing at night to escape the heat. She continued to thumb through the pages, engrossed in the information over the Draconians. Nothing on their blood so far, but there was plenty on their diet, origins, ability to hide in the sand dunes, and how to make peace with them. Ernimoens were mentioned sporadically, so Thea made sure to ask Blythe about them tomorrow.

Hours passed, and Thea felt the soreness creep into her thumb. She'd tossed and turned, held the orb up in the air to read as well as tucked it close to her face. Her eyes were becoming dry and heavy, but she kept promising herself *one more page.*

Finally, she got to the chapter reading "Blood of the Beast." She sat up straighter against the pillows, eyes flying over the words. "'...the blood of a sand wyvern is a sacred gift that cannot be taken by force. It must be freely given, for if blood is drawn from a wyvern against its will, the blood will turn to sand. Should one obtain an offering, the magic properties imbued will heal any illness, magic or otherwise...'" she continued to mumble the words aloud, eyes drifting over the image until one passage stopped her cold. The glass slipped from her fingers and fell against her chest. It rolled off her body, but Thea didn't feel where it landed.

She blinked. No. She'd read that wrong. She was tired, after all. The letters were tiny—they'd blurred together, and she mistakenly read it as something else. Numbly, she felt around for the orb and grasped the cool crystal. She brought it back to eye level and read it one more time.

The dark arts plague the human body and violate the soul. Once a caster has delved too deep, there is often no mercy outside a swift death to be found. A sand wyvern's blood can purify even the blackest of hearts, but there is always a price for the path a magic wielder chooses. Should the wielder embrace the darkness and let it riddle their being, the blood will nonetheless purify this evil, but the soul will ascend to the beyond and leave the body behind.

Thea leaned back against the pillows and let the glass ball drop from her grasp once again.

Cressida was going to die?

A sharp knock on the door of her room startled her. She scrambled to grab her orb and dismiss the images on the glass, plopped the sphere back in its cradle, and scooted back on the bed. "Yes?" she asked, trying her best to sound calm and normal. She quickly ran a hand over her hair to smooth the flyaways as if she'd been doing something she wasn't supposed to.

The door swung quietly open, and Thea wondered if Namara was going to come in and request more attention. It was Rafe, though, who walked through the door. He held his favorite brass candelabrum in one hand. The thin, milky white candles flickered and cast shadows along the sharp planes of his face.

Rafe had always been a little old school when it came to...well, everything. The man didn't own a single lamp, and the candelabrum he was currently holding had been handed down to him by his late grandmother.

Her heart squeezed pleasantly in her chest at the sight. She watched his eyes drift over her quickly, knowing he was taking in her in silky soft shorts and loose shirt, and her heart repeated the action. It was nothing scandalous. It was something she'd feel comfortable wearing around the house, but in the quiet, cozy atmosphere of the bedroom where it was only the two of them, this felt...intimate.

"I was wondering if you were still awake," he finally said. "I saw the candlelight and didn't know if you forgot to blow them out."

She huffed a quiet laugh. "Between you and Namara, it's a wonder you let me eat without checking to see if I've died."

"Careful, you'll jinx yourself," he chuckled, propping himself up on the frame of the door.

Thea rolled her eyes. "I was just about to go to bed. You?"

"Yeah." He nodded, looked like he wanted to say something, but instead straightened and said, "Well, we have to rise early. I'll leave you to it."

"Wait." The words were out of her mouth before she could stop them, and her eyes must have been just as wide as his. "Um..." Why had she stopped him? Rafe leaned back against the door frame and smiled gently at her. She only felt her face growing hotter under the look. But she was not a little girl. She could tell him what was on her mind, what she wanted. Taking a deep breath, she asked, "Will you stay?" then, to clarify, "With me? Tonight?" By the time she finished speaking, her heart was pounding in her chest. She didn't want to be alone, but it was more than that.

Rafe appeared stunned at her request, but it was smoothly overshadowed by the same gentle smile. His eyes lightened in the flames' flickering lights. "Didn't get enough attention from Namara earlier?"

Thea's fingers curled into the covers. "It's not...the same. I," she licked her lips, mouth suddenly dry, and noticed Rafe following the movement before flicking his eyes back up to hers. "I want you by my side." There. She said it. She looked away and let a shaky breath of air escape her. "I don't know what to expect from this mission. I told Namara the same thing. I wanted to promise her that I won't die, but I can't. You can't promise me that either, so...for tonight..." she let the words trail off, eyeing everything in the room but the man in the doorway.

Rafe didn't answer her right away. She heard him blow out the candles, and the light from the threshold died. He shrugged off the frame and nudged the door closed before his quiet footsteps brought him deeper into the room. His bare feet found their way into her view, and when she looked up, blue-green eyes filled her vision. His forehead found a place to rest on her own, his breath mingling with hers, the emotions in his gaze matching her own. She found herself unable to speak, for there was nothing worth saying.

When he climbed into bed, they said nothing. She found solace in his embrace, ear pressed against his chest while listening to the calm force of a strong heartbeat. She envisioned a future where it would beat solely for her before her eyes closed, and they didn't open again until the next morning.

Chapter Eight

Sometimes Things Do Go According to Plan

The start of their last day in Tolvade was an early one. The stars were no longer out, but the sky was transitioning to that in-between color of midnight and baby blue, broken up by golden rays of light. It was warmer, and while normally Thea would have been elated to finally be rid of the cold, her impending mission was weighing heavily on her mind. That and the news she found out last night.

"We travel light," Rafe announced over their meager breakfast. An egg, some spinach, a handful of nuts, and some fruit would be enough to sustain them while being light enough to not spoil in the heat they'd soon be facing. "One change of clothes, two at the most."

Thea wrinkled her nose. She had packed as many pairs of underwear as she could. She was not about to develop rashes from the Summoner's survivalist methods. She said nothing though, merely nodding as she munched on apple slices. She caught Namara's gaze on the other side of the butcher block island and smiled faintly when the kelpie made a similar face.

"We'll have all our weapons once we stop by Smithson's, I've packed two canteens, our pouches are full of dusts..." he kept going, but Thea tuned him out. This was the second time he'd gone over their list, and rather than nag him, she let him reconfirm everything in his head aloud. She was convinced the mental checklist was more for him than her anyway.

"Does he do this with all his missions?" she asked Mokana quietly to the side, sliding the rusalka her ration of raisins. She had only gone on a handful of missions with him before.

The creature greedily stabbed them with her dagger-like claws and sucked them off each nail. "Yeah, but he tries to hide it from the others. His squad is used to it, but he's still self-conscious about it." Mokana went back to munching her portion of walnuts, cracking them open effortlessly in her demonic grip. "He told me once he was the most organized out of all his older brothers in keeping up with his younger siblings."

Thea snorted. Her eyes tracked the Summoner as he went over the last details of their operation, imaging him mother-henning his little brothers and sisters so none of them got lost on a family outing. She reached for her breakfast mug, a blend of sliced fruit, yogurt, and milk, spelled with a protection enchantment as well as a dash of long-lasting endurance magic.

Mokana cracked another walnut with ease, swallowing the pieces whole, shell and all, as she said, "He'll be like this with your children, too."

Thea choked. Chunks of pink smoothie spewed all over the table, and she nearly fell out of her chair from the convulsions of her sudden coughing fit. Rafe was at her side in an instant, but she only waved his concern away, croaking "water" at him when he refused to leave. While he rushed to fetch her some, she leveled her best glare the rusalka's way. Mokana winked casually and cracked another walnut.

A glass of water was shoved in her face, and she nodded her appreciation at Rafe before cautiously sipping some of the liquid. "Thanks," she grit out after a minute, voice still scratchy.

"What was that all about?" Rafe asked, his attention still on Thea, but when she refused to answer right away, he turned his scrutiny toward his pet. The rusalka simply shrugged with a wide grin, unperturbed by his gaze.

Rafe sighed and carefully picked up the mug, avoiding the spittle clinging to the glass with a grimace. "I'll have to make you another one if you want to survive this journey."

Thea cleared her throat. "Fine by me."

They left soon after with Mokana and Namara in tow. Thea had her sickle strapped to her back, a sling with her clothes and essentials over one shoulder, the leather canteen bag over the other, and her pouches full and secured to her hips. She wore a light, long-sleeved shirt, corset, and thin, cotton pants. Her outfit covered her skin from head to toe because the more revealing the clothing the more water would evaporate from the body. Surviving the desert was akin to surviving the jungle, only Thea had kept all those clothes on to combat insects sucking at her blood and possibly gifting her with some disease. Lastly, her hair was pulled back into a low ponytail to cover the skin on the back of her neck but keep the strands out of her face.

Rafe wore something similar with his staff holstered on his back, his own bag and canteen over his shoulders, and his new boomerang clipped to his pouches. To combat the cold, they adorned their Coven grade cloaks and set out. They were approaching Smithson's just up ahead, close by the public library, the small Raen & Bowes Banking branch, and the Coven's back training area. The runesmith workshop shared a wall with Spellvana, and as they neared, Thea noticed a group of Summoners exiting the herb store with pouches now filled to the brim. They weren't anyone she recognized, but they nodded in greeting at Rafe and, by extension, her as well.

Rafe opened the door and allowed the three women accompanying him in first. The tinkling noise reached their ears as the warmth of the shop seeped into their bones. The smell of coffee mingled with the scents of geranium, almond butter, clove, and white musk from the spell shop next door. Early mornings meant potion brewing for Spellvana.

A man the size of an ox with light brown hair cropped short and streaked with silver throughout came up to the reception desk. He had what looked like a permanent scowl chiseled into jutting cheekbones. Bridget must be out.

"How can I help you?" His deep baritone voice asked.

Thea stepped up the counter, fishing her coin purse out of her belt. "I'm here for a pickup? Thea Bauer."

The man picked up the clipboard and flipped through a few of the pages, the object dwarfed comically in his huge hand. "You had…" he squinted at the dainty writing Bridget had written the information down in yesterday, "the arrow launcher runed with fatal enhancement?"

"Yeah, how's she looking?" She wouldn't admit it out loud, but she was nearly trembling with excitement, eager to get her hands on the new weapon. She kept her face a neutral mask, though, even as the man turned toward the back of the shop and brought out the arrow launcher.

"Nice, basic model. It'll get ya through a few battles before the rune needs a recharge. That'll be seventy-two gold and six silver even," the man said as he laid down the weapon.

A steep price but a fair one. Thea still winced as she ran her crystal card through the merchant processor.

"Ugh," she groaned as they exited the shop. "Winona better pull some strings and get us a bonus incentive."

"No one told you to pick the arrow launcher," Namara piped up from behind her owner, quickly fixing the strap on Thea's left thigh that now held the new weapon. There was no more room on her back.

"It felt right," she defended. "I can't wait to try it out." She shifted so she could see her leg better, and her eyes practically gleamed as the light hit the rune piece affixed just below where the arrow would materialize.

Rafe nodded as he rested his hand on his holstered, tri-bladed boomerang. "When we get out in the open, we should practice a bit. I've never liked depending on a weapon before I can get a feel for it."

Thea hummed her approval, and the rest of the walk to the sanctuary was quiet.

"And that's why we need your help," Thea said as she ended her long-winded explanation. They all stood in Cressida's parlor, perched in various positions on the twin sofas. Blythe wore a wide-eyed expression, mouth dropped into a little "o" before the woman launched off the couch with a squeal.

"*Se keterael i!*" then hastily translated with, "This is perfect!"

Thea blinked at the unbridled enthusiasm. "So, you'll come with us?"

Blythe threw her hands up in the air. "Of course! You will not believe me, but I have my bags packed to leave for home already!"

Rafe's brows scrunched. "You were planning to go to the desert by yourself?"

"You are never alone in the desert," the sorceress held up a finger, pointing at the Summoner with a wide smile. "And, *eau*, I was. I knew the *evez voshep*—sand wyverns—held magic properties from the legends I learned as a child." Her sparkling brown eyes dulled and the excitement in the air practically fizzled. "If I had known earlier about…" She let go of a shaky breath. "I could have convinced her to let me go looking for them, but once I found out, she had already summoned Asmo." She appeared ashamed, and Thea bit her lip to the point it nearly bled.

She couldn't tell Blythe. She couldn't let her know of Cressida's impending demise. They needed her guidance, and Thea understood how selfish that was of them, of her, to withhold such vital information. Blythe deserved to know, but if she did know, would she still accompany them? Would she still leave her oath-bound's side, knowing it was all for naught? It wasn't something Thea was willing to gamble on.

Cressida would die, yes, but others—many others—would live.

"When did you find out?" Namara asked, pulling Thea from her internal battle. She glanced up from her spot on the couch's arm and watched Blythe shyly tuck a stray lock behind her ear. It must have fallen from the ram horn updo.

She peered at Thea from under her long, thick brown lashes framing to her large doe eyes. "It was actually when you came to visit the kelpie—er, Namara. You two started fighting, and I did not want to intrude. I left, but I wanted to make sure everything was alright…and I overheard everything."

Thea paled. "Everything?" she queried quietly.

"*Eau,* everything." Blythe appeared ashamed again, but a small smile that didn't reach her eyes managed to surface. "I tried to bring up the Draconians to Cressi afterward, but I did not want to be too obvious. She placated me, but I understood she was not seriously interested."

Thea bit her lip again. "I'm sorry you had to find out that way."

Blythe nodded in return. "As am I."

A tense quiet settled around the group. No one really knew what to say, and just as it was about to become unbearably awkward—Thea could see Rafe shifting in his seat—a knock on the door startled them all.

Blythe's face brightened, and she bounced out of her seat. "*Ú*, this day could not have been planned out better if we tried! She is right on time!"

Thea watched the sorceress bound over to the door and leaned over the edge of the couch, hoping to see who had come to visit. Her jaw dropped when an imp walked through the door.

"Ma?"

Chapter Nine

Ma is… A Lot of Things

Leslie's mother strode through the door with a wicker basket hanging from the crook of her arm, looking like Adalith's most influential agricultural tycoon. She was decked out in a large, bright white fur coat with a hood that was three times the size of her head sheltering her from the elements.

Ma whipped her head around and dislodged the hood, and the imp's short, white pigtails sprung up in the air. "Thea, baby, what a' you doin' here?" She put the basket down on the desk and shrugged out of her coat, revealing a long-sleeved velvet dress embellished in white frill. Her signature pearl necklaces and jeweled rings glinted in the light. Blythe swooped in to grab the furry garment and placed it on the coat rack by the room opposite of Cressida's.

"I was just going to ask you that, Ma," Thea jumped up from the couch and hurried over, bending down so the imp could give her a firm hug. Ma was such a hugger.

When she let go, she peered around the Spellweaver and narrowed her black, beady eyes. "Don't think I don't see you in there, Rafie. Get in here and give mama some suga. Wait, you cut your hair!"

Thea snickered at the put-out sigh she heard coming from the office but did Rafe a service of not watching him get his cheeks pinched. Instead, she looked to Blythe for answers over Ma's arrival.

Blythe giggled at the scene going on behind Thea, impartial to the Summoner's suffering, but she addressed Thea's silent question, nonetheless. "I informed Ma the other day that I was going back home, and that I was looking for a sitter to watch over the sanctuary. Someone trustworthy that could handle the ins and outs of Srbeveara, and she graciously offered her services."

"Oh, darlin', I owe ya for what you did for my poor Sammy." Ma abandoned Rafe's cheeks to turn around and place her leathery hand over her heart and she exhaled in exasperation. "That nephew o' mine. Can't do anythin' wit' 'im. I told that imp too many times to quit pokin' Quincy's amoni demon, but *oh no*, no one listens ta Ma. Got his hand burnt to bits for his troubles."

Thea's eyes widened. Amoni demons looked cute with their owlish bodies and serpent tails, but they vomited flames when provoked. Not Hellfire, thankfully, but their fire was fierce enough to cause third-degree burns regularly.

"It was no trouble at all." Blythe smiled sweetly and waved away the imp's concern. "Let me go grab my bags, and we'll be out of here shortly."

"Sure, sweetie. Take ya time. You got nothin' ta worry about." Ma turned to the group of Coven members loitering in the hall. "So, where ya guys goin'?"

"The desert," Rafe mumbled, using his thumb and forefinger to rub his sore cheeks. Thea twisted around to seek out Namara and found her wringing her wet hands while Mokana fiddled with her hair.

"You two staying here?" It would set her mind at ease if the two pets were in a place guarded against ferals, but she would understand if they couldn't. Wouldn't want to make the guests uneasy.

"If it's no trouble," Mokana piped up while Namara shrugged her shoulders. She was still pouting, but at least she wasn't pitching a fit.

Ma's rings clinked together as she clapped her hands excitedly. "Oh, we can have girls' night! Don't you worry, I make a mean soggy cockroach casserole!"

Thea had to look away lest Ma see the look of disgust clear as a crystal ball on her face, but she was saved when Blythe came bounding down the staircase with a couple of bags slung over her shoulders. She was in a different outfit, too. In place of the blue dress, she wore red harem pants and a loose, baggy, and see-through red top that covered her arms and torso. Under it, a white crop top. Her shoes were open-toed sandals.

Thea's eyes widened. "Are you going to be warm enough in that?"

Blythe only grinned. "I managed to equip a warming spell. Although, I believe I made it too warm. I'm already sweating," she said as she fanned herself with her hand.

Rafe rubbed the bridge of his nose and sighed. "I should have thought of that. We can't keep our cloaks with us once we hit the desert."

Mokana skipped over to her owner, a wry smirk forming on her ghostly lips. "Why don't you leave it here and equip a warming spell then?"

Warily, Rafe stepped away from the rusalka and lifted his thick cloak away from her reach. "I don't have the specific dust for it." Thea watched them curiously, not understanding what was going on. She knew Mokana to be crafty, but even she couldn't understand what the demoness was plotting.

Oblivious, Blythe set down one of her bags and began digging through it. "I have more than enough! You can leave your cloaks here." Finding the right thing, she pulled out a gold drawstring pouch and tossed it the Summoner's way.

"Look at that, Rafe, she has more than enough," his pet said in mock-surprise as she slipped closer to her owner.

Catching the pouch one-handedly, Rafe had let down his guard. Mokana struck while she could and dug her fingers into the part of the cloak covering Rafe's broad shoulders and yanked the garment off of him in one fell swoop, choking him in the process.

"*Gah*—you little—!"

She laughed at his furious glare and danced out of his reach, waving the cloak at him as if he were a bull. When he took a threatening step in her direction, Thea intervened before he could strangle the rusalka back, but even she could not hide the amusement in her eyes.

"All right, all right. If we're all done acting like children, we should go before the sun climbs any higher in the sky."

Rafe rubbed his neck and continued to glare over Thea's head. "I'm not going to miss you," he stated angrily, to which he only received another girlish giggle.

Ma let out an airy sound, propped up on her elbows over the desk she stood behind with a wide smile. "You young whippersnappers remind me of my youth. What I wouldn't give ta be three hundred years younga again."

Thea, naturally, was up to date on the lifespan of a lot of creatures, including imps. She hummed as she slipped out of her cloak and said, "You don't look a day over four hundred and fifty, Ma."

The imp's cheeks dimpled, and she waved a flashy hand the Spellweaver's way. "Thea, baby, flattery will get ya everywhere." She sighed again, but it was more exasperated this time. "If only my Leslie would settle down wit' a nice girl like you an' give me gran' babies."

Handing over her cloak to Namara, Thea contemplated telling Ma just where they were taking her only son while Rafe conducted the temporary warming spell on her. She nibbled on her lip and decided to remain quiet, unsure of what Ma's reaction would be and added it to the growing list of secrets she felt guilty about. She knew she'd get an earful when they all got back…*if* they all got back.

She sent a sympathetic smile the imp's way but quickly changed the subject, directing her next comment at Namara. "Keep the cloaks hidden. In fact, you two stay hidden altogether. We don't need someone else from the Coven dropping by and seeing unattended pets hanging around. Blythe," she turned to the sorceress, who'd been gazing off toward Cressida's office. "We're teleporting to the edge of town. Can you help Rafe set up the teleportation spell?"

"Of course!" Back to her chipper self, Blythe skipped over to the big Summoner and sank down to the ground to start setting up with the ingredients handed to her.

"Ma," Thea turned to the imp again. She was watching curiously, beady black eyes sparkling, but her large ear twitched and she angled her head in Thea's direction to let her know she was listening. "Do you have anything we can use to teleport to the other side of town? We were going to walk, but since you're here..." she hoped she wasn't overstepping, but she figured Ma liked her well enough.

The imp's eyes brightened, and she straightened up a little, though she stood no taller than Thea's hip. "Oh, sure. Lemme see, lemme see…" Her little, weathered hands frantically searched her body for something until she pulled out a little black booklet and flipped it open. "Where ya headed? Adalith, Lorvo, right outside the Coven? You name it, sweetie."

Thea pulled at the strings of her tunic around her neck, already feeling a little hot from the warming spell. The loosely fitted corset over it might have been a mistake. "Actually, right outside of Borlimane would be ideal."

Ma looked up from her booklet in surprise. "Ya know," she began in her high-pitched voice, "I usually got beings wantin' out'a Borlimane, so this is a first for me. But if you're sure, Thea baby." She flipped the pages of the booklet, each with a small item taped to the inside, but frowned when the last page she reached was blank.

Thea peered over the desk. "Something wrong?"

Ma hummed. "I don't have anythin' here, but wait just a minute..." She patted down herself again before raising one of her hands up to her face. "How 'bout a hangnail? I'd give ya some of my hair, but Mama needs every one of 'em to keep her lookin' this good."

Thea tried not to grimace. "That'll work."

Rather than just the part that had been torn, Ma pinched down and ripped the whole nail right off her finger without so much as a wince. She tossed it in Thea's direction, but the Spellweaver dodged the bloody claw and watched it fall right into the pile of ingredients on the floor. Rafe jerked back out of disgust and even Blythe looked a little queasy. The two water demons off to the side were each holding their clawed hands to their chest with wide eyes.

Ma was something else.

Thea whirled around to shout, "Ma, what in the—" but stopped when she saw the imp inspecting the new claw that had sprouted out of the nail bed, shiny and white in comparison to others that were painted blood red.

The imp flexed those deadly weapons and grinned. "That feels so much betta." She peered over her shoulder at everyone staring at her aghast. "What?"

Blythe swooped in to rescue them, and gently pulled a stupefied Thea over to the circle. "Ms. Ma, you're welcome to any of the nail polish I have in my room right there. Please take care of Cressida while I'm away."

"You're too kind, sweetie!"

Namara hurried over before the spell could take place and pulled Thea in for one last hug. Neither would ever admit it, but as Thea squeezed the kelpie without fear of hurting her, anyone could see that there was more than the owner-pet bond between them. Namara was the sister Thea had yearned for growing up, rather than the true demon she'd been dealt with. She closed her eyes and held on a little longer, silently vowing she'd get that water spell to work when she got back.

"You should hurry," Namara softly whispered and pushed her owner back. Before Thea could question her, the kelpie continued. "You jinxed yourself earlier. I can feel something powerful coming, but it's not feral. Something that monstrous can only be tethered to a Coven member."

Thea cursed but nodded in agreement. "Go hide in the healing waters." She turned to Rafe and Blythe and held out her hands, closing her eyes when she felt their warmth clasping her palms.

Chapter Ten

Battle at Banshee Bog

Thea was weightless for only a moment before her feet hit pavement. She blinked the blurriness from her eyes and took in her surroundings. As expected, they were right outside Ma's apartment and where Thea had asked Leslie about a tethering stone a few weeks ago. Across the road a little ways was the Grim Bean, and while the coffee shop was busy like it normally was, the street they were currently on was dead. Not even the imps or the other assimilated creatures were wandering around in the back alleys.

"I'll call Winona. It shouldn't take long," Thea said to Rafe as Blythe eyed the coffee shop curiously. "Do you want to go get something?"

Rafe nodded, eyeing the sorceress and the growing excitement bubbling out of her. "Might as well. No coffee, though," he directed at Blythe who deflated slightly. "It dehydrates you."

Her dark eyes regained their sparkle even as her thick brows pinched together. "We do not have this drink in my village. I see why now."

Thea watched the two cross the street and snorted at the wide-eyed looks Blythe was gathering by those who hung around the establishment. Oblivious, Blythe continued chattering the Summoner's head off, though Rafe didn't look like he minded. Thea pulled out her crystal ball and pictured Winona's arrogant face, and the orb lit up in her palm. The Second Chosen answered immediately.

"I gather you've collected the sorceress without any troubles?"

Thea's lips thinned into a grim line. "Just barely. Namara said she'd sensed someone from the Coven headed our way. There's no doubt they detected the teleportation spell, but I'm hoping Ma is able to cover for us."

Winona nodded with eyes sharper than silver knives. "She's craftier than most give her credit for. Do you know who was arriving?"

"No," Thea said with a shake of her head. She felt rolling anxiousness churn in her stomach, and she could only hope that Winona would keep them out of trouble. A lot of things were riding on hoping, she knew, but it was the only thing she *could* do.

"Relax, Spellweaver Bauer. I'll handle any reports involving Srbeveara personally. What's your location?"

Thea swiveled the crystal ball to face The Grim Bean's direction. "Just send Leslie on home." She brought the orb back to face her.

"Very well. He's already been briefed on the situation. You and Summoner MacBain are well within your rights to act accordingly if he steps out of line. Good luck out there." The lines around Winona's eyes relaxed, and she appeared the most content Thea had ever seen. However, before Thea could see if smiling was within the Second Chosen's capabilities, the connection cut.

"What did she say?"

Thea's eyes snapped up to see Rafe approaching her with drinks in his hands. Blythe bounded over to Thea with a gleam in her big brown eyes, her dainty hands holding a weird looking concoction of blended berries.

She shoved the crystal ball back in her pouch and took the drink offered to her. "She's sending Leslie over now, and she'll handle any paperwork regarding Srbeveara that comes in. Which there's bound to be considering we teleported right before they arrived. That just screams suspicious activity." She took a casual sip, but her eyes widened in surprise at the flavor that burst forth onto her tongue. She furrowed her brows at the cup as if looking at it more closely would divulge its secrets. "What is this?"

Rafe's lips quirked upwards, highlighting the twinkle in his eyes. "It's just a smoothie," he paused for a moment. Then, "with unicorn milk."

Eyebrows raised, Thea took a second look at the drink in her hand. "You got that ornery unicorn to produce some milk?"

Blythe butted in with a look of confusion. "He did not seem very ornery at all. Are there two unicorns at this shop?"

Now Thea was the one who was confused. She'd only been there once recently, so she couldn't say for sure if there were two unicorns working there or not.

Realization washed over Rafe's face. "Oh, I forgot, you haven't seen the inside since we went undercover. The Grim Brean was shut down for poor food preparation and hygiene, and now it's under new management. Did you know gremlins have OCD?"

This was not helping Thea's confusion at all. "OCD? It sure didn't look like it. I saw one chuck a cup onto the floor—which was disgusting by the way."

"Oh yes, it is a fact," Blythe stated with an eager nod. "While technically it is a human-only ailment, gremlins are born with brain functions that closely resemble those that suffer from OCD."

"What does that have to do with anything?"

"Well," Rafe said after another sip of his own drink, "after I filed a health inspection request form, a buddy of mine went and took a look and had the whole place shut down. We uncovered Sheldon had been faking the assessment grades since he came into management."

Thea wrinkled her nose. "That's disgusting."

"Yeah," he concurred. "You should see the place now. It's probably cleaner than HQ's medical wing. I never thought gremlins could look so...non-gremlin-like."

"What do you mean?"

Rafe rubbed his chin as words seemed to escape him. "I don't know...happy? Content? You know like...not how gremlins usually act."

"Are you guys jabbin' about tha Grim Bean?" A new voice slid into the mix, full of scorn, and Thea fought the urge to rub her temples.

"What I wouldn't give to be happy or content right now," Thea muttered to herself before turning to see Leslie strut up the sidewalk in his typical garb. His long leather trench coat was weighed down with faulty items he tried selling to the poor souls wandering the streets on the wrong side of town. His toady-skinned hands were shoved into the pockets of the coat, and his beady black eyes were trained not on them but on the cafe.

"What have you got against the Grim Bean?" Rafe asked when the imp joined their rag-tag team. He appeared genuinely curious.

"We can talk and walk now that you've finally decided to join us," Thea quipped and turned to lead them down the even shadier parts of town into Borlimane's borough, Herbon. She may not have Namara by her side, but her reflexes were quicker without the extra weight of her cloak, and the two Coven-exclusive weapons on her person made for a clear enough warning to the people here.

Leslie scoffed behind her, the rough drag of his trench coat accompanying his words. "It ain't like I took my sweet time gettin' here, toots. I had ta walk all tha way from tha Coven on foot! You'd be su'prised at how many beings refused ta give me a ride! I look like an honest imp, don't I?"

Thea snorted. "Leslie, you're the most dishonest imp I know, even after meeting Sheldon."

The creature made a scandalized sound, but Blythe was quick to come to his rescue. "I think you look very handsome," she said with a beaming smile.

Leslie's black, beady eyes widened and glanced over the sorceress before turning back to Thea, pointing his thumb back at Blythe. "I like her. Why can't ya be more like her?"

Why can't you be more like her?

Thea grimaced at the sharp echo of her mother's words that rang loudly in her head. So the ghost of her family wasn't gone like she'd hoped, after all.

"Why can't you be more like Ma?"

"Ouch, ya bringin' out tha claws, ain't ya? Still a honey badger, through an' through."

Thea felt her eye twitch, but she remained silent and took a sip out of her drink. She only half-listened as the imp started back up on the Grim Bean, complaining about the state the establishment was in and how the new manager was going to lead it to ruin.

"Have you even been inside the Grim Bean yet?" Rafe asked seriously, to which Leslie grumbled something unintelligible at first.

"Does'en matta. That new managa don' know what he's doin'! Mark my words, that dump'll be undawater by next week!"

Thea glanced behind her to see Rafe's secret smile as if he knew something they didn't. He caught her eye and winked at her, and she felt her face heat at the gesture. She quickly turned away.

As they walked past the tattered sign welcoming them into the place that was more or less a dark stain on the map of Aeristria, chipped cobble roads and shabby stone houses spread out before them. Stone architecture was the norm in much of Borlimane's borough as wood of any kind would rot away in the humidity and occasional floods that sprang from the heavy rain. The large wall that ran along Herbon's entire border and separated the town from Banshee Bog helped stop feral first-tier demons and wild creatures—such as banshees, obviously, rusalkas, bunyips, and bog trolls—and prevented mass flooding coming in from the swamp. However, flooding still happened here more than it did in Tolvade.

Herbon was a poor, rundown town and reflected most of the people within its borders. That didn't mean they were all bad, just desperate, but that could be equally as dangerous. It was why it was so vulnerable to blood mage activity. People wanting off the streets and warm food in their bellies turned to the bloody craft when promised these things. Once a blood mage, always a blood mage though. There was no getting out of the cult once you were swept in. If practicing blood magic didn't kill you or you weren't eliminated by a Summoner, the blood mages would hunt you down if you tried to escape.

"I want eyes looking out at all angles," Rafe commanded from behind her. She heard the slip in his tone. He was now the man she went to the Dark Market with; a leader, on alert, and merciless. He had to be because this was blood mage territory. "Blythe, Leslie, that includes you two. We're down two comrades so you will act in their place." His voice brooked no argument, though Leslie looked like he wanted to make a snide comment.

"Eyes out," she hissed at the imp without looking his way, and she heard his teeth clack together as he shut his mouth. Out of all of them, he looked the least concerned. As he should, considering this was basically an imp playground. No one bothered the assimilated creatures that left the Coven after their owners died, but humans—especially those ranked in the Coven—were given less hospitality than the stray dogs that prowled around alley dumpsters.

The cobblestone streets of Herbon were covered more in half-melted, mushy snow puddles than actual stones. The Cleansers didn't even bother coming out this far, and rations were handed out by the old rickety welcome sign rather than on the front stoops of the townspeople. Some hooded figures were headed that way now, but they would be disappointed to find out the Cleansers were not there at the moment. Thea felt the urge to tell them so, but she remained quiet. You only spoke to the beings you knew in Herbon, and Thea didn't know anyone. That was a lesson she had learned personally.

Rafe nudged Thea's right arm twice, and she moved with him as he spoke. "We'll take the next right and pass by the Coven's outpost. It's a straight shot to Banshee Bog from there. I'm not sure who's patrolling today."

Herbon needed Summoners patrolling it at all times. Because of the large population of blood mages that mingled with the other less than innocent populace, the Coven built a separate outpost out here where Summoners not on the roster for summoning spells or Dark Market raids were stationed.

"Chances are you'll know them," Thea commented off-handedly and took a sip of her drink, keeping her gaze on two people whispering to one another by the mouth of an alley. Suspiciously, they fled as soon as they spotted the group, but Thea resisted following after them. She'd leave all questionable behavior to the Summoners on duty.

"It pays to have connections," he said seriously.

Thea went to reply, but before she could take her next breath, she caught movement darting out of the corner of her eye. A blast of white light engulfed her vision, and then she was slamming headfirst into one of the rundown buildings with such force her whole body was immediately overwhelmed with searing pain. She felt everything in that moment. The throbbing on the side of her head, the sharp scrapes along her chin and right cheek, every nerve fizzling with adrenaline that had her fingers burning hot at the tips.

Her scream bordered on an enraged growl as the pain was swiftly replaced with hot anger. She heard her name being called, but it was muffled by the ringing in her ears. Her hearing was shot.

She shoved herself away from the brick and whirled around, coming face to face with a person charging full speed at her. She couldn't see their face, covered by the dark hood of their cloak, but they were not someone she knew. Instincts took over, and the thoughts in her head silenced. She dodged their attack and threw a punch directly at their jaw. She felt the bone connect with her knuckles, felt the skin split on her hand, but the pain didn't register. Before she could think out her next move, she whipped her leg up and slammed her heel into the side of their head.

Someone else took their place, a man with stubble on his chin, but his eyes were covered just as the last person's was. After he was down, another person appeared. More and more were starting to swarm her, striking out and clipping the edge of her ear with a blade and one person delivering a swift punch to her gut. Her corset softened the blow, but just barely, and it was difficult to fight in it.

She grabbed a fist full of dust from her belt and flung it into the air, screaming "Emblaze!" and watched as the silver dust ignited into burning embers and pelted her assailants with fire. Her fist connected with a man's sternum, sending him careening into two other figures, and then she was whipping out her dagger. She locked eyes on the men righting themselves from the ground and growled, "This was my favorite corset," before slicing the strings down the back and ripping the destroyed brace from her body.

She felt her lungs expand as she heaved a large breath of air. Just as the trio stumbled on their feet, she flung herself at them. Hooking her arm around one's neck, she threw him back on the ground with a hard thud and brought down her boot, snapping his ankle. His screams went unheard as she rounded and grabbed the arm that was reaching for her with a sword in hand, twisting the wrist painfully back. The person dropped to the ground along with their weapon, their wails joining in with their comrade's, but he too went ignored as Thea tunneled her focus on the remaining foe. He rushed her with a scream of rage, and she dodged, light on her feet, pivoted, and grabbed the man from behind. Swift as a river, she twisted his jaw up in a way that would send him into an unconscious slumber. None would die, but they'd be down until the Summoners showed up. Then they'd be carted off to jail.

She turned and ran. Her eyes had begun to burn from the smoke that had come from her emblazon spell, and she felt blood dripping down her chin and the split skin of her knuckles, which throbbed in pain. She could feel the scraped skin of her knees as she ran back to where she heard more fighting.

She found Rafe around one of the closest buildings, surrounded, livid, with ice-blue eyes blazing. He grabbed a fistful of cloak from one figure around the back of the neck and hurled them into the nearest building with one arm. A pained howl and gasps for breath left their mouth. Rafe spun, collided his heel with another assailant's jaw, and swung his sharp staff into the body of another figure that came at him.

Thea shoved both hands into her dust pouch and dove into the fray without a second thought. She cast a blinding spell and then a weakening effect on their attackers by flinging plum and sapphire dust, but it wouldn't last very long. All she could do was rely on her training to keep herself alive. She ducked, punched, dodged, and as a last resort grabbed her amulet. Murky purple encased her body and sent one assailant flying back when they went to jump her. When it faded, she grabbed her blade, and it was like an extension of her arm.

Pain flared in her left leg where a knife had been suddenly lodged. She pushed past the intense stinging and gripped the handle, ripping it out of her body to prevent it from hindering her further in battle. It hadn't been deep, and it hadn't struck somewhere vital. She'd heal when she had the time to dig out her blue dust. Now, she'd send the amateur who did this to her into an early grave. She found the man at the edge of the battlefield running in her direction. Fast as a spell, she flung the knife right back at him. It sunk into the flesh of his neck, and down he went.

"They keep coming!" she heard Rafe yell at her side. She turned quick enough to see for herself and—Goddess above—he was right. Hordes of cloaked black magic users were pouring out from every alley, crevice, and corner.

Thea ripped off the arrow launcher clasped to her leg, and the rune that was enhancing the weapon glowed a deep, blood red. Relying on her swift reflexes, she shot down three figures before they could reach them. She grabbed Rafe's bicep and yanked him into running with her. "Where's Blythe and Leslie?" she shouted over the noise, never taking her eyes off the path in front of her. Someone jumped out ahead of them but took an arrow to the heart before he could make a move.

Rafe peered over his shoulder and aimed his staff at something behind him, and a ball of energy shot out of its razor-sharp hoop. One of the buildings took the most damage, collapsing down into the path and blocking their aggressors from reaching them. It would only slow them down, though.

"I sent them up ahead and told them not to stop running until they reached Coven base!" he yelled back, and with a destination in mind, they hunkered down and sped off in the direction of the outpost.

"Why are they attacking us?" she bellowed in frustration, knowing Rafe couldn't possibly know the answer to that any more than she would.

"I don't know," he answered, throwing his arm back and blasting another building with a ball of golden energy. She felt sorry for whoever was living in the stone hovels, but this was the price to pay for living in one of the worst places in Aeristria. "But if they think we're going down easy, they've obviously never dealt with the Coven."

"Or if so," she gasped as she ran, "they probably picked on Hunters fresh out of the academy. The next guy I get my hands on is going to wish he never signed up to that cult!"

Rafe shot another ball of energy, and it demolished an already abandoned, crumbling house into nothing but chunks of stone. "I don't think they're blood mages!"

"I don't care who they belong to! It's obviously organized, whatever it is!"

A cloaked figure jumped out in front of them and cut them off, forcing them to skid to a stop. Thea raised her arrow launcher and Rafe his staff, but the golden emblem on the man's chest was his saving grace.

"Aaron!" Rafe sighed in relief, but there was no time for a happy reunion. Aaron lifted his hand, dusted in green pigment, and shot out a glowing blast of light. The gold, jewel-encrusted armlets on the man's wrists glowed, amplifying the spell. A huge firebird—similar to a legendary phoenix—blurred past them, the heat of its feathers leaving baked air in its wake as its terrifying screams echoed through the destroyed borough. Screams, human this time, erupted behind them, and all three Coven members were on the move again.

"We'll hold off most of them," the gruff man said. He already had a bloody wound forming on his tanned face and dripping into his amber eyes. "You guys get out of here!"

"We can help!" Thea insisted, incensed he would even think they weren't going to stay and aid the others.

"Every Summoner in the Coven is on their way, and from what I gather from your little foreign friend, you're on a top-secret mission. Plus, you don't have your partners with you. So go, but I expect you to take out those that slip past us. Got that, MacBain?"

"Wouldn't dream of letting them escape!" was his quick reply.

The large rock wall separating Herbon and Banshee Bog lay ahead, and as Thea and Rafe sped toward it, Aaron fell back and began blasting the black magic users that were after them. There was no time to stop and help each other over the barrier. Relying on all the strength she had in her, Thea launched herself at the wall. She bit back a groan as her forearms scraped against the rough surface, and her fingers ached as they bit into the sharp crevices as she hauled herself up to the top. She slung her non-injured leg over the edge and straddled the stone structure, taking only a second to survey the drop on the other side before she jumped. She landed with a roll and grimaced as her clothes now clung wetly to her back from the soggy marsh ground.

She spotted Blythe in the distance, trying her best to hold off a reddish-brown, stump-like bog demon with glowing silver palms raised in defense. Leslie stood in front of her with a large tree branch and swung aimlessly at the creature.

"What's a matta wit ya, ya braindead or somethin'!"

"Run!" Thea called to them desperately and grabbed Blythe's hand as she sped past the two, jerking the sorceress into running with her.

"What is happening!" Blythe's panic-stricken voice cracked.

"I don't know," Thea replied, "but help is on the way!" She could already hear more explosions happening behind her, a sign that more of the Coven was coming down in all its fury on Herbon.

"We got company!" Leslie panted from behind them.

A blast of white light barely missed them, only confirming that some of their assailants had managed to slip through the Summoners and climb over the wall.

She could hear labored breathing behind her and the extra footsteps speeding up to her. With as much strength as she could, she hurled Blythe ahead of her and spun around. Her fist connected with the figure trailing them, sending him flying back from the momentum. Her eyes widened when more—a lot more—could be seen scaling the wall. Why were they after her and Rafe so badly?

She couldn't answer that question now. Running blindly would only get them killed, and a shared look with Rafe affirmed that they would need to stop and fight. She took out her sickle, let its weight steady her, and aimed her arrow launcher and began shooting. Down one, down another. Their screams echoed throughout the forest. She swung her arm back and sent her sickle flying, cutting down a man trying to go around them and get to Rafe, who was preoccupied with blasting energy orbs out of his staff and slicing through opponents. Blinding light brought luminosity to the dark swamp over and over again.

Thea wrapped the chain of her sickle around her arm and let the weapon drop close to the ground. When a black magic user reached her, she swung her fist again, the chains biting into her skin as they made contact with her attacker. She kicked out and booted them into the nearest tree. Just as she was about to end the fight, the massive roots came alive and constricted around the person's body. Her black, clouded eyes were revealed, bulged out in horror, and her screams were swallowed up by the ground as she was dragged under.

Thea froze at the scene. This was exactly why people didn't venture out past the wall. She snapped out of her daze and began screaming, "Don't touch the trees!" Someone else was getting caught up in another root trap and, fearing it was Rafe, shot her arrows at it until it broke off and the body came falling to the ground. Only then did she realize that was *not* Rafe.

The man shot a beam of magic at her, and she jumped, landed on her hands, and bounced back onto her feet. "Seriously? I just saved your life!"

The figure didn't hesitate to try and shoot her again, but a blur from behind him took away his chance to act, throwing him to the ground and revealing that his eyes, too, were blacked out entirely. A howling swamp troll made of moss and gray skin, no hair, and red eyes bellowed above the man in victory before it tore into his shoulder.

Someone grabbed her from behind, and she reacted blindly by swinging, but her wrist was caught, and ice blue eyes stared into her own. "We need to run! More of those are on the way!"

She didn't need to hear anymore. All the activity must have alerted the bog dwellers, and they were soon going to be well fed for the rest of the night. Without another word, they took off running into the swamp. The further they distanced themselves from the sounds of fighting, the more the sounds of swamp surrounded them. Guttural croons of creatures cooing played against their eardrums. Hissing, spitting sneers erupted as they dashed through green puddles, the sounds of squelching as loud as the disturbing trills of birds overhead.

Bark cracked and groaned as the massive trees around them came to life. The branches that had coiled down low to the ground swung at Thea and Rafe as they passed. Thea shrieked as the mossy limb slammed down behind her. The splinter of wood echoed through the swamp and mingled with the chirrups of crickets screaming their hollow songs in the underbrush.

Thea skirted another walloping tree branch and jumped over roots tearing themselves from the ground. She landed with a splash into a murky pond, and something gurgled threateningly from under the surface. A webbed hand, gray and mottled, shot out from under the water, but a blast of energy knocked it back. Thea sprang over its sizzling and smoking flesh and didn't look to see if it was coming after them as she continued to run.

She spotted Blythe's brightly colored clothes in the distance. The trees were coming to life around her, about to swallow her up, but she was holding them back with her magic as best she could. Her palms were now red, and fire flickered in her hands, leaping from her to the branches that tried to attack. Leslie was holding a measly dagger and waving it around like a madman. A perfectly aimed vine slapped the knife out of his hands, and the sound of tearing reached Thea's ears.

Rafe aimed his staff at the trunk just before it snatched either of them, and Leslie swore loudly at Blythe's side from the splintering explosion of bark. Thea reached out and snatched the imp up in her arms, and they tore through the rest of the forest in their flight.

Her heart was beating so fast, practically pounding against her rib cage, and she didn't think it'd slow down until she could no longer hear the demonic warbles of the swamp or the wails of her assailants being ripped to shreds in the distance.

Chapter Eleven

What Shines More Brightly?

Thea dropped Leslie in the dirt as soon as they burst through the treeline. She didn't even see the filthy—quite literally—look he sent her as she collapsed to the ground. Her chest heaved in exertion, and her open mouth gasped loudly as she desperately tried pulling air into her lungs. The pain was coming back to her now that her adrenaline was draining, but the tremors in her fingers made the digits nearly useless at the moment.

They were still covered by the trees' shade, but the sun was out with a vengeance. The bright blue sky was blinding to look at after just exiting the dark cave that the deadly forest tried to imitate. Thea sluggishly threw her arm over her eyes to help block out the light.

After what felt like forever, her breathing began to slow, and her heart began to calm. She could still feel the spikes of adrenaline course through her body in tiny shivers, but she could curl her fingers at will more easily, could feel the coolness of the metal chain still in her grasp, and could feel the throbbing ache in her leg much more intensely.

"Not a good start to our journey," Rafe griped from somewhere off to her side. She hadn't lifted her head yet to find out where he sat, and she didn't have the desire to remove her arm just yet, but she heard in his voice just how winded he was.

She let out a breathless laugh. "To think I've been bored the past couple of days." She winced as the throbbing in her hands, face, leg, and pretty much everywhere else was becoming more pronounced. She hauled herself into an upright position with a grunt and blinked at the intensity of the brightness all around her. Her tawny curls had flopped over her shoulder, and now more hair was loose than tied back. She pulled the ribbon out but left her hair down for now, instead reaching for her canteen.

"Is your job always this dangerous?" Blythe piped up from Thea's left. She had fallen in an exhausted heap as well, though she looked a little more out of breath than the two Coven members did. Thea supposed that was due to Blythe's job—whatever that actually was—being less physically demanding than either of Thea or Rafe's.

Thea chortled and Rafe looked exasperated as he rooted around for a healing spell, but they both nodded regardless. Blythe's eyes widened.

"It's a wonda none of yous a' dead yet," Leslie, the least winded out of all of them, snippily remarked from slightly behind Thea. She could still hear him patting himself off, trying to get rid of the debris sticking to him.

"It's not ideal," Thea continued, digging through her belt for her own healing spell and grimacing at the wet, disgusting state of her shoes and pant legs. "But danger comes with the territory. We're here to protect the beings of Aeristria first and foremost. It's not a productive day if someone isn't coming home without a broken bone or healing from a harmful spell hurled at them."

"It's not always so bad," Rafe amended when Blythe paled.

"Don't lie to her. It's not like she's joining the Coven herself," Thea said as she finished up her healing spell and jumped to her feet. She ran her hands through her curls and began combing them back into a low ponytail once again.

Rafe, also done with his healing spell, rolled his eyes and began shortening his staff until it could properly fit on his back again. "No, she's only joining two Coven members on a classified mission that could likely get us killed." He winced when he realized what he said, but Blythe actually looked a little better now that she was on her feet.

Her chocolate doe eyes observed the landscape surrounding them, and a reserved smile graced her features. "The desert is dangerous, and we all must respect the power it has. However, my family and I have crossed it many times. If you two know Tolvade like the back of your hand, it is the same with me and the Golden Sea."

Thea squinted as she took in the land properly for the first time. It didn't look like a golden sea right now, despite its name. The ground beneath her boots was packed, solid, and crackling from the sun. Banshee Bog's treeline stopped abruptly, stretching both right and left until disappearing from her sight, but not one tree encroached from the pack into the desert. It was like an invisible barrier kept the two ecosystems separated.

What trees were out in the desert were few and far between with skinny branches that didn't look like they had the strength to pull anyone underground. Dry, yellowed grass was the only other vegetation abound, but it wasn't rolled out like a lush carpet like Thea was used to but rather clumped in splotchy patches that left room to walk in between. Past it all, in the far distance—so small Thea had to squint her eyes to see it properly—was some kind of rock formation jutting up into the air.

Blythe brushed off the dirt clinging to her outfit and looked around. She peered left, nibbling her dry lips as she said, "I believe that way is marsh territory. That is where you will find the lions. They rarely come out this way, but I would much prefer to not test that theory by staying here for much longer."

Thea had never seen a marsh lion before, but she also didn't want to anytime soon. Seeing Helena's manticore was close enough, though at least normal lions didn't have wings, spiraling horns, a spiked tail, and a corpse face. She strapped her arrow launcher back onto her leg, and the rune that had been softly glowing faded completely, situated her sickle back in her holster, and hiked her rations bag higher over her shoulder.

"Well, I'm ready."

Rafe nodded and hiked his own bag over his shoulder, and Blythe picked up her belongings from the ground. Leslie was the only one still dusting himself off, but since he didn't really have anything packed, he grumbled that he was ready to go too.

"What's out there?" Rafe asked, gesturing with a nod of his head, presumably in the direction of the distant boulders.

"Please tell me there's food," Leslie pleaded, groaning up at the cloudless sky. His head lolled to the side, and his beady eyes squinted at Thea's canteen. "Hey, Honey Badger, lemme have some of that wata."

Thea grimaced. Just the thought of Leslie's lips wrapped around her canteen was enough to send shivers down her spine regardless of the sweat that was starting to build up from the heat. "No way."

Leslie gaped at the Spellweaver, clearly offended. "C'mon, I'm dyin' ova here!"

"I carried you most of the time we were running. Besides, can't imps like...survive without water, or something?"

"Another stereotype? Really? We camels now?"

Blythe pointed dead ahead, toward the rock formation. "That is where we will be going. Those rocks may look really small now, but it is the canyon where my village resides," she answered amidst Thea and Leslie's bickering.

Rafe was also ignoring them, humming in thought. "I thought Ernimoens were nomadic?"

"I'll 'ave you know imps do need wata ta live. In a pinch, we can suck on fresh eyeball juice ta get us by. What's it gonna be, Honey Badger?"

Thea tossed the imp a dirty look. "That's disgusting."

Blythe giggled, whether over Rafe's query or Leslie's ridiculousness, Thea wasn't sure. "You are partly right. Large groups of us travel the desert looking for food and items we can craft into wares or tools, but some of us have to stay behind to watch the children and elderly. There are other nomadic people like us, but they are much further out in the desert. We probably won't see anyone on this side."

"I'm gonna keep complainin' until ya hand over that canteen," Leslie persisted, earning himself another dirty look. He only shrugged in the face of Thea's anger. "It's your fault I'm here in tha first place."

It's your fault he's here in the first place. It's your fault any of you are here in the first place.

It's your fault! Her sister sneered.

It's all your fault, her mother chimed in.

It's always your fault!

"Urgh, fine!" Thea shoved the canteen into the imp's stubby arms, glowering as she did so. She looked away and muttered, "Don't put your lips on it, and don't drink it all. You wouldn't be so thirsty if you got yourself something to drink at the Grim Bean."

Leslie *tsk*ed, uncapping the canteen and muttering, "Says tha one hurrien' us ta go."

"What was that?"

"I didn't say nothin', Honey Badger. Ya might need ta clean ya ears out every once in awhi—ow!" Leslie kept his grumbles to himself after that and quietly nursed his surely bruised arm. Who knew honey badgers could pack such a punch?

As they continued walking, Blythe prattled on and on about information on the desert. Thea understood some of what she was saying when it came to the hardy flora due to the book she'd skimmed over the other day, but mostly it went in one ear and right out the other.

"I do not know about these trees in particular, but the ones near my home look similar, and they produce many fruits in the spring and summer months. I have not seen them in the city, which is a shame, because pomegranates, figs, and apricots are some of my favorite delicacies. Although, we may arrive in time for the almond harvest, but I believe you have those already…"

Thea didn't mean to tune out Blythe completely, but her mind had started traveling elsewhere. Why had they been attacked back in Herbon? Why had they been pursued so adamantly? Their assailants were clearly under the influence of black magic, but she had never seen a user's eyes completely black as if they were a demon pulled straight from the underworld. All of them had been that far gone. They had appeared to be mindless, working on basic instinct, and their goal was to kill. Yet, that had clearly been an organized attack. Were the two figures Thea spotted before the attack the masterminds behind it all? Were the cloaked figures heading up to the town's border in on it, too, or were they innocent in this? It still didn't make sense why she and Rafe had been targeted so viciously.

"I can't wait for you to see them. Moje and Gitk' are a sight to behold, especially at sunset. They look like they could come to life."

Thea came back to the conversation, but she didn't say anything, even as she was totally lost to what Blythe was talking about now.

"Ahh," the sorceress suddenly sighed loudly and twirled about with her arms up over her head, spreading her fingers wide as she reached for the sky. "I missed the sun. It does not feel the same in the city." She looked right at home with a genuine smile on her face.

Thea merely hummed in agreement. It definitely wasn't as sweltering as she expected it to be, but it was very hot. She was almost thankful she had shed her corset. What had she been thinking?

"I'm surprised it's not that hot," she mused aloud. "Isn't the desert supposed to be hot enough to bake blood?"

"Ya got a weird obsession wit' blood, Honey Badger."

"No one was asking you, Leslie."

Blythe interrupted before another bickering spat could commence. "Just be glad it is not summer. If it was, you would be correct. However, because it is not so hot during the day right now, it is dreadfully cold at night."

Thea nodded, indeed thankful. The air was exceptionally dry as it was, and the wind was like an oven being opened against her face as it blew over the desert. Still, the sun was nearly at its peak in the sky, and Thea was enjoying the warmth on her skin. She rolled up her tunic sleeves and loosened the drawstring at her neck, basking in the heated breeze that was much more forgiving than the icy fingers that skittered up into the openings of her clothes back in the city.

She didn't seem to be the only one enjoying the change in temperature. Leslie had his arms up too, crossed behind the back of his head with a pleased glint in his bottomless eyes, trench coat dragging behind him in the dust. Even Rafe, who much preferred the cooler spring and fall seasons, ran a hand lazily through the short hair on his head and sighed contently.

They hadn't been walking far, but Blythe, even amidst her frolicking, had sidled up front and had become the leader of their ragtag team.

"You headed somewhere in particular?" Thea asked after they reached the top of a grassy hill. Her eyes widened at what stretched out before her. The desert had transformed from dusty loam and scattered, dead-looking foliage to sand the color of melted gold. It rose and dipped in peaks and dunes, and the wind whipped across the granules and created dizzying patterns.

Blythe laughed lightly and gave Thea an exasperated look. "You were not listening when you were arguing with Leslie earlier, were you?" Thea had the decency to look sheepish. Blythe only waved it off like it was nothing. "We are headed to my village," she said easily, gazing out into the desert with familiar recognition painting the lines of her face. "We will not be there by nightfall, so tonight we sleep under the stars."

Thea watched with rapt attention as the woman began her descent down the hill, her sandaled foot sinking into gold. The woman's face twisted a little in what appeared to be pain.

"What's wrong?" Rafe asked, joining the sorceress in the sand. He frowned as his balance seemed to falter when the weight of his shoes separated the ground under him. Leslie waddled his way down the bank, but he did the strangest thing and shucked his shoes clean off. His gross, grubby toes scrunched in the sand, and a most pleased expression tugged at his weathered face.

"I forgot just how hot the sand could be," Blythe giggled, watching the imp bask in the heat.

Leslie tossed back his head and sighed. "I think I'm in love."

Thea made her way down last and crouched, scooping up a handful of granuals in her palm and hissing as the heat kissed her flesh. She shook the rest out of her hand and glanced at the imp. "Does that not hurt?"

Leslie rolled his head around until he met Thea's gaze and gave her the most deadpan stare he could manage with his all-black eyes. "Born in Hell, toots, rememba?"

Rafe snorted.

Thea rolled her eyes and stood. "I've never seen you ditch your clothes in the summer back in the city," she quipped, then shuddered at the mental image that conjured before adding much more quietly, "and thank the goddess for that."

The imp shrugged and went back to basking. "Eh, city's too humid for my tastes. Ain't no moista in Hell. It's a dry heat."

Thea nudged the creature as she passed by him but paused in her rebuttal as the sand shifted oddly under her feet and took her by surprise.

Oh, this was going to be *so* much fun.

"Enjoy the dry heat while you walk," she said as she regained her footing, only for it to be momentarily lost again when more loose sand shifted and sunk away from her feet. She groaned in annoyance.

Blythe laughed, walking like a natural through the terrain, her footprints light over the yellow, grainy substance without sinking like a stone. "You'll get used to it soon enough. You should have seen me walking around when I got into the city. The ground there is so hard and solid, and I kept tripping for a solid week." She laughed again, this time at herself as the memory seemed to tickle her pink.

Rafe joined in her merriment, adding with a smirk, "You say that, but watch us get used to walking on sand and forget how to walk on solid ground when we get back."

"Oh, goddess above, don't say that," Thea griped, but her small smile betrayed her annoyed tone. "The last thing I need is to be waddling around like a duck Tassie got ahold of."

Rafe threw back his head in laughter, Blythe tried stifling her giggles behind her hand but failed, and even Leslie snickered at the image of fearless Thea Bauer waddling down the streets, quacking madly.

Hours passed. The sun now hung low in the sky, transforming the pale blue into hues of berry wine and scarlet and marigold while the intense light of dusk made the already golden sand glow as if molten magma brewed below its surface. Thea paused to take it in, eyes landing on the scarce desert plants dotting the landscape. One plant she had read to steer absolutely clear of was the cacti that jutted out from the ground. Their flowers were beautiful, bright pink or red or some in-between color that contrasted starkly against the arid background, but they were sharply guarded by thousands of long barbs just waiting to prick a finger.

"We should camp here for the night," Blythe announced, speaking for the first time in a while.

"We'll have to split up into teams of two—Leslie, you're with me—and use the last couple of hours of sunset to bring back any sort of kindling for a fire," Rafe said, Summoner mode on. Thea nodded at the order and dropped her belongings onto the sand with the rest of them. The arrow launcher was heavy and starting to weigh down her leg, so she unhitched it and left it behind too. Her sickle would be more than enough to reap dead bushes from the ground.

"I believe we can find something that way," Blythe said and pointed off to the right. A golden dune was currently blocking their field of vision, but she trusted the woman's judgment. Blythe may normally act carefree and airheaded, but this was her homeland. She probably had names for every dune out here. So it wasn't surprising when they climbed the sandy hill that there was, in fact, a bunch of dead-looking grasses clustered together. Thea made sure to stay far away from the cacti that were present as well. The ground was far more level here than back where they dropped off their things.

Thea grabbed the first prickly bush and used her sickle like a scythe to chop off a good portion of it. "We should make camp here instead."

Blythe was busy wrangling a bush from the ground, but she stopped to look up and smile hesitantly at the Spellweaver. "While normally I would agree, we did not bring any sort of tent or barrier against the desert. Things like scorpions, biting beetles and fire ants prefer level ground like this that has plenty of hiding places." She nodded toward the bushy grass in her hands. "Like this."

Thea blinked owlishly. "Noted."

Blythe managed to finally yank the prickly bush from the ground, but by the time she had, Thea had already collected four more. The sorceress merely giggled and helped pick up the extra bundles.

Rafe was compiling his and Leslie's findings, a bunch of similar dry bushes and dead twigs, together when they arrived.

"Ugh," Leslie groaned, inspecting his hands with an unimpressed frown. "My hands ain't hurt like this since Ma locked me out. I had ta scale tha apatment buildin'." He flopped down onto the ground with a huff.

"Set that off to the side for now," Rafe directed, ignoring the imp's complaints. "We'll use it to keep the fire going throughout the night."

Thea nodded, dumping her kindling on the side of the encampment and watched as Blythe did the same. "I'll take first watch tonight."

The sorceress perked up as she was dusting herself off. "First watch?"

"It's where we take turns sleeping to ensure the safety of the group," Rafe informed whilst sitting down with his legs folded in front of him. He began rummaging through his pouch and brought out a dark brown bundle of what appeared to be dry leaves wrapped in twine. "That's not something you do when traveling through the desert?"

He placed the bundle in the center of the kindling and then dug out some of his dust, whispered the emblazoned spell into his hand, and sprinkled it over the firepit. The dark bundle of leaves was the first to erupt in flames. Golden flaring light, tinged with sparkling chartreuse and shimmering teal, grew steadily until a healthy size fire burned brightly in the darkening evening.

Leslie's eyes widened, and he turned his suddenly suspicious gaze on the Summoner's bag. "What otha' kinds a' doo-dads ya got in there?"

Rafe gave him a patronizing smile. "That's a secret."

Blythe had begun spreading out things from her bag, daintily plucking a large rolled-up matt, socks, a beautifully ornate comb, and several pins for her hair. She paused in her rummaging to ponder over Rafe's previous question and hummed. "Hmm, no not really. Every time my people and I have crossed the desert at night, we all fall asleep together. Sometimes we use the camels to shelter the fire and us from the wind blowing sand everywhere if the weather is particularly unsettled that night. They would surely start bellowing if there was something approaching. We're all very light sleepers, though, and most of the large predators here in the desert usually don't come this far out. They prefer stiffer hunting grounds.

Much easier to run around on." She shrugged. "But I will take part in this watch if it assures the rest of you."

Thea couldn't help the smirk that surfaced. "Guess it's just a habit of ours. We'd appreciate it. I know Rafe sleeps like the dead over there." She nodded in his direction, receiving a playful glare from her partner.

"As long as you stay on your side of the firepit I will. Namara mentioned you like to kick in your sleep."

Thea actually laughed at that. "And she still wanted to sleep in the same bed when I was out cold for that week."

Rafe sobered a little at her words, but his smile remained. "She said it was the most still you'd ever been when sleeping."

A soft silence settled around the group, but it was short-lived when Blythe finally rolled out her mat and settled down on top of it with a relaxed sigh. "Cressi used to say I slept like a vampire with my arms over my chest and on my back all the time."

Leslie snorted, lounging on top of his spread-out leather jacket. His hands propped up the back of his head, and one stubby leg was crossed over his other bent one, swinging gently in the air. "Ma sleeps like a troll—all gangly limbs out an' snorin' loud as eva. Wears this fluffy lookin' sleep mask like she's some demon princess, and boy if she don' act like one if ya accidentally wake 'er up."

Thea had picked up her canteen and taken a sip, but upon Leslie's admission found herself choking from the laugh that burst forward. Her reaction sparked a high-pitched giggle from the sorceress beside her and an exasperated look from Rafe. Leslie wasn't bothering to hold back his smug grin.

"Honestly, Thea," Rafe sighed as he propped up his bag for a suitable pillow, "can you drink something without making a mess at least once today?"

Thea wiped her mouth with the back of her hand, cheeks burning from embarrassment, and she stuck out her tongue in a childish taunt. "I just didn't expect Leslie of all beings to say something that was actually funny—"

"I resent that, Honey Badger."

"—and it's not like I expected a fight to break out in the middle of Herbon today. I really liked that drink. And, furthermore, it was *your* rusalka that caused me to cough up the first drink."

A playful little glint entered Rafe's sea-green gaze. "What was that she said again? You never told me."

Thea could feel that sweltering, heady feeling engulfing her entire face, and she looked away to settle her gaze on something, anything, but the blasted desert landscape didn't offer much to look at. She swore Rafe loved just messing with her.

You're never going to find a man who'll love you.

Ouch. Her lips twisted into a frown, and her brow furrowed at the mental dig.

He'll be like this with your children, too.

Mokana's voice was a clear whisper in her mind, just as mischievous as it had been that morning. The image it conjured had Thea chewing her lip and her scowl dissolving. She glanced at Rafe out of the corner of her eye, watched him laughing and conversing with the rest of their entourage. His eyes sparkled in the ever-changing lights of the magic flames crackling in the pit, and one would never know from looking at him in that moment the dark images he had to live with just as she did. No one would know how dead his eyes could look, glamoured or not, while doing his raids in the Dark Market.

He caught her gaze and held it for a moment, a sense of knowing transacted in that breadth of time before it was broken by something else Leslie said.

Thea startled when Blythe leaned over and tapped her gently on the shoulder. She met curious dark irises, momentarily reminded of Namara in that moment, and a pang of longing settled in her chest. She kept the emotion from showing on her face, but she allowed a questioning brow to raise.

"Will you help me get ready for bed?"

Both eyebrows were now high on her forehead. She stuttered as she tried to understand what Blythe could possibly mean. "W-What? As in…?"

Blythe giggled again and held up a thick, bundled cloth up to her. "I just need you to hold this up while I let down my hair."

Still not really understanding why, Thea merely nodded and stood up. She took the cloth and shook it out, holding the rectangular fabric high and shielding Blythe from the others while she herself turned her head and looked away.

"Thank you," the sorceress said kindly, and Thea accidentally looked down and caught sight of her undoing her hair from the elaborate creation she'd spun it in. Feeling as if she were spying on a private moment, Thea quickly switched hands and turned around fully.

"Um, yeah...no problem," she assured awkwardly. Leslie was curiously eyeing the fabric, but Rafe was now sprawled out on his back with his eyes closed. The soft crackling of the fire would lull him to sleep soon, so Thea used a soft voice when she spoke again. "Why...um, why do you need the shawl to hide your hair? If you don't mind me asking," she added quickly, hoping the topic wasn't something taboo.

Blythe was heard brushing her long brown locks and hummed quietly as if in thought. "Hair in my culture is...how you say, *sacred*. Women in our village learn at a young age to style it into wonderful and intricate updos, and the complexity increases with age. Men keep the hair on their head short, but they grow out their beards very long. Sometimes they decorate them with carved beads or braid sections."

Thea eyed Rafe's haircut, then down to his chin where only stubble remained after the shave he gave himself the other day. She smirked at the thought of the men in Blythe's village reacting to his lack of facial hair. Then her smile disappeared when she thought about how the women would react to seeing her curls loose and around her shoulders. She wondered if she should put it up into a bun before they arrived. Wouldn't want to shock the locals.

Blythe's rhythmic brushing paused for a moment before she continued. "Women do not show their hair down to just anyone. Only immediate family and those they are intimate with get the privilege. It is why..." She sighed, and Thea assumed she put down the brush. She heard fabric being shaken out, and then the only sounds in the camp were Rafe's gentle snores—asleep at last it seemed—and the soft *pops* and *clicks* of fire burning at dried twigs. "It is why I knew something was wrong when Cressida said she had never seen my hair down before... You may lower the shawl now."

Thea dropped down next to her bag and crossed her legs, handing the material back over to Blythe. The woman now had a bright green cloth around her head. It contrasted sublimely against the deep tan of her skin and dark brown eyes. She was looking up at the sky and smiling, lost in thought. Thea lowered her arm and fiddled with the edge of the shawl's material.

"I always wanted to show Cressi the lights."

Thea's brows scrunched in confusion, and she glanced up at the sky. "What ligh...oh. Wow."

The sky above them bled out in dazzling colors now that the sun had sunk below the horizon, the likes of which was unlike anything she'd ever seen. She had always enjoyed stargazing as a child, but what she was seeing now couldn't compare to all the nights she'd climbed the manor lattice and slept under the stars after a particularly hard day with her family.

Powder blue sapphire washed over the world and acted as the backdrop against the dark midnight tendril that arced over the sky like an old battle scar, spattered with billions of brilliant white stars that trickled off into the night and twinkled all around them. A contrasting tendril of cosmic light bowed over the other, a wash of swirling lavender and milky white. They appeared like giant swords crossing in a magnificent battle. Embers from the fire glowed in the darkness, swirling up into the sky and reaching for the dazzling pattern of stars in stunning gold, green and blue.

She opened her mouth, but it only hung there as her eyes darted across the sky. Words couldn't express what she was seeing, what she felt seeing something so beautiful. Words were trivial in the face of something like this. She glanced over at the sorceress beside her, but whatever words she did plan on saying died on her tongue.

Blythe... was crying.

Thea felt her breath stutter out of her. She could feel the heavy silence surround them. The breeze caressing her skin was suddenly very chilly.

Blythe sat motionless against the fire's luminous light. The warmth of the flames reflected in her dark eyes became smothered, drowned out as tears glittered wetly along her thick eyelashes before falling and splashing onto the sand below. Every promise, every whispered confession, every "I love you" was broken on the panes of her heart-shaped face and mapped out in the lines of melancholy that bleached her skin of the smile that often radiated there like it was her own personal sun. Her small hand was twisted in the fabric over her heart, squeezing when she released a shuddering breath.

Thea felt the guilt from before crawl up her bones and nestle within her chest, dagger aimed at her heart. She couldn't tell her. She wanted to tell her, but what would she say? What could she say that would make it all right? Her mouth bobbed open and closed, but she had nothing. There was nothing she could say.

Words were trivial, after all.

Chapter Twelve

Confessions Under the Stars

"I'm sorry," Blythe whispered and began wiping her face. "I do not know what came over me. Sorry, sorry," she sniffed.

Thea watched her apologize a few more times before she sighed and scooted closer to the sorceress. She lifted her arm, paused, and chewed her lip a moment before continuing to wrap it around Blythe's shoulders. Blythe tensed for a moment before more tears started escaping the corners of her eyes.

"You don't have to be sorry. There's nothing wrong with showing your emotions."

Blythe clasped her small hands over her eyes as a shudder wracked her body again. "Still, I do not wish for others to see me this way. I'm sorry."

Thea felt at a loss for words. Watching Blythe struggle was like peering into a mirror that reflected a younger, wearier version of herself. "I never wanted anyone to ever see me cry either," she said at last, continuing when Blythe's teary eyes were revealed again. "I was perceived as weak because of it. My family...they groomed me for a life I never wanted so, when I started voicing my opinions, they tried breaking me down any way they could."

Thea, what do you really think you're going to accomplish on your own? Without money? Without connections? People are nothing without those two things.

"Every time I cried—every time they made me cry—they'd turn around and ridicule me for it."

You may look like a man, but Goddess above do you cry like a baby.

This is getting pathetic, Thea. Stop crying already!

If you would just listen to reason, darling, I wouldn't have to be so mean. Can't you see your future is already decided? All you need to do is sit back and let me take care of everything.

Thea sighed and looked away from Blythe's gaze. "When I ran away, I started figuring everything out on my own. I realized that being strong didn't mean I couldn't have emotions." She nodded in Rafe's direction. "I saw him lose it once. We lost someone we both knew from our academy days." Her lips thinned at the memory. "For a man revered amongst his peers, I expected some sort of backlash, but no one poked fun at him, laughed at his pain, or told him to man up. I learned a lot from him that day."

Blythe smiled softly and wiped at her eyes again, the tears finally drying up. "I have never seen Cressida cry. I think she must have thought the same. That crying was weak. I cannot count the number of times I cried in front of her." She hiccupped, giggling afterward. "I stubbed my toe once on the coffee table, and I started tearing up. The look on her face..." She broke off into more giggles, and Thea snorted at the vision.

"Cressida is strong," Thea murmured with pursed lips, annoyed at having to admit that, "but so are you, and even though I have my moments of weakness and even though I cry, I'm a strong person too."

Blythe hummed, nodding as she stared off into the colorful flames. "Yes, I very much admire those in the Coven. I would never leave Srbeveara, even now that I have magic, but back when I was magicless, I wished very much that I had some sort of power so I could become part of such a wonderful organization."

"It's not without its downfalls." The Dmitri and Isolde catastrophe being a major one.

Blythe only huffed a laugh. "Neither is the sanctuary. I have a large scar on my upper thigh from trying to assist a mermaid who did not want my help. I think in the moments following Cressi was far more terrifying. That poor creature..."

Thea threw back her head and laughed. Tears of her own sprang to her eyes, and soon they were both laughing hysterically.

A grumble from the sleeping imp had both women hushing themselves with cupped hands over grinning mouths. Thea removed her arm around Blythe's shoulders to rub warmth back into the limb. She tossed another cluster of twigs onto the fire and watched the flames engulf the offering in a burst of teal flames and sparkling dust.

"You should go to sleep soon," she advised around a large yawn that took hold of her. "I'll have to wake Rafe here in another couple of hours for the watch."

Blythe caught her contagious yawn for herself. She shook herself and said, "I will stay up. You can go ahead and go to sleep if you want."

"Are you sure? You've got to be tired."

She shrugged. "Not really." When Thea continued to give her a reproachful look, Blythe waved off her concerns with another giggle. "Really, I will be all right. I want to continue seeing the stars while they are at their most beautiful." She gestured to the sky with an eccentric wave before leaning back on her palms. "I have missed this sight. It is not the same in Tolvade, and the trees around Srbeveara do not allow me to see much even in the winter."

"Well...okay, then."

Though she was still wary about leaving Blythe alone with her thoughts, knowing full well what that felt like, she acquiesced and stood up, dusting off the sand that had collected in her lap. She picked up her bag and made her way over to Rafe, dropping it beside his stuff and settling once more on the ground. It was warm from the heat the fire put out, and Rafe acted as a nice shield from the wind.

"Wake him in a few hours. I'm sure I don't have to tell you that staying up all night is not a good idea," she said lastly, resting her head on the sack and watching as the sorceress humored her with assurances. Thea didn't have the energy to reiterate the importance of a good night's rest as she felt the pull of sleep tug at her eyelids. The warmth of the fire, the sand, and Rafe's body heat at her back lulled her to sleep quickly.

Blythe watched the scene fondly, even more so when Thea started lightly snoring. Her gaze drifted back to the sky she knew so well. The stars were truly beautiful. She had hoped that the next time she got to see them would have been…with Cressida.

Can we go see your village one day? You keep talking about the stars.

The tears began to fall again. She huffed at herself and wiped them away with the heels of her palms. Her breath quivered as she remembered beautiful green eyes gazing at her. Laying on their sides, they'd whispered to each other until the hours of the night bled into those of the morning. The first night they'd said *I love you*. Back then, Cressida's eyes had been softer. Her hands had been warm, her fingers eager to clasp between Blythe's.

We will one day, she remembered saying. *I would love to show you my family.*

Promise?

Only if I get to meet yours.

Cressida's smile had been so soft, but her eyes had been full of ghosts. *I don't have any family. You're my family. The sanctuary is my family.*

She fell back into the sand and watched the stars twinkle. She let loose a soft breath, closed her eyes for a moment, and pictured herself standing under the same sky as stardust swirled in dizzying designs up above. Cressida was standing beside her. Her expression was full of wonder, eyes soft and mesmerized. Not hardened and lined with exhaustion like they had been for the last year. She'd take Cressida's hand, twirl her around, and dance to the quiet tune she would sing, the one her people sang to their loved ones, and they'd laugh and dance and fall to their knees when their legs gave out. Just like they used to.

The scene flashed, and Blythe was standing in the entryway of the sanctuary. Cressida was there, holding her hands down by their waists. She was wearing the green gown that complimented her eyes so well. Lace detailed in the shapes of leaves graced her bodice, over prominent collar bones and down her arms. It trailed down the dress and scattered around her feet. Cressida's hair was pulled up and pinned by the same lace. Wisps of copper hair framed her face. She was smiling, pulling Blythe along in circles as a beautiful lorelei sang atop the rocks of the waterfall. Her lilting voice echoed throughout Srbeveara.

Marked by their union as oath-bounds, it would continue to echo as long as they both lived.

You are so beautiful, you know that, right? She had said with a smile, another twirl that sent both their skirts fluttering.

Blythe had giggled right back. *Not as beautiful as you.*

The vision changed as Cressida scoffed.

They were laying back in bed again. It was the first time she noticed something strange about the woman beside her. Cressida rolled over, and her eyes were shining so brilliantly in the light of crystals surrounding them.

You know I will do anything for you, right?

Another pang in her chest gripped her heart, and she gasped. The stars above her were blurred when she opened her eyes. She pulled in a deep breath and her eyes hardened at the sky.

I will do anything for you, too, she promised.

The vision of them dancing under the stars swept through her mind. She would see that vision come to life, no matter what it took. This she vowed to herself.

"Finally, the little witch sleeps," a slithery voice said in her ear.

Blythe's blood froze, and she let loose a high-pitched scream—one that was quickly muffled by a clawed hand. The hand disappeared once her lips slammed shut, and she was whirled around to face her aggressor. The moment she locked eyes with endless blackness, the fear gave way to anger.

"Asmo?" she whispered hotly.

The demon sucked at his sharp, obsidian teeth and lounged back in a naturally seductive pose. The moonlight gleamed off the skulls on his shoulders and along his twisted horns. The illumination from the fire added sinister shadows under his cruel, bottomless eyes. However, his complexion was a lot more pale than usual. His platinum blond hair cropped above his shoulders seemed ruffled and out of place as well.

"Don't tell me you're going to continue carrying on that obscene butchering of my beautiful name." He crossed a long leg over the other, and Blythe scrunched her nose up in disgust at his immodest clothing.

She stuck her chin out in defiance. "I may not have practiced magic up until recently, but I have memorized most spells known to man. I know the formulas for the most complex incantations ever created. I would think I should know better than to say a demon's full name and give it more power over me."

Leslie's grumbling had both of them snapping their heads in his direction. One beady, black eye opened, a large ear twitched, and then both eyes shot open. The imp bolted upright in alarm, but Blythe launched herself over to the creature and clamped a hand over his mouth before he could make a sound.

"Shh! It is alright. I know this demon. He will not hurt you."

Asmo grunted in annoyance. "I would not go making false promises of protection, little peacock griffon."

Another pang of sorrow settled in her chest, but she refused to shed another tear in front of this creature. Thea had been one thing, but this monster was not a comrade. She turned and sent him a dirty look over her shoulder. "Why are you even here, Asmo? Should you not be in Hell?"

With a rueful smile full of black daggers, Asmo stared up at the sky and said, "No one dares touch my throne right now. All those who defied me are no more. As for what I'm doing here..." He dropped his gaze to meet hers, and his smile disappeared. "I am here to stop you from partaking in this little adventure. Go back home to your...oh, what did you call her? Your *keresela*? Go back to her."

A fresh wave of pain and longing washed over her, but she strengthened her resolve and glared at the demon prince. "I will when I complete this mission. I am going to save her."

Asmo sniffed haughtily and glanced away, expression bored as he watched the other members of the group slumber away. "You won't make it in time. She's dying. I give her another day."

Blythe gaped. Her bravado disappeared and images of Cressida came crashing through the forefront of her mind. "You're lying!" she whispered fiercely, fists tight in her lap.

The demon merely shrugged, tilting his head as he glanced back at her. "Am I? Are you willing to take that chance?"

Blythe's heart thundered away in her chest, and she was so close to jumping up and sprinting through the sand dunes, cure forgotten. If she wasn't going to make it in time, then she would rather be there by her oath-bound's side in her last moments. She was just about to spring into action when a weathered hand clasped onto her arm. She startled, looking down and meeting Leslie's dark gaze.

"Hold on, toots. Sumthin' ain' addin' up." The imp brought his attention over to Asmo but faltered under the prince's heated glare. In the underworld, Leslie probably would have been a loyal follower of this prince. Would have quaked in fear as he passed by. Would have done his bidding, whatever it may have been. But this wasn't the underworld. "Why you care so much if Zippy 'ere goes back home?"

Asmo stiffened, but the action was so quick Blythe wasn't sure if she really saw it. He only sucked at his teeth again and looked away. "Seems I'm not the only one here with a stupid nickname. I just thought I'd let my *master* know." The word 'master' practically dripped with scathing sarcasm.

Blythe settled herself more firmly in the sand and crossed her arms. Her eyes raked over the creature with disdain evident in the way her brow ticked, the flattened line of her lips. "I do not believe you. Why are you really here?"

She couldn't hold back the flinch she made when Asmo surged upright and gnashed his sharp teeth together. "I already told you, you stupid little—"

"It is not out of loyalty, Asmo. I am not stupid."

"Could have fooled me."

"Why do you not want me finding a cure!" she demanded, voice rising just the slightest.

Asmo launched himself to his feet and snarled. "Because it is going to take my possession away from me!" he hissed. "She's too far gone. It will kill her!"

Blythe froze. Her wide eyes took in his furious expression, the way his hunched form shivered as if possessed, the hard scrutiny in his gaze. She shakily stood to her feet as well, hands trembling and memories of the ceremony in the dungeon unfolding in front of her all over again. Tears threatened to spill, but she held them back. "You are wrong."

"I would not lie about this," he growled lowly.

"Maybe we should all just calm down," Leslie interrupted, standing between the two taller beings. How he hated his short stature at times like this.

"You have to be!" she hissed, ignoring the imp tugging at her harem pants. "You are nothing but an *enbertevem, perrkets khurdyburd!*"

"Whoa!" Leslie chided, expression twisted with astonishment. "I ain't translating that."

Asmo whistled as if impressed, but his bottomless black eyes narrowed dangerously. "Tell me how you really feel, little peacock griffon, but only after you get your colorful hind end back in the city."

It was on the tip of her tongue to lash out at him for ruining what was once a beautiful pet name, but she pulled back and once again crossed her arms high on her chest. She felt her anger dissipate as her rationale returned to her. This was *Asmo*. A demon prince who had schemed his way back onto his throne. The same being that knew Cressida would end up the way she did all along.

Coolly, she stated, "You do not want me to obtain the cure because you want to continue feeding off of her pain."

Asmo looked about ready to pull his hair out. He was clearly used to demanding something and having his order carried out without question. What a spoiled creature. "Of course!" he barked harshly, shoulders hunching in a dangerous display. "Why else would I be here? If you think that makes what I said any less true—"

"You cannot fool me anymore, Asmo. A cure *cures*. That is its purpose. Your purpose is to lie, steal, cheat, and scheme. Why would I believe anything you say?"

The demon prince glared, but rather than fight her anymore, his jaws snapped shut with an audible *click*. He looked positively drained, but his aloof nature came coiling back around him and his shoulders dropped. His smile bled into the confines of his features, and smugness dripped from the arrogant grin once again. "Fine," he allowed, the coy nature of his voice returning. "It's not like you'll make it back alive. You'll be walking straight through blood mage territory at the peak of the blood moon." He pointed to the sky, specifically the pale white moon hanging there. "The night after tomorrow marks the Blood Moon Festival. This time you will be stopped."

Blythe blinked, peering up at the moon above her. If that were true, they would need to hurry their mission along to avoid that. No one would be able to tell just from looking at the moon now, but if there was indeed a blood moon coming up soon, the sky would bleed red from its crimson hue.

Something about what Asmo said nagged at her, though.

"What do you mean *this* time?"

His arrogant grin grew, and he looked immensely proud of himself. "Who else do you think orchestrated the little fiasco in the borough today?"

Leslie swore and Blythe's eyes widened. "That was you?"

Asmo dropped graciously down into the sand, a loud sigh escaping him before sprawling out like a cat in the sun. "But of course," he breathed out, eyes closing. "Took a lot of my power, too, but I was able to feed off their pain and suffering before the possession broke. Now, I've got some pretty little souls to accompany me down under for an eternity."

"But I have not read anywhere that demons are related to black magic. Are you saying it is true?"

The demon blinked and propped himself up on his elbows. "Are you deaf? I just said they were under possession. That is not black magic. Even I would not be foolish enough to meddle in *their* business."

"Whose business?"

Asmo groaned loudly and tossed back his head in annoyance. "I grow weary of this conversation. I have still not regained my full strength, and I only came here to convince you not to continue on this foolish quest. The souls I gained and the pain I fed from are the only things keeping me going as it stands, and I only have enough power to sift back to the sanctuary. I suppose I shall take my leave now."

Blythe stiffened, and the anger she felt cooling earlier resurfaced with a vengeance. "You leave Cressida alone," she snarled through clenched teeth.

Asmo's eyes were practically shining. "Hmm? Now, why would I do that? She is absolutely delicious...but you would know that already, wouldn't you?"

Fury like none she'd ever felt before boiled her over the edge, and she launched herself at the cackling demon with an enraged howl, but she landed in the sand rather than on his wiry body. She whirled around, ready to string the prince up by his horns and flay his mottled, hoary skin from his bones. He was gone, though, and the only sign of his presence having been there was the remaining anger burning hot in her veins.

Chapter Thirteen

Are You a Memory, or Are You but a Dream?

Asmo slunk out of the air in Blythe and Cressida's shared bedroom with stubborn ease, not there one moment and visible the next. His limbs trembled at the drain of his essence and whispered up his skin in little reminders that he was fatigued. He pulled back a lock of white-blond hair with a sharp ebony talon and clicked his tongue in disgust at the shaking digit. Then his deep, chasmous gaze flitted over to the writhing form on the bed. A slow smirk danced across his pale features, even as waves of fulminated energy were clamoring around his very being.

His hands sunk into the mattress on either side of Cressida's head, and he leaned down close, nosing a limp lock of ginger hair out of the way and closing in on the woman's ear. He blew on the flesh slowly and grinned manically as a high-pitched whine escaped Cressida. A grimace twisted her growing ghost-like features.

"Your little peacock griffon is playing hero," he murmured into her ear, following her movements when the woman subconsciously jerked away from him. "She thinks she can save you, but nothing can. Nothing will. Why won't she let me keep you? I know she's the one tethered to me, but I'd much prefer you to be my little pet. You people like to think it's the other way around… Coven members, non-Coven members, what difference does it make? You *humans* are not as smart as you like to think you are," he hissed, throwing back her own words at her.

She flinched, eyes screwing shut as another wave of pain rolled through her body. She felt the fire in her blood, the ice locking up her bones, and the grip of both taking turns squeezing her heart. Already, Asmo could *feel* the power returning to him as he breathed in her suffering.

"This bed must be so cold since she left, *Cressi*. How 'bout I keep you warm for the night?" He gracefully slipped behind her and drew her into his arms, grinning madly as she desperately tried fleeing despite her unconsciousness. Eventually, after only a few frantic moments, her exhausted body gave out. Her eyes never opened, but if they were to, would she even see what was happening? Would she ever see this room again, even if her eyes blew wide and she took in everything? Was her mind even here? Even Asmo didn't know.

"You're going to die," he whispered to her. "If not by that little kaleidoscope, then by your body giving out. You don't have much time left." More pain rolled off of her. His claws walked up her bare arm, the fingers attached to them no longer trembling. "You're going to die, Cressi. Maybe you'll reunite with your little lover when you do because she's going to die too. The blood mages will make sure of it. Or, maybe for all your misdeeds, I'll get lucky and get to keep your soul in the afterlife? Wouldn't that be fun, *om keresela*?" He laughed quietly at the thought. The anger conjured by the thoughts of his possession being taken from him vanished at the prospect of a more permanent possibility.

"You're going to die, you're going to die," he sang softly into her ears. "And I can't wait."

Cressida squirmed, only for her body to slacken when a pale arm reached out and snatched the air above her just as before. Her panting slowed, her limbs numbed out, and relentless twitching of wild eyes under closed lids ceased. Still, the whispers of *die, die, die* penetrated something deep inside her mind. Die? She wasn't afraid of dying. Death had always been a shy friend, constantly present but lingering just a little ways off. Had been since she was a little girl...

A child with frazzled red hair, round cheeks, and gem-like irises stood over the single bed in her home and watched the life fade from her mother's eyes. Ginger hair, the same ginger locks the girl had been gifted with—the mark of the Katsaros gene—was frizzy and as lifeless as the color of skin stretching tight over some parts of her mother's body and loose over others.

"Mama," she cried quietly, basket of fresh market vegetables and bread tossed forgotten on the floor. Tears blurred her eyes.

She knew, even as young as she was, that her mother was dying. The medicine man had said something about Medusa's Kiss, whatever that meant. She hated him, that stupid doctor who couldn't fix Mama. He was just lazy, or maybe he was like some of the other people in town who didn't like Mama because she was so powerful. Tons of other people could use magic but not like Mama could. Mama was "gifted."

She didn't understand why being gifted was so bad. It wasn't like being gifted had saved Mama from this fate. Being gifted hadn't stopped the scornful looks or the calls from the important people at the Coven. Being gifted hadn't stopped her father from leaving. Gifts were supposed to be good things, but nothing about being gifted was good.

She wished her mother could have had an easier life, a life where she hadn't been so special, but as she grasped her mother's too-stiff hand and cried tears into a too-dry palm, she wished more than anything her dad was here to comfort Mama. She never knew her father, but hearing Mama talk about him made him sound so handsome, so nice.

Her mother gasped something, the sound dry and weak and wordless. Cressida rubbed her eyes of the stupid tears that kept welling up in them and grasped her mother's hand tighter. "Yes, Mama? What is it?"

Eyes once the same shade of bottled green glass glinting under a summer sun were now the color of expired olives sitting on a dusty shelf, and they rolled in hollow sockets to lock onto her daughter's gaze. She made no noise, but Cressida thought she felt the twitch of fingers. Then she was dropping to her knees in soundless agony, the hand of her mother now death-gripping her cheek.

Flashing images, too many to count, exploded inside her mind. Someone fleeing with books in their arms, running back and forth under the cover of a dying sun. A huge fire encasing an enormous building while screaming people ran for cover, coughing on the black smoke billowing into the air and darkening a city. Weathered hands digging through ashes, ashes, *ashes*. A giant library of magic and water hanging suspended, large rats in robes, a dark shape swimming through stars. The flash of green eyes and ginger hair of her grandfather as a small boy with a hand cupping his face as pain and memories filtered through his eyes. Her mother screaming as a child when the same thing was being done to her. A lifetime of knowledge and formulas and equations. More information, more magic knowledge.

More.

More.

More.

Blackness hazed the edge of her vision, swimming as the images faded, looped again in her mind, then faded once more for good. She blinked away the pain, panting as if she'd just run through town on the hottest of days. Her eyes landed on the hand hanging off the bed, unnaturally stiff and skin gray, blotchy. She shot up and clawed desperately at the bedsheets, hauling herself up to look into the unseeing eyes of her mother.

Sand Dunes & Blood Moons

Cressida spat blood onto the alley's floor. Her clothes, not having been properly washed in years, were now ripped and hung awkwardly around her thin shoulders from where they had been grabbed and yanked at. Talk about bad luck. She'd been bound to run into it, but she'd gotten cocky. Pickpocketing that one man had been a stupid decision, regardless if her skills in the trade of stealing had gotten so good they rivaled that of imps. The man had had buddies though. Buddies that didn't care if she was a little girl growing up on the streets. She spat more copper-tasting spit onto the ground and wiped her mouth with her dirty sleeve. At least he hadn't called the Coven on her. They would have thrown her into an orphanage fast. Tried to on multiple occasions the few times an overzealous Hunter had spotted her.

She peered at her reflection in the standing puddle of trash water and frowned at the cuts and scrapes on her face. Her brassy red locks, cut short and blunt from a dulled knife, looked lifeless even in the muddled reflection. A bruise was starting to form around her neck. She sighed, and the action hurt. Wiping her lips again, she ventured back out into the bustling market. Some people gave her weird looks, but for the most part, she was ignored. Fire red hair or not, no one noticed a person in need. That was how she liked it, though. She slipped between the various beings of the marketplace and disappeared into the crowd, ready to try again.

The market was alive with opportunities. It was always packed, and every being that walked, scuttled, or plodded through was easy pickings in the highly distracting bazaar. Food stalls were shoved up against one another, creating long lines of beings waiting to get some grub, and pop-up tents offered trinkets and cheap crafts from the local villages just outside the city center. Wagons advertising services pushed through the crowd while the establishments that horseshoed around the market had their doors propped open to entice more business. Humans and creatures of all kinds crowded the busy streets, but Cressida was used to it. That meant she could stow away items and money from those swept up in the chaos. So that's exactly what she did.

Later that afternoon, after a successful day looting, she was leaning up against a bricked building in the shade and out of the suffocating sun when she saw something strange. A man who was *obviously* not from around here was wandering through the market, seemingly lost. He got a few looks too, but they were nothing more than curious passing glances. A wide, wicker-woven hat covered his head and shadowed his features, but it didn't stop the longest black hair Cressida had ever seen from spilling out and swaying behind him in a heavy-looking curtain. He kept stopping, looking around, maybe rubbing his eyes?

His head swiveled in her general vicinity and she froze. Why did she feel so uncomfortable under his gaze? She got looks all the time, but this man wasn't looking away like everyone else always did. Maybe he wasn't even looking at her? She couldn't see his eyes, so it could be the shop she was leaning on that had caught his attention.

He started walking toward her, and Cressida had the briefest feeling that she needed to flee, but curiosity was also nagging at her to see what he wanted. Was he one of those who saw a kid all beaten up and wanted to get them back to their mother's? She snorted. Her mother had been dead for years. Was he going to grab her and drag her to the Coven? The nearest orphanage? He could try, but she'd wriggled out of stronger holds before. Had she stolen from him and he recognized her? Nah, she would have remembered him.

When he stood in front of her, he gingerly pulled off his hat and stared at her. And she stared back. He didn't look like anyone she'd ever seen before. His eyes were different. The color was intense, too, dark like smoke clouding black from a roaring fire. His skin was tanned, even, like he worked in the sun constantly. His hair without the hat trapping it down now drifted behind him in the breeze like ink-stained waves of a lapping sea.

He was looking *around* her when she focused on his gaze after she was done with her own assessment. She raised a ginger brow, but it wasn't taunting. The action was more of a silent question, and it had the man looking *at* her now.

"You're not like the others," his soft accented voice said, and, again, it was like nothing she'd heard before. His statement, however, caused both eyebrows to now raise.

"What do you mean?" she found herself asking.

"Your aura…it is contained, yet I sense great magic within you."

She still didn't understand what he was talking about.

He rubbed his eyes again with one hand, the fingers drifting to massage his temples next. "These people in this city. They let their magic run amuck around them. They're like brightly colored flames and the colors are driving me insane." He dropped his hand and looked at her again, looked *around* her again. "You are so young. Yet, your magic is under better control than those around you."

Brightly colored flames? Color her confused, she still didn't really know what this man was prattling on about. And her magic? Yeah, she knew a lot *about* magic. Sometimes she would be kept up at night filtering through the algorithms in her head, formulas for spells, or rigorous equations that took hours just to complete. So yeah, she knew a lot *about* magic, but she never practiced. Didn't ever have the tools to. Besides, why waste what little coin she gained on amplifiers for magic that wouldn't aid her in acquiring her next meal?

"Would you like to come with me?" he suddenly asked, but she had a feeling he wasn't talking about to the Coven or to the nearest orphanage.

"Where?"

"It is a sanctuary. I run it for magic creatures to escape the harshness of this world when they need to." He looked at her again, but now his dark eyes were traveling up her arms and features. "I have a feeling it will be as much a sanctuary for you as it is for them."

When he reached out his hand, something told her to take it. So she did. She didn't think of the possible dangers this man could have posed, what horrible things he could do to her that she may never recover from because anyone that ever could have taught her these things were dead. And as she walked out of town with a strange man, they got a few weird looks, but no one noticed her missing when she was gone. No one ever had.

Cressida spent the days of her youth bounding through meadows with half-human, half-goat fauns and making intricately woven crowns out of the wildflowers that bloomed as if it were an eternal spring. She rolled down the side of hills with them and even though new bruises formed on her body, they didn't hurt as much as her old ones had.

She got lost in the endless maze of a forever forest while playing hide and seek with a leshy, a forest guardian spirit. His sides and face were no longer the mottled color of green and gray but charred black from a small forest fire. As a guardian, he had stayed behind to make sure all the woodland creatures made it out alive, but he'd been badly burnt as a result. When he caught her hiding behind a large boulder, as he always did, her giggles rang throughout the faux forest, and she settled into his lap and played with his mossy beard and ivy hair as he retold his great adventures in his home, of how he couldn't wait to get back to woods that were more familiar.

She spent nights in the made-up habitats of the moss folk, the low lighting in the pocket dimension a constant, and it made nodding off to sleep while listening to the chitter-chatter of mossy-faced, lichen-haired, elderly looking beings easy as they braided flowers and long blades of grass into her hair.

When the creatures at the sanctuary had been introduced to her, they had taken one look at her bruised soul, cut up body, and the flickering fire in her verdant green gaze and had taken her in, sheltered her, and taught her what it meant to love. To trust. She'd cried the first night in the arms of a brownie mother, wishing it were her own.

And when she wasn't jumping from one dimension to another, she was learning about the magic that pulsed through her veins with her new instructor Enzou. He knew more about magic than she had given him credit for, and his lectures were not boring or drawn out. There were days where she'd demanded he teach her more. He would ruffle her hair and smile, tell her she's done enough for the day, and excuse her from her studies. He looked at her like her mother used to. Was this what having a father was like? The pride in his voice when he told her she got something right or the smile in his dark eyes when she countered his teachings with her own formula made her feel like she wasn't so lonely anymore.

The first few days she'd learned the most.

"Magic-wielders have an aura around them, and it's brighter depending on how much magic they possess. My people have trained ourselves over the last few centuries to be able to see this aura, and because we can see it, we can see when it is leaking out of us," he said as they sat around a large table in the first room off the sanctuary's entrance.

"Your people?" she parroted. She was idly running her fingers through her ginger locks, momentarily distracted when she pulled out a leftover flower and smiled at the soft blue petals. "What color is mine?"

"I hail from the mountains," he answered softly, and she noticed a faraway look in his dark eyes. "I left to seek something new." He glanced at her quickly, then answered, "As for your aura, it is a bright and lively green. Though, it's still leaking out a little bit."

She looked down at herself, but she saw nothing. She admitted she was a little jealous she couldn't see her own magic. "What's so bad about that?"

"When you rein your magic back in and train yourself to keep it from leaking out, you become stronger because your magic is condensed…" He looked a bit confused for a moment as if searching for the right word, "It's more properly controlled. When you suck in your magic into your being, it also hides its presence from others."

Cressida's brow scrunched in confusion. "Why would I want to do that?"

Enzou smiled at her and while it wasn't a scary smile, it wasn't *not* a scary smile. "Your people can sense the magic of others even if they can't see it. If they sense you are powerful, that will only invite trouble for you. You will also be able to take anyone by surprise once you release your magic. Now, try imagining your magic as a body of water inside you, overflowing."

She still didn't understand why it mattered if people knew she had power or not, but she closed her eyes and cleared her mind of all the formulas, magic incantations, and mathematical equations jumbling up the space in her head. She pictured a river, and green, lagoon-like water was flowing in an endless direction. She looked down, and a large stick lay at her feet. She looked back at the river, then down to the stick again before picking it up. She walked over and placed it down into the water, and as if by magic, some of the current slowed. She looked back at the riverbank, and more sticks lay by the water's edge. One by one, she laid limb after limb into the water until a dam was created. The water she was standing in on the other side disappeared.

When she opened her eyes, the first thing she noticed was the proud glint in Enzou's eyes. The second thing, and by far the most astonishing, was just how clear her mind now was.

He was dead. Just like her mother. Medusa's Kiss hadn't taken him, though. He had passed peacefully in his sleep. A heart attack. Of course, it had been the one where the victim doesn't wake. Doctor said the left main artery had gotten blocked, but "he died with a smile on his face." Was that supposed to make her feel better? He was gone. Over the years she had come to know him as her instructor, her mentor, her *father*. The most important person in her life. Gone.

The creatures in their habitats, both new refugees and old, had wept for him. News spread. The sanctuary quickly became surrounded by spirits that had once resided within the walls of the refuge to mourn the loss of the one who had given them aid when no one else would. Many faces she knew; some were before she'd come into Enzou's care. She was reunited with the leshy, the brownie mother, the fauns, and the moss folk. Each held or held onto her as her tears fell. Soon, she wasn't the only one who cried. Howls, pitching calls, bellows, and wails, all sorrowful, crested into the night as the moon peaked in the sky.

Cressida joined them.

A knock on the door startled Cressida out of the conversation she was having with a mermaid. She glanced at the large doors of the sanctuary, gaze wary before she looked back at the creature poking its head out of the smooth stone circle on the floor. The waterfall cascaded down around her teal hair, washing away the blood that flowed from a giant gash on her back. Cressida sighed when the knock repeated itself. She opened the large tomb she was holding and presented a blank page to the creature, dribbled a drop of ink into a webbed palm, and let the creature slap a messy handprint onto the page. The mark glowed within the pages and vanished.

The sorceress waved a hand over the creature, and the water bubbling and splashing around the mermaid took form. Slowly, the mermaid was raised into the air while a large bubble of water surrounded her. Her fire orange tail flapped in surprise, but a soft murmur from Cressida caused the creature to calm.

"I'm sending you to your room," she stated, ignoring the knock on the doors even as the mermaid's finned ears twitched at the sound. "Up the stairs, third corridor, second room on the right side. It will open if you have the right room."

The mermaid nodded and responded with a noise, but the bubble of air that escaped her mouth drowned out the sound. Then she was flapping her tail and propelling the suspended bubble of water up the stairs and disappearing from Cressida's line of vision.

She heard the knock again and sighed. She really doubted it was a creature on the other side of those doors. She didn't feel any trace of magic coming from the entrance, but, now that she thought about it, that was odd in itself. Cressida was now able to see what Enzou had been talking about all those years ago. She saw and felt other beings' magics easily, regardless if they were human or creature.

She crossed the short distance to the doors and opened one just enough to get a look at who was on her stoop. She blinked. The woman standing on the other side was beautiful. Her skin had been kissed by the sun, her face was delicate and adorned with freckles that danced under wild eyes. Her *eyes*. They were so dark, so clear. Pangs in her heart had her reaching a hand out to soothe the sensation in her chest. Her eyes were the same color as Enzou's, and—like Enzou—this woman, too, did not hail from around these parts.

Her dark brown hair was a braided bun with no loose strand in sight, her makeup was vivid and colorful with splashes of purple, blue, and glittering gold, and her clothing was foreign. She was draped in silk robes that wrapped around her lithe frame in sheer mauves, turquoise, and saffron.

She noticed the woman looking at her and taking her in too.

"Yes, how may I help you?" she asked softly.

"My name is Blythe Castel," the woman stated carefully. She looked a touch nervous. Her accent was thick, but after nearly a decade of listening to the garbled noises of various creatures and trying to discern what they wanted or needed, understanding what this woman said was as easy and enjoyable as looking at her. "I would like to help you improve your sanctuary. I have always…" but Cressida wasn't listening anymore.

Improve her sanctuary? This place had been her home and the home of many creatures longer than this woman could even guess, and she thought it needed improvement? Every creature around knew they could come to this sanctuary and receive aid, and the far-reaching reputation she'd established amongst the magic fauna had granted the respect of even the wariest of creatures.

Cressida's eyes did a once over of the woman a second time, her gaze more critical. She saw nothing. No magic aura. This woman didn't even *have* magic, and she was telling Cressida how to run *her* sanctuary? Preposterous.

She hummed, cutting off the nervous babbling the woman was spewing and said, "I'll take that into consideration. Have a nice day now," and closed the door. She huffed.

The woman was cute, but she didn't need *cute.*

Cressida turned and walked up the stairs, thinking she'd never see the woman again.

Fortunately, she was wrong.

Cressida collapsed in her bathroom and gasped. She'd just been getting out of the bathtub when she felt something whisper up her skin and attach itself to her like a vile embrace. She looked down at her body and let her magic go free. Years ago, she would have had to picture the rickety dam she'd built in her mind and pull off one large stick at a time before she could release her energy. Now, the river that was her magic built until it flowed over the dam like a waterfall, releasing itself from the hold she kept on it. Her magic, beautiful and alive and color of life itself, flowed out of her body, but something was different. Something was not right.

A soft knock on the wall had her looking up. Blythe was on the other side of the bathroom, not looking in out of respect for her privacy despite them being together for over a year now. "Cressi, *k'iz hit emin onch' kergon i?"*

k'iz hit emin onch' kergon i…everything is fine with you?

"Um," Cressida swallowed before continuing, "Yeah, I'm fine."

"What? I cannot understand," Blythe playfully said, moving away from the open arch in the wall.

Cressida scowled. "Uh…*ais lev aim,*" she tried, cringing at the awkward words that rolled off her tongue.

Blythe's tinkling laughter could be heard in the bedroom, and Cressida relaxed at the sound. The river in her mind receded until the dam was dripping but visible and containing the magic within her once again.

Yes, she *was* fine. She had to be.

Medusa's Kiss. She had Medusa's Kiss. She was going to die. She wasn't going to see Blythe's smiling face anymore. She was never going

to hold her again. She was going to lose out on the years to come with her oath-bound.

A new wave of more sinister thoughts bubbled up in her mind.

Who was going to protect the creatures in the forest surrounding her home? How would Blythe deal with it all? On her own? Not having magic to aid her? How would she keep the amplifiers running? The ones specifically tied to Cressida's own life force? Who was she going to trust to run this place when she was gone? The Coven had cut funding for the sanctuary yet again, so there was absolutely no way she was going to reach out and ask them for aid. The only one she could count on was herself, but now only certain death shadowed her future.

Cressida took a long, deep breath, lit the letter from the doctor's on fire, and dumped the ashes into her cold teacup. She looked at the extensive mass of books on her shelves, and another pang throbbed in her chest. She'd poured herself into her studies after Enzou died, collecting various archives in the form of scientific novels, scholarly journals, dossiers, and transcriptions of famous incantations. Turned out Blythe was incredibly talented with formulas and spells as well. She was able to understand magic in its highest complexity despite not being able to practice.

It had been one more thing they had connected on. One more thing that made falling for her so easy.

The books on her shelves had answers in them, she knew. Alchemists scrawled abbreviated notes along page borders. Scholars documented every detail. Common practitioners that had been perfecting their craft for decades had formulated the perfect spells, camouflaging them into things like cooking recipes and how-to manuals in order for their work to remain secret from the world...except for those that could decipher them. The answers were in these books, somewhere, even if they were not printed in clear directions. Even if it meant reading between the lines and decoding simple clauses to uncover the true meaning of the text within, or even...dare she think about it?

No matter what, you must never, ever practice the dark arts. You are strong enough to survive its urges for a very long time, but that will only lead you further down its path. You will be condemned. You will die, Cress.

Tears stung her eyes. *Oh, Enzou. I'm going to die if I don't.*

Never, ever practice the dark arts.

She stood from her desk and took another deep breath, walked over to the large collection of books, and waved her hand at the top shelf. A large tomb was plucked from the bookcase and floated down to her.

I'm sorry, Enzou. But I'm not going to die. I've finally gained happiness. I've finally found someone to share my life with. I love her. I'm not going to leave her like mom left me. Like you left me. I hope you can forgive me. I don't want to die.

"You're going to die," Asmo whispered again and again. He loomed half over her, his sharp black daggers for teeth inches away from her ear.

Cressida jerked away, and trails of tears glistened as they slipped down her gaunt cheeks. "I don't want to die," she cried, and the demon prince knew he'd broken her. He breathed in her pain and laughed.

Suddenly, the door to the room burst open, and in the threshold, there stood Ma.

Chapter Fourteen

Do You Have Any More Wine? We're Going to Need it.

To say Ma was flabbergasted would have been the understatement of a lifetime, and she had lived through several. She'd been minding her business, raiding Blythe's parlor, dayroom, hoarder's paradise, whatever the woman wanted to call it, trying to find the wine the sorceress had mentioned in sweetening the deal to come look after Cressida when she'd felt a heavy oppression weigh down on the sanctuary. Now, she was standing in the doorway of the woman's bedroom staring down a blasted demon prince.

A *demon prince*.

Last time Ma had laid her sore eyes on one, it had been nearly half a millennia ago. And was he ever a sight for sore eyes. He still terrified the fire and brimstone out of her though.

His black eyes narrowed at her, seemingly peeved he'd been interrupted, before he glanced back down at Cressida. In the blink of an eye, he was gone without a word. Cressida's hunched over form relaxed slightly, but the woman was still curled up in a pitiful ball as whimpers escaped her chapped lips.

Ma laid a shaky hand over her heart before taking a deep breath to calm her nerves. Now, was not the time to be having a fright, not with what she'd just discerned. She stepped into the room and neared the large bed, peering over the mattress and laying a motherly hand on the ex-sorceress's head. Cressida's tears fell and dampened the sheets below her in rapid succession, but her taut form relaxed a little bit more. The twitching under her eyelids ceased, and her furled fingers unclenched when Ma's soothing shushing broke the quiet, heavy tension in the room.

"Shh, shh," the imp cooed, but inside the creature was a whirlwind of warring emotions. "What have ya done?" she asked carefully, quietly, but the woman on the bed didn't respond. Not that Ma thought she would. "Scratch that, I don' wanna know," she sighed gustily.

A tinkling chime accompanied by a soft whirring against her skin had her looking down and shoving a hand in her dress pockets. She pulled out her crystal ball and answered the call, schooling her features with ease into the stern expression she rarely wore. It wasn't hard to pull off the look at present.

"This betta be good, Herman," she warned, accent thickening in her displeasure.

A shady figure with a square face and beady blue eyes took up the ball's surface. His scruffy goatee was patchy and a shade more orange than the close shaved hair on top of his head. His smile was off-putting, and his teeth were thin and shaped like that of a rat's, and they were a gross shade of yellow and green from improper care. Ma swore she could smell his breath through the glass. Sad to think he was human through-in-through.

"All the preparations are in order," he hissed in glee as his blue eyes twinkled like shattered glass. "The Blood Moon Festival is nigh upon us, and we have prepared the finest amplifiers and ingredients for the cult."

Ma pursed her lips, looking unimpressed. "Ya wanna gold rune fo' ya effets? Make sure ya start the biddin' off high. We tha only supplia fa this kinda stuff, an' if they wanna take the Coven by su'prise they'll fork ova the coin."

Herman straightened his spine and nodded hastily. "Yes, yes, of course, Mother Queen."

She cut the call and massaged her temples and let loose another sigh. The woman beside her groaned in pain and Ma cut her a look. "You ain't makin' my job any easia,'" she snipped quietly. Then she picked up her crystal ball again and made her own call.

Winona's face filled the glass, but neither female looked pleased to see one another. The Second Chosen had bruises starting to form under exhausted eyes, and Ma could see around the edge of the sphere that there was a mountain of paperwork around her.

"This can't be good," Winona griped in clear annoyance. "What is it?"

"You catchin' an attitude wit' me?"

Winona swallowed carefully. "No."

"That's what I thought. Now, listen 'ere, I got some infa'mation fo' ya."

It was Winona's turn to rub her temples, exhaustion clear in her silver gaze. "About?"

"The Blood Moon Festival."

Winona halted mid-action and cursed. "Blast it with hellfire, I've been so busy I forgot about that sadistic, cultist celebration." She groaned loudly before taking a deep breath. "All right then, let's hear it."

Ma quickly relayed the information she'd gotten from Herman, along with her own knowledge of the items on the auction storage room: blood siphoning daggers, illegal powder enhancements, skin runes that tattooed themselves to the flesh of either the caster for power or to the victim to weaken them, and flasks of elixir to numb and corrupt the minds of small creatures for the purpose of sacrificial slaves.

"Torro's lil stunt didn' do as much damage as planned. They recov'ed in less than a week," Ma said with a deep frown.

Winona growled lowly, but her eyes were diverted from the crystal ball. "We charred that place to the ground. The only thing left standing was the auction house itself."

"Yeah, I *know*. I had ta convince Herman and tha others not ta warp dimensions. Again. Ya lucky. Resettin' pocket portals are a pain in tha horns I'll have ya know."

The Second Chosen shrugged. "We would have just gotten the new access points." She then pursed her lips into a scowl. "We destroyed as much of their wares as possible. How did they bounce back so fast?"

"Performers of tha dark arts be crafty like that. All right, I ain't got all night so put me on a private connection with tha Celestial."

Winona floundered, exhaustion cleared from her gaze. "What? I can't do that. The proper protocol is—"

Ma cleared her throat, and the woman's teeth clicked shut. The imp leaned further into the glass and watched as, from the other side, Winona settled stiffly back in her seat. "Do I look like I got time ta be playin' games, Winni?"

Winona tried to swallow around the lump in her throat. "No, but—"

"Good, we undastand each otha. In fact, ya don't have to get her on the line. Tell her ta bring her pretty lil self on out here to Srbeveara."

"Wait, I have to—"

"You gotta report ta Torro everythin' I just told ya right afta ya get the Celestial out here. I expect her in tha next hour, sweetheart."

She cut the connection and huffed into the darkness of the bedroom. *As if bein' the undercover ringleader of the Dark Market wasn't drainin' enough,* she thought to herself. She knew everyone referred to her as Ma, but she was getting real tired of cleaning up these kids' messes. She eyed Cressida beside her. She didn't even know how this child created *this* mess, and what a mess it was.

Ma opened the doors to the sanctuary just as the High One passed the barrier. Though the Celestial was sexless, a being of pureness and magic and older than most even knew, Ma, and many like her, referred to the Celestial as a "she." The being was unbothered by any title given, smiled, even, as if amused. As long as ill feelings were not directed toward the Celestial, the High One remained uncaring.

"How ya been, darlin'?" Ma began with a warm smile. She hadn't liked the Celestial at first—her being the exact opposite make-up of the High One and all.

"To what do I owe the pleasure of this late night affair?" The High One asked softly. She was like a beacon of light in the darkness the way white, glowing light emanated from under the deep blue cloak swathing her delicate body. She was a little hard to look at directly, but Ma could tell she had long golden hair and milky, iridescent, all-knowing eyes.

"I think it's betta for you to discern that yaself, High One. Trust me, you'll know when ya get in 'ere." Ma opened the doors wider and allowed the Celestial to pass by her. The being froze no more than a few steps into the building and whirled on the imp.

"What is the meaning of this? Why do I sense…" she paused, looking around and letting her words die off. "I do not like what this means," she finally said after a short moment.

"What's it mean?" Ma knew somehow a demon prince had gotten loose and was able to blip in and out of existence within the sanctuary…and no doubt other places as well, but she didn't know how, and she didn't know for what reason.

"Someone has tethered themselves to a prince."

Ma's burly brows rose as shock gripped her. She didn't have time to ask how in the inferno *that* was possible before the Celestial was turning around and sweeping into the cave. The trickle of water did not wet the being's form or stick to her skin as she passed under the rivulets, but it sure made Ma's white pigtails droop. The Celestial paused at the healing pool's edge as she spied two sleeping forms cuddled together under the water but pressed on quietly with Ma steadily following behind. The imp was too busy muttering about scuffing up her new heels to pay attention to where the two of them were going, but when the Celestial spoke, she looked up.

"Yield to me," she demanded to the face of a stone wall. The rocks fell away and unearthed a hidden stairwell. The torch sconces within blazed to life and lit up the steps as if it were daylight. Ma's mouth dropped, but she scurried after the High One when the being swept inside with composed haste.

The stairwell seemed to go on for a while, but eventually, they stepped onto the bottom floor. Ma squinted into the dark chamber, but there was nothing out of the ordinary. The High One took slow steps into the room, holding up a hand behind her when Ma went to follow.

"Stay back," she warned gently.

Ma still poked her head in further. "Why, watcha doin?"

"We have company."

An intense, swirling storm of energy imploded inside the room as maniacal laughter bounced erratically off the stone walls. Ma sucked in a sharp breath as the demon prince that had been upstairs appeared in the middle of the dungeon. His roguish features were pulled into an amused grin, and his sharp black teeth glinted in the light of the torches. "I should have known you'd be called in to come deal with me. How precious."

The Celestial reached up and popped the clasp of her cloak, and the material slowly fell away from her shoulders. Light, blinding in its intensity, erupted from the being and washed the entire room in pure white energy. Ma ducked behind the stairwell wall and rubbed her eyes. Being a demon, especially a low-level demon, affected her more than it would a human. She'd have to content herself by staying out of sight, but as her large ears twitched, she was hearing plenty.

The prince hissed, and his amused grin faded, but his overbearing power still remained. However, it wasn't as oppressive now that the Celestial was there.

"I would like to know your business here," she stated directly, never taking her luminescent eyes off the being before her.

The prince gave a hard laugh. "Ha! My business is none of yours, sweetheart. Now, I usually don't object when someone takes their clothes off in front of me, but I'd take my things and go if I were you. There's nothing you can do to me as long as the tether remains." Laughter rang through in his voice, and his smugness was nearly as palpable as his power.

The Celestial was right? Ma's eyes grew wide from the other side of the wall.

The Celestial did not flinch at the crude words spoken to her. She did not show any emotion at all to the prince. She simply said, "Then I will have to erase it," and held up her palms.

Asmo's facade fell away. His aura shifted, the room's temperature snapped to ice, and his black teeth revealed themselves in a terrifying snarl. "I'd like to see you try." His hands reached out, fingers curled, and from within his grasp, black liquid oozed out and dripped onto the floor.

The Celestial flung her arms out and closed her eyes, and from within her, an even more dazzling light burst forth.

The demon prince roared, and an equally fearsome light surfaced. Crimson like the blood of the innocent, as pitch black as the deepest pits of Hell, his aura exploded outward and collided with the High One's, forcing the being back a step. Shadows thrashed and writhed inside the depths of the inky, bubbling sickness that had fallen to the floor and spread along the stone.

"You WILL leave this realm!" the Celestial bellowed, pushing her arms out in front of her shoving the purification magic onto the prince.

"I WILL destroy you!" Asmo countered, laughing as the shadows under his feet rose up into tall, bodiless figures. Eyes of saffron and molten rock glared out of the darkness before launching themselves at the Celestial. Asmo's sick laughter belted out into the dungeon.

The High One was forced back again. She grunted as the shadows latched onto her arms, dying away from the light she emitted only to be replaced by more, each sucking away at the magic she wielded. She opened her iridescent eyes and locked her gaze onto the prince's glee-filled chasms.

"I will not allow you to trample upon that which I have kept protected for so long!"

Asmo threw back his head and laughed so hard the skulls on his shoulders danced in the dueling lights. "And how are you going to stop me? You can't even fight off the Shadows of Sin! All those little black witches and possessed mortals who died today sure have a lot more power in the underworld, wouldn't you say?"

The Celestial gasped as more began to latch onto her body, disintegrating much slower as they sucked her magic dry.

"I have no choice it seems," she grunted out.

Asmo's ebony teeth gleamed. "Oh, what's this? Have a little trick up your sleeve? Do your worst!"

The Celestial glared. "I will have to call upon Mother."

Asmo balked, jerking back in disbelief, and the shadows vanished at the break in his concentration. "You couldn't possibly call on her! You do not remember how!" he roared, and even Ma felt rattled by the fierceness of it.

"I do not forget the core of my existence, Prince, no matter how many times I drink the Elixir of Echoes." The High One countered, her voice hardening. "I never forget I am a true descendant of this world's great mother and ruling goddess, *Saellah,* born of her womb and a gift to this world, a High Elf." Power swelled in the room at her words, snuffing out the prince's little by little and replacing it with pure, untainted energy. The Celestial raised both hands in the air again, outstretched with palms facing up as she shouted into the air, "I call to you, Mother. Lend me your strength. Lend your child, your progeny, the gift of your love, the power I require. I call upon your merciful ways to rid the world of this demonic oppression, to rid your far-child of the tether that binds their soul to a void. I call to you this once, most merciful mother, knowing I forfeit your guidance for the rest of this life. *Undo what had been done.*"

The prince was bellowing his anger, but his once overwhelming power and dark essence were slowly being dwindled until it was nothing more than a candle next to a blazing inferno. Roaring static buzzed angrily in Ma's ears, and she clasped her weathered palms over her head as a bright, white light engulfed the stairwell and pierced the imp's eyelids no matter how Ma twisted away. Then...

Silence.

Ma unfurled from her doubled-over position and scrubbed at her now sensitive eyes. Spots danced in her vision for a moment before clearing up. Cautiously, she peeked into the chamber. The prince was gone, and the Celestial lay crumpled on the floor.

Across the desert, Blythe had distanced herself from the campfire to try and calm the anger that still clamored deep in her heart. Leslie was by her side, fretting and not knowing what to do when the sorceress dropped to her knees as pain ripped through her soul. Her jaw unhinged, and a silent scream was pulled from her, and she felt the sensation of *something* vanish inside her. Leslie had caught her as she fell, and now he watched with wide black eyes as the woman on the ground began giggling even as tears fell from the corners of her reddened eyes.

Her gaze landed on his, and she smiled. "I think...I think Asmo is gone."

Chapter Fifteen

Dinner was, Decidedly, Not Barbecue

The light emanating off of the Celestial was much dimmer than before, and Ma rushed over to the High One's side as worry pulled her mouth into a hard frown.

She helped the being steady herself as the Celestial attempted to sit up. "What in tha three worlds did you do? Is he gone? I thought you was just gonna detain 'im until we could figua out how to desummon 'im." Ma had so many more questions to ask, but the Celestial didn't look like she was feeling too good. Elixir of Echoes? True descendant of the goddess *Saellah?* High Elf? And what was a far-child? Did the Celestial just desummon a demon herself?

The being sighed and, with Ma's assistance, stood to her feet once again. She swayed slightly but caught herself before she could trip. "Even I cannot detain Asm—" Her lips thinned. "I dare not even say his name lest I undo everything I just went through." She looked down at the imp before her, saw Ma's confused, all-black eyes staring up at her, and let a small smile surface on her pale face. "I can tell you are confused. Come," she held out her hand, "there is much you do not know. As someone so trusted and doing so much for the Coven, and after what you have just witnessed, I believe you deserve some answers."

Ma scoffed softly and took the being's hand. "Ya best believe I do. Tell me everythin', but wait till we get upstairs. Mama needs a drink."

The Celestial laughed quietly. "If you are offering, I shall partake as well."

"Ooh, I'm finally gettin' girls' night," Ma sang with glee as she practically pranced up the stairs. The two only paused at the edge of the pool to inspect the demonesses still curled up and dead to the world asleep in the water. "Ha, kids these days. Don't wake fa nothin'."

It was only when the two beings were settled into Blythe's daybed with a glass of red wine in their hands that the Celestial spoke up.

She cleared her throat, then...

"I do not remember what I said in the chamber."

Ma squawked in disbelief. "Wha—"

The Celestial held up a hand to silence her, and a small, amused smile surfaced. "I never do right away. The power that banishment took and the power I asked to receive has left me drained. I only know I unlocked a part of myself that I had once forgotten. What did I say while I was speaking to the demon prince?"

Ma could not believe what she was hearing. Was the High One pulling her ear or something? "Uh, ya said somethin' along the lines o' bein' the true descendant of the great mother and tha rulin' goddess *Saellah*. Well, first ya said somethin' about some Elixir of Echoes. Oh, then afta' that ya was all like 'I am a gift ta this world, a High Elf' or whateva. Then ya made Mista Big Bad disappear. Somethin' about asking fa ya ma ta lend ya some power—oh, what was that thing ya said? Fa'-child? I neva heard that before."

The Celestial's mother-of-pearl eyes were wide, and she gazed off into the distance as she idly swirled her glass of wine. "It has been a long time since I have heard that name. I forgot her, just as we all did." She raised the glass of wine in the air and studied its contents. "That is the purpose of the Elixir of Echoes. Every millennium, I drink it to stop myself from descending into madness." She locked eyes with the imp sitting across from her. "That is what it means to be an immortal."

Ma swallowed around the dry lump in her throat and took a swig of her wine. "I thought ya told princey ya neva forgot."

"In truth, I do not. It is more like…the memory is repressed. It is only called forth when I ask for mother's power. And, no, I cannot call upon it again. Not until after I drink the Elixir of Echoes, and it has only been a few centuries since I last did so. Drinking the elixir too soon…well, let us just say it will have the exact opposite effect." The being sighed and took a small sip of her drink. "I did not think I would have to call upon her so early. But a released demon prince? I could deal with the old Coven burning down. I could deal with my brethren running amuck in the Black Forest. I knew the prophecy would eventually be fulfilled and would put an end to their ways and magic would be restored to the land."

"Eh? What prophecy you talkin' 'bout?"

The Celestial's gaze wandered again as recollection clouded aged eyes. "It is coming back to me now. Mother came to me right before I was to take the elixir. She is the creator of us all, the one who birthed magic into the land. She foretold the end of days when magic would cease from this world, and I was to make sure that did not happen. Time was of the essence, and I could not come forth with the information to just anyone, for I could not have known who would use it against the very Coven I established. I had my suspicions with some of the members of the Council recently, but even I could not have guessed as to how far Isolde and Dmitri's corruption ran."

Ma, enraptured in the information she was receiving, didn't even look away to gulp down some more of her wine. "Then what happened?"

"I wrote *The Fairy Fall* under the pen name Darion Black. My mind was going numb after existing for so many hundreds of years, and the epic poem was a release of everything I felt in that lifetime while also acting as a guideline for the events of the past, what had transpired between the humans and the elves, and the prophecy to bring magic back to the realm."

"Darion Black…Darion Black…why does that name sound so—oh!" Ma gasped and let a gnarled hand fly to her mouth. "That was *you?*"

"Yes. I only know for certain I was the one who wrote it because I left a note for myself to read after I took the elixir." The Celestial hummed and took another sip of wine. "What else did you say? High Elf?" She did not wait for a response. "That was my original title, long before my brethren were ever born. The elves you know of were born of mother's tears while I came from her womb."

"Why was she cryin'?"

The Celestial stopped, mouth opened in a soft "o" as a gust of air left her. "I…do not know."

Ma's brow furrowed. "What da ya mean ya don't know? You should ask 'er. That's ya motha."

"What?"

"Look, alls I'm sayin' is if I was cryin', my Leslie would be tha first ta ask. Oh, that reminds me. What was that thing you said about a fa'-child? Like I said, I neva heard of that one."

The Celestial blinked out of a daze that had settled in her luminous eyes. "Oh. That is what mother, I, and other Celestials refer to humans by. The humans of today are descendants of elves and first-generation humans. That is why humans today can practice magic. It comes from their elven bloodline, and it is why some bloodlines are stronger than others. It is sometimes not inherited at all. Humans that come from elven bloodlines are the goddess *Saellah's* children by extension, but they are so far down the bloodline that they do not even remember the name of their creator. It is why we call them far-children."

"Wait ah age-old minute now, you mean there'a more of ya?" Ma went to take another sip of her wine but found the glass empty.

The Celestial appeared… wistful? Ma couldn't put a claw on it, but the High One appeared a bit sad. "I have many siblings, but they are… far away from here. In another part of this vast world."

Ma whistled and slumped back into the daybed cushions. "Well, ya just a fountain of infamation ain't ya?"

"It seems that way now that some of the veil has been lifted."

Ma reached over to the flask on the table and poured herself some wine. "I'll drink ta that. Want some more?"

The Celestial smiled softly and offered over her glass to the imp. "I think I shall take you up on that."

Thea woke to the gentle caresses of strong fingers in her curls and dawn's first light. She groaned at the feeling of her head hurting and eyes feeling heavy from exhaustion, and the deep massage to the back of her neck and scalp was enough to nearly pull her back under. She knew instantly that she was propped up in Rafe's lap, but she regained awareness of her actual surroundings as the warming sand under her shifted with her every movement.

Right. Desert. Find the cure for an incurable disease.

She pulled herself up with another groan and grimaced at the feeling of sand sprinkling down her arms from within her curls. She wiped her hands over her shirt before rubbing at her eyes, careful not to get anything in them.

"See anything last night?" she yawned.

"Pack of camels in the distance," Rafe replied, voice on the edge of a yawn himself.

She nodded sleepily, thinking having a pack of camels might have been a benefit while traversing the sand dunes while she glanced around the encampment as her body began adjusting to being awake. Blythe was passed out flat on her back, snuggling a snoring Leslie. The imp's eyes were crusty, and his mouth was open wide, drool clinging to his thin lips.

"When did they get so close?" she murmured, nodding over to the still slumbering duo.

Rafe stood and stretched, releasing a hearty groan as he reached for the brightening sky. His baggy tunic rode up the smallest bit, but it was enough to reveal the man's well-defined stomach underneath. Thea was able to pry her eyes away, but not before peeking a little. "Couple hours into my shift." he was saying before he dropped back down to the ground and began rummaging through their bags. He brought out the canteen and sipped modestly from it, eyeing the reserves before allowing himself to take another sip. "Maybe it got cold sleeping alone or maybe it was just Blythe's...natural magnetism."

Thea wrinkled her nose. "Blythe is too intense to draw people in that quickly."

"Yet she bagged the iciest sorceress in the country."

She rolled her eyes, flicking her gaze back over to find Rafe applying a minor healing spell over the back of his neck and then covering it with a piece of fabric like a short scarf. "What are you…?"

"Ah," Rafe chuckled and sent her a sheepish look over his shoulder. "I'm so used to having long hair that I forgot about the possibility of sunburns." He glanced down at his tanned arms. "I haven't had to deal with one in years."

"I'd feel sorry for you," she said with a smirk, "but I never would have told you to get rid of your hair in the first place."

"The truth comes out at last. You only ever really liked me for my hair."

Thea giggled. "What did you say before? That *I* was going to regret not getting my hair cut?"

The Summoner took the opportunity to hurl a handful of dust at her.

Thea threw back her arms up with a shriek and started laughing. Her loud cackles, mixed with Rafe's grumbles, were what roused Blythe. She inhaled heavily before blinking dark eyes open, sitting up and stretching around a heavy exhale.

Leslie gave a loud, abrupt snort before jerking awake. "Huh?" he mumbled sleepily, dazed eyes looking all around him.

Blythe yawned next, raising her arms above her head before her eyes flew open and she gasped. Her hands immediately scrambled over her body before she was jumping to her feet and spinning around as if looking for someone.

Thea had stopped laughing at the abrupt change in the sorceress's demeanor, and she nearly flinched when the woman's intense gaze landed on the Coven members. "What...what is it?" She had barely gotten the question out before Blythe was staggering over to her and dropping to her knees.

"What is it like? What does it feel like? To have it disappear?"

Confusion quickly masked the Spellweaver's features, and her mouth bobbed open. "What?"

"The bond between you and your demon," Blythe clarified. "What does it feel like when the bond is broken? When the tether breaks?" Her eyes were dancing wildly, bright and glinting off the fractures of hope Thea saw there.

"Why do you ask?" Rafe came to sit beside them, face suddenly serious.

Thea finally shook off her stupor and sat up straighter. "What happened last night?"

"Ugh," Leslie groaned from his spot by the firepit. "What happened last night? Fah! I tell ya, yous guys sure know how ta pick 'em."

Thea blinked at the imp's input, but Rafe's gaze never wavered. His voice was grave, pressing. "Did it feel like it was slowly disappearing? Fading?" He frowned as he noticed Thea's hand go to her chest. She felt the familiar pang thrum through her as memories of Namara drying out in the snow flashed in her mind.

Blythe took a steadying breath and calmed the spark in her deep brown irises. Her small hands also reached up and massaged the area around her heart. With another deep breath, she said, "Last night Asmo came to visit me."

Both Thea and Rafe froze, mouths open in shock. Thea snapped into a rigid, upright position, about to drill the sorceress with no doubt a hundred questions. However, Blythe was carrying on, voice now much deeper and accent thick.

"He said...He said Cressida was going to die. If we gave her the cure. She would die either way, but..."

Thea felt her breath leave her in a small, explosive huff. Asmo actually knew about the cure. He knew it would cleanse Cressida's soul and—why had he bothered telling Blythe that? What was his angle?

The sound she had made was enough to gain Blythe's attention, and Thea continued to hold her gaze for a long, silent moment. This was her chance to come clean. This would be her only opportunity to tell the woman the truth. Cressida was going to die. Thea didn't know of any other way of stopping the ex-sorceress's impending demise. What was Blythe going to do? Turn around and walk all the way back to the sanctuary? Without having gotten the cure? Without having achieved anything?

She just might.

So, instead of telling her the truth, instead of taking the chance to tell Blythe, someone she now considered a friend, she asked instead, "Do you believe him?" as carefully as she dared.

The woman's shoulders sagged, and she heaved a heavy sigh. "No, but he must be desperate to keep me from curing her." She glanced at the Coven members and bit her lip, guilt suddenly visible in the dark depths of her eyes. "He was the reason why we were attacked yesterday. He possessed a massive amount of people in order to stop us."

Rafe swore. "That was Asmo?"

Blythe nodded, adding quietly, "He was still drained from it all when he sifted here to talk me out of continuing this...mission." Her lips twisted as if that wasn't quite the word she was looking for, but she didn't say anything else after that.

Thea shared a look with her partner. "That would explain their appearances. It was like nothing I've ever seen before."

"Also why they were as relentless as they were," Rafe agreed, chin in his palm. "Instead of focusing on the incoming Summoners attacking them, they continued after *us* despite the dangers of Banshee Bog." His eyes widened and he sat up straight. "Is that why you were asking if the tether was broken? Has he overcome the tether with his will power?"

Would it be so surprising if he could? So much was still up in the air when it came to demon princes. No one could ever really study them because anyone who ever encountered one always ended up dying a slow, torturous death. Only documented evidence on tier-three demons came from the Summoners who—a very long time ago—tried summoning them. The intelligence spell all demons are blasted with (which would bless the creature with morals as well as basic intelligence) had been repelled by a soul eater. After multiple attempts, it was desummoned. That data was some of the oldest remaining in the Coven.

Blythe's eyebrows pinched together in thought. "I do not think so. Shortly after he left, I felt this horrible pain in...ah, *vuch' om hugon, vuch' om sorta…*" She huffed, the language she wasn't familiar with failing her. "Not my heart," she tried again, "but in here." She tapped her chest where her heart lay all the same.

"Your soul?" Thea offered. She knew whenever she thought of the tether, she pictured it as a cord between souls...even if demons didn't technically have souls.

"*Eau!*" she nodded quickly. "It was like nothing I have ever felt before. The pain was so intense I could not even scream."

The Summoner was frowning, mouth pulled down tight as he rubbed at his chin. "That sounds like the tether was forcefully removed."

Thea perked up beside him. "Who would even be strong enough to—" She paled. "I have to call Winona." She scrambled to her feet and patted her person before diving to her pouches that had been clustered close to all their other belongings. She found her crystal ball and put some distance between her and the rest of the encampment.

Her crystal ball was pulsing a soft white light, glowing brightly before fading repeatedly. Weird. She thought nothing more of it as she pulled Winona's face into the forefront of her mind. The Second Chosen immediately answered.

"Do you know how many times I've tried calling you?" Winona seethed without greeting.

Thea blinked at the hostility. Maybe that was why her orb was pulsing. "Uh—"

"Let's get one thing straight, Spellweaver," her superior snapped, "if I had not burned all that incriminating evidence against you, you both would be in shackles the second you stepped back into the city. You better be lucky I—" She cut herself off and took a large, shuddering breath and closed her eyes. When they reopened, they were sharp, steel knives, and Thea found herself the target of those serrated edges. "Whatever happened in that dungeon, it took the power of the Celestial to undo it. She's keeping it under wraps, but I was thoroughly questioned because of my investigation on both you and MacBain's involvement. As it stands, you both are innocent—inept and incompetent at your jobs but naive of what went down at the sanctuary. Your little stunt has not only put my position under scrutiny, but Councilman McTaggart's as well. For your sake, Bauer, come back with the cure or don't come back at all." The connection winked out, and Thea was left feeling a little numb. She turned around, jumping at the sight of Rafe standing so close.

"Well, that explains Asmo's disappearance," he said grimly, handing her a large broadleaf in the palm of his hand. It was slightly brown with the edges curling, and in the center were three egg-sized balls. All were some sort of shade of tan with clumped combinations of toasted seeds, oats, dried fruit and molded around some oily, buttery paste.

"What is this?" she asked softly, but it didn't stop her from popping a whole one into her mouth. Big mistake. Her eyes widened, and she nearly choked. Whatever it was, it was incredibly chewy and sticky. The nutty, sweet flavor was nearly overwhelming.

Rafe snickered when she went to claw the roof of her mouth with a finger. "They are energy-rich trail mix drops. Blythe had them prepared sometime last night."

"We should get moving as soon as we can, and something for on the go seemed ideal," Blythe piped up, a small smile gracing her delicate features.

Thea agreed, but she couldn't very well say so with her mouth full of the tacky substance. It tasted good at least.

The sun was high in the sky and burning hotter than it had the day before. The only one unaffected was Leslie, who was basking in the rays as if it were a pleasant spring day. The four had kept quiet so as not to run out of breath quicker, and Thea would be the first to admit she was not built for long treks across shifty surfaces. The landscape was also much the same—sand, blue skies stretching endlessly over them, more sand, the occasional desert plant, a lot more sand, a scurrying lizard or snake shimmying under all the...sand. Thea sighed.

"How much farther?" she asked petulantly, and she didn't care if she sounded every bit like a tired, fussy child wanting to go home. The imp strutting beside her tutted and shook his head. Thea sent him a dirty look.

"It is honestly not th—" Blythe started to say with a giggle, but her footing slipped, and her dark eyes widened. She dropped to a low crouch while a hoarse "Duck!" tore out of her throat.

Years of working in the Coven saved Thea as she dropped to her knees. When someone yelled 'duck,' there was usually no time to question the act. Instincts forced Thea to flip onto her back, sand now hot against the fabric of her thin tunic and the skin underneath as the sun was now over the horizon and streaking red fire across the sky. Her arrow launcher was gripped tight to her chest in the blink of an eye. Her fingers had dexterously unholstered the weapon as soon as she had hit the ground.

A large shadow flew over them from above as a piercing caw rang throughout the desert. A large bird circled overhead menacingly, and it was by far the biggest flying fowl Thea had ever seen. With feathers the color of burnt flesh, its one wing was big enough for all four of them to fit comfortably on. It swooped around them, and a huge gust of wind tore through their clothing and carried cool air onto their heated skin. It would have been a blessing had the bird not been trying to kill them.

"What in tha seven sins is that!" Leslie shouted from his squatted position.

"How good is your aim?" Blythe cried to Thea over another of the bird's blaring calls. "Rafe, do not blast it with your staff! It will char it, and I'd rather bring my family something edible to eat!"

Rafe looked at the sorceress as if she were nuts, but this had not been the first time.

Thea only huffed at the Summoner's low curse and brought her arrow launcher up higher on her chest. She fired an arrow once, twice, but the insanely large creature dodged her magic shots effortlessly, and the wind it generated with its massive wings propelled the arrows into the infinite desert beyond. Thea narrowed her eyes and snarled. Moving targets were obviously a lot more difficult than something sitting still.

She didn't have the chance to calm her breathing and trace the bird's trajectory before it pierced the skies again with its ear-shattering cry and dove at the group. Her heart jolted as she watched talons as large as her head plummet down to her. She fired another arrow, but the beast's wing tipped and swung the creature out the arrow's path at the last second. She saw out of the corner of her eye Rafe raise his staff, burnt flesh the least of his concerns, but before either of them could try, a huge net flew over their heads and swallowed the bird whole.

The creature released another ear-splitting squall before crashing gracelessly to the ground. The vibrations rattled Thea's bones. Heart in her throat, she scrambled back in the sand with her arrow launcher pointed at the netted bird. Sand was flinging everywhere in the bird's desperate attempts to flee, pelting the onlookers with hot golden glitter. Somehow, its talons weren't cutting through the rope binding it, and it flapped around and fumbled in the trap endlessly.

"Blathi?"

Four heads jerked up at the top of the dune they were crouched into. A man stood there, deep umber skin swathed in colorful teal and dark blue robes while a dazzlingly gold scarf wrapped around his head and shadowed his dark eyes. A long, dark beard sprouted from the man's chin, but the hair looked to be very fine and soft. It wasn't coarse or scraggly like all the ones she'd seen old men wear back in the city. It was also decorated in waterfall braids and shining beads while the loose strands curled in waves, like the endless rise and fall of the dunes surrounding them.

A soft, surprised gasp left Blythe, and Thea, Rafe, and Leslie swung their attention to the woman and caught the recognition in her eyes. *"Soles? Dy de ais?"* she shouted up to him, flinching when her voice caused the large creature close to them to start flapping vigorously again.

"Eau!" he called back with a large, blinding smile. *"Bero virederdz! Onch' ais enym eastigh? U, aiv dyk' kerugh aik' nkeril rruka."* He paused for a minute and took in the other three that had accompanied his former tribemate warily. *"Perzepis mo gendzik' ean."*

Thea whipped around to the imp who was cowering by her side like a second shadow. "Hey," she hissed, "what are they saying?"

Eloquently as always, Leslie let out a, "Huh?" before pinching his brows as he tried remembering. "Uh, well, I think he said her name, and then she said his and asked if it was really him." Leslie scratched his head with a grubby finger, looking up and flinching at Thea's intense, expectant gaze. "Jeez, ya puttin' the spotlight on me, Honey Badger, I wasn't payin' attention!"

Thea scoffed and whispered fiercely, "The whole reason we brought you with us was to translate, Leslie!"

Blythe giggled behind her, and Thea glanced up to see the woman now standing. "It is okay. He simply welcomed me back home and asked me why I have come back. Then he said you can go ahead and shoot the rok...just don't char it."

The Spellweaver blinked. She glanced over at Rafe, who merely shrugged as he slowly put back his weapon, and then up at the man still standing at the top of the dune. He seemed friendly if the small, awkward wave he sent them was anything to go by.

Guess they really don't like barbeque, she thought before her eyes drifted to the rok still flapping angrily in the unbreakable net. She raised her arrow launcher and shot.

Chapter Sixteen

The Village Protected by Deities

"O'nch' ais yzym dyrs gel eastigh `bulurod onk'nyryan?" Blythe was saying, the words flying out of her mouth at an incredible speed. She almost sounded angry, and perhaps the pinched look on her face was a bit stern, but there was a sparkle in her dark brown gaze that couldn't have been ire.

"'What are you doing way out here by yourself?'" Leslie glumly quoted. Thea's hand was latched onto the demon's skull, keeping him from looking away and losing focus. She would probably be like this until common tongue was the predominant language spoken again.

The man, Silas, furrowed his brow in a confused look. *"Ais onk's ch'im,"* and then he pointed over the sand dune he'd been standing on a moment ago.

"'I'm not alone,'" Leslie parroted around a sigh. Then it seemed to register what he had just translated, for he and the others all looked up toward the dune Silas had pointed at. He waved for them to follow before the man was jogging up the dune as if the shifting sand weren't an obstacle at all. The rest struggled, Blythe the least out of them all.

When they reached the top of the dune, Thea's eyes widened. Silas was most definitely not alone. Six other men and women, three camels, and two small camel-like creatures were also in attendance. The animals were all loaded down with bags of wares, fabrics, and dried goods. Upon seeing Blythe, the others' eyes went wide, and their mouths dropped open in shock, jumping into a frenzy of wild gestures and loud, foreign words. Hugs were exchanged between the sorceress and her people before they were quickly surrounding Rafe, Thea, and Leslie.

"What are they saying?" Thea hissed down at the imp, but Leslie was too busy being picked up and prodded at by the Ernimoens surrounding him.

"Ay, ay, ay!" he cried out with arms flailing around him. "*Ondz ts'ets dror!*" A collective gasp left the villagers, the one holding him nearly dropping the imp on his head before they all burst into laughter. Blythe looked close to tears as she exchanged hugs with everyone who wasn't harassing Leslie, and when they were done with the imp they gathered excitedly around Thea and Rafe.

It didn't take a translator for Thea to figure out that the two women crowding around her wanted to touch her loose curls. She smiled politely and bent her head toward them. The woman standing closest had taupe-colored hair pulled to one side of her head and swirled into the shape of a coiled snake from hundreds of microscopic braids. She was swathed in sparkling midnight and fuchsia robes, and she gingerly reached out and touched Thea's spiral locks. Surprise morphed her features, spreading over cheeks splattered with large, clustered freckles and lighting up her soft, chocolate brown eyes. The other woman seemed to teeter between being nervous and being jealous of her fellow villager. Thea thought the shy woman's hair was perhaps more intriguing than all of them. She too had hundreds of tiny plaits close to her scalp, but the further from her head the more they grew in size, fanning out over her like a wide-brimmed hat. She wore bright green and rich, dark brown robes that complemented her onyx eyes and fairer complexion. She was still tanner than Rafe would ever hope to be, but even compared to Blythe the woman was the lightest of all the villagers.

Thea glanced over to Rafe, who was surrounded by the five men in the traveling party, Silas included. Blythe was helping translate for him as he explained his lack of facial hair with a large, goofy smile on his face.

"You should see how long my hair used to be," he continued, pausing only briefly so Blythe could repeat his words in her own tongue, "it came all the way down to here." He gestured to his lower back, turning slightly to better show where the length used to be.

"Ean embughj cheneperhuv hesev eystigh," Blythe stated, giggling when the men in her old village gasped and fell into loud, barking laughter.

"Erdau'k' bulur tghemerdok eadk'en airker ain echym orints' mezira?" An older man spoke, his voice rough and deep. He looked to be the oldest of them all. His eyes were dark yet exceptionally clear, surrounded by smile lines. He wore pure white and light blue robes, and his beard was streaked with white and decorated in hundreds of gold beads and sparkling trinkets.

Rafe looked to Blythe.

She was giggling again. "He asked if all the men where you live grow their hair out."

"Oh, no." He laughed and shrugged his shoulders. "I didn't see too many people with hair as long as I had mine...unless they were women."

The group of men burst into another round of uproarious laughter as soon as Blythe relayed his words.

Introductions were quickly made and gotten out of the way, the rok was hauled up the dune and secured to the three camels, and Silas began leading the way back to the village. Leslie was placed on top of one of the allocamelus, an odd creature that looked like a mashup of a donkey and a camel, so that he wouldn't slow the party down with his short, stubby legs. He had appeared freaked out for all of about thirty seconds before his features smoothed out (as smooth as they could for such a bumpy, toad-like face), and his demeanor changed into that of a small lord being carted on the backs of his peasants.

The sun was now high in the sky and burning Thea's skin pink, but she relished the heat that warmed her bones. She could deal without the sweat that was working up under the mane of curls she had, but the hot breeze that blew by every once in a while was nice. She felt a tap on her arm and blinked up at the woman with the mass freckles adorning her cheeks. Chaska was what her name had been translated to, and she was offering Thea a piece of lilac fabric and pointing to her head.

"Oh, thank you," she said, hoping that even if her words didn't reach the woman her sincerity would. Chaska beamed, and her freckles danced across her features as if they were alive.

Blythe was ahead of them all, keeping pace with Silas and one of the allocameluses he was leading. As she tied up her curls, she observed the two. There was really nothing else to look at, and she couldn't exactly converse with her foreign acquaintances.

I guess I'm *actually the foreigner here,* she thought absentmindedly.

She kept her eyes on the two as the group continued to walk along the spine of a particularly long dune. Blythe seemed to be reminiscing about something, but Silas…his gaze was nothing short of adoration. Thea bit her lip. Maybe she was misinterpreting his expression. It wasn't her place to worry about something that didn't concern her anyway. She and Blythe were not *that* close, after all. How would Blythe even handle a conversation like that?

Hey, I know you're still in love with Cressida, and you're bound and determined to save her…but she's not going to make it, so...if you're into guys, maybe give Silas a shot? He's clearly infatuated with you.

Thea grimaced, and guilt settled heavily within her soul and left a bad taste in the back of her mouth at just the thought of speaking those words aloud.

The group had remained relatively quiet throughout the journey to the village. Small, translated chit-chat mingled between them all on occasion until the dune they had been traveling along veered sharply eastward. Now, before them, the desert transformed from shifting mountains of golden sand to dry, compact dirt the bleached color of wheat stalks. Brown clumps of hardy grasses, tall and spiky bushes, and sharp, flowering cacti jutted up from the cracking loam despite the arid temperature and blazing sun beating down on them. The dune had also given way to an aerial view of a large, gaping canyon a couple hundred paces away from where they stood. Silas pointed and spoke in short, sharp words.

"That is the village," Blythe easily translated. As the group began moving toward the deep gorge, she continued speaking. "We'll be going around and entering from the front." Then she clapped her hands and tossed an excited look over her shoulder at Thea, Rafe, and Leslie. "You're going to meet Moje and Gitk'! I cannot wait to see your reactions."

Thea vaguely remembered Blythe speaking about those two yesterday, but she couldn't put faces to the names. Maybe they were the village leaders? Did they not have translated names?

Her feet connected with the hard, compact ground, and she nearly lost her footing. She scowled down at her ankle, peeved she had to actually think about how to walk properly on solid ground.

Anticipation was heavy in the air the closer they neared the canyon. Everyone had hushed, eyes set straight ahead. The heavy drag of the rok over dirt and rubble, the hefty sighs of the camels, and the snuffles of the donkey were the only sounds accompanying them at the moment. They were nearly a mile away when Silas diverged left and followed a natural decline, walking parallel to the canyon now. The rough, stone wall rose higher and higher into the sky beside them. Its dry cliff face bore the brunt of the burning sun. The further they walked, the lower the elevation, the narrower the path. Masses of thin-branched, barren trees grew on the other side of the path, keeping the travelers in a line that allowed no more than two people to stand shoulder to shoulder.

Quite a ways in front of Thea, the trail stretched on and let out into a large desert valley. It was wide, oblong, and rocky mountains and huge sandy dunes jutted up from the horizon. The canyon came to an abrupt stop just up ahead, but they hadn't come around to the face of it yet.

When they did, Thea felt her jaw drop.

"Whoa," Leslie commented from atop his little steed.

"That's...something," said Rafe after floundering for words himself. Thea didn't even try. She just gaped. Beside them, Blythe was giggling and clapping like an excited toddler.

Moje and Gitk' were not people. They were not even living beings but rather enormous stone statues carved out of the face of the canyon. They were ten times larger than the statues sitting outside HQ, their forms soaring into the air like mountains. Both were cat-like, sitting back on wide haunches while their faces were a unique mix of human and grimalkin. They both were nearly identical; pointed ears, human-esque facial features, cat mouths, barrel chests, and long, feline front legs. The paws of the beasts were as big as her duplex. The one on the right rested one paw on a circular orb, and the other statue held one paw up in the air.

"Welcome to *Gaygha Peshtpenvets i Estvetsyt'aynniruv,*" Blythe said with a wide grin, sweeping low in an introductory bow. Silas snickered beside her, muttering something only she caught.

"Oh, right." She eyed Thea and Rafe's blank stares. "You can just call it *gaygh.* Much shorter."

"Thank you," Rafe chuckled.

"The Village Protected by Deities?" Leslie parroted in common tongue after a moment of consideration.

Blythe gushed happily, "Correct! Moje is the Patron God, and Gitk' is the God of Rain. One protects our village and the other ensures its survival. Come, come! I have much to show you!" She waved enthusiastically for them to follow her before forging into the canyon.

The sounds of a marketplace reached Thea's ears the nearer she got to the monumental statues. She came to a stop before she passed them, and Rafe came up beside her. The rest of the party, along with the rok that was drug behind them, passed them by with encouraging smiles and waves to follow them. Leslie was swept along with them, bouncing on the little donkey as he went.

Warm fingers slipped in between her own, and she steeled herself. The villagers so far had been extremely friendly and welcoming, and Thea didn't think for a moment she would be met with open hostility. But venturing into unfamiliar territory was as unnerving as it was exciting. She squeezed Rafe's hand and took the first step into the entrance of the canyon. Above her, she swore she felt the eyes of the enormous deity statues watching her.

The canyon entrance was broken by a bend in the natural rock walls but reaching the short distance around the bend allowed for Thea to see straight through the marketplace for what looked like miles. Everywhere was packed with *something*, and Thea was immediately brought back to Blythe's eclectically packed room in the sanctuary.

The canyon walls that jutted seemingly forever into the sky were spaced large enough apart that HQ could fit snugly within twice, and on either side of the canyon were mazes of etched in steps that led to carved out bungalow houses within the rock. Up the wall and down, along every available surface were stairs that wandered this way or that, up to more homes and down to the market below. Lines of brightly colored flags in dazzling shades stretched from one side to another, as did clothing lines on pulley-devices.

Women were shouting out of the dug-out, glassless windows, children were running barefoot in the street, and hagglers were bickering back and forth with those wanting to buy from them. Vendors in pitched tents crowded up against their neighbors beckoned to the loud passing crowd before them while musicians strumming strange instruments danced between onlookers. Merchants tugging camels or donkeys crowed to customers, bragging about the wares they collected on their journey across the desert. No one was dressed dully. Everyone sported every color of the rainbow and all the shades in between.

Oddly shaped jars in jewel-toned colors glinted in the light of some of the open canvas shops, hung from above and over the crowd. Soft silk robes and scarves dangled betwixt them and swayed in the cool breeze that weaved through the canyon.

Pungent odors blended and crashed together the further in Thea walked. Incense burned in one tent, grilled meat smoked out another, and a makeshift stable for animals rankled the air in the desert heat. Animals Thea had never seen before prowled through the market alongside the people who had tamed them. Outside of the camels, donkeys, and pigs, there were huge birds bigger than any human that walked upright. With elongated, naked legs and a neck that was just as bare and lengthy, it had Thea nearly breaking her own neck to keep an eye on it as it passed. Small rabbits with unproportionally large ears bounded past her feet and kept pace with the shrieking children of the village, and reptiles like large lizards and tortoises bathed in the hot sun that pelted their backs along the walkways and on the steps of the cave walls. Among them all, large cats Thea recognized as the *kereselas* she saw in the Skrittish Library book were the most common. Their red-tinted, golden fur glowed under the rays of daylight, and they were joined at the hip with nearly every other human in the vicinity. They were more common than the dogs back in Tolvade by the looks of it.

A loud cheer rang throughout the crowd, startling Thea out of her musings. Up ahead of them, people had gathered around what she believed was the captured rok while loud, foreign words belted out into the market.

"Eas airiku mink' tunym aink'!" Thea didn't recognize the words, but she recognized the voice belonging to Silas. Whatever he said, the village was now going wild with boisterous jubilation, piercing whistles, and people banging things together like pots, pans, and musical instruments in their excitement. *"Aiv emin onch' mir hayriro shnurhov i!"*

With that, the crowd went quiet, and hundreds of faces turned to Thea and Rafe.

Chapter Seventeen

Family is Not Always Defined by Blood

Thea felt the hairs on her arms raise as the silence stretched on. Camels grunted, donkey's brayed, the hanging jars swaying in the breeze clinked together, but not a sound came from the masses surrounding her. She felt Rafe's hand tighten on her wrist while his other inched for the boomerang on his belt.

Cheers erupted around them as swiftly as the silence had descended, and before they could blink, they were swarmed by the townspeople. Thea was grabbed and pulled this way and that, given rough shakes and hard pats on the head, arms, and back. Rafe was receiving the same rough treatment, but some of the affections had him stumbling forward or backward from the intensity.

Blythe and Leslie appeared by Thea's side out of nowhere, and she batted away the rowdy hands pummeling the Coven members' bodies with a joyful smile. "*Lev, lev, de beverer i!*"

"She said 'that's enough,'" Leslie automatically supplied when Thea glanced his way.

She nodded and looked around at the sea of faces now circling her. "What's going on?" she muttered at Blythe.

The woman giggled. "Silas may or may not have given you credit for taking down the rok."

Rafe tilted his head her way. "He's the one who threw the net."

"*Eau*, but it was Thea that shot the killing blow. It was much quicker and easier than if they had used a sword or ax. Now, because you are the first guests we have had in a long time and because you brought us a magnificent feast, *Udoni-petroerk'* wants to have audience with you."

Thea looked back and forth between Blythe and the fellow villagers, but no one stood out. "Who?"

The sorceress giggled. Her excitable energy was nearly palpable as she stood amongst friends she hadn't seen in years. "Call her Madam Odine. She is our village's matriarch, but you will talk with her later. For now, let us give you a tour! *Uv i yzym errejona gnel?"* She shouted the last bit to the crowd surrounding them.

The village came alive once again with cheers and choruses of *"ais, ais, ais,"* and other words Thea had no hope of understanding. She was swept along in the tide and brought to stall after stall. Each individual wanted to show off their livelihoods or their families off to new eyes.

Silas was the first introduced. Blythe went on to describe that he was swiftly becoming the village's main hunter, and he was constantly out in the desert using his keen senses to kill and capture creatures to bring back for meals.

Silas looked down at the ground and scratched the back of his neck. *"Ais p'vurdzym aim emin onch' enil, beats' kertsym aim, vur perzepis bekhts biril i."*

Blythe waved away his words and rolled her eyes fondly. "He says he's an amazing hunter."

Leslie snickered.

Thea was listening, but she couldn't help but be distracted by the warm look in Silas's eyes whenever Blythe translated what he was saying. It was clear she was embellishing his words, for Silas was by far too shy to be talking about himself so highly.

Next, there was Jorah, a middle-aged man with a shine to his midnight eyes, who hand-crafted beads from the unique glass sculptures formed from lightning striking sand. The beads were beautifully painted in different patterns, colors, and shades.

"It takes him hours to carve one bead and paint it," Blythe translated as Thea and Rafe marveled over the massive variety. Leslie was straining on his tiptoes to see.

The man was still talking, but now he was holding a few brightly colored pieces and urging the sorceress to take them.

Blythe's eyes widened, and she blinked a couple times before she found her voice. *"Onch' o nketo ynis?"*

Jorah was smiling, and he gently took Blythe's hand and dropped the beads into her open palm. *"Virts'ry nrents' aiv mo murrets'or miz."*

Thea looked back and forth between the two. Surprise morphed her expression when Blythe's eyes began to water, but she nodded and held the beads close to her heart. When the Spellweaver glanced at Leslie, the imp merely shook his head. It was none of her business what was said.

They moved on to Niran, a stone sculpture whose age was unknown even to those around him. His smile was crowded with wrinkles, and his light brown eyes held wisdom in their depths. Streaks of gray decorated his beard, along with the main braids and beads, both wooden and glass, woven into the dark hair. His granddaughter, Zemira, was his ever-helpful assistant. Her hair was parted in small buns across her head, leaving her scalp in a zig-zag pattern, and she wore pale green harem pants and yellow blouse that was modest but left her arms free to work with. The younger woman skirted the imp-sized statues of the two deities outside the canyon and hurled herself into Blythe's arms.

Blythe groaned in exaggeration as she hugged the girl back and lifted her off her feet. *"Vea, dy eanken' mits ais derdzil!"* she laughed. She glanced up and smiled at the two Coven members and clarified. "This one used to give me such trouble when I was tasked with looking after the children."

Rafe laughed fondly. "I can tell. She has that look in her eye."

Thea instantly thought of Rafe's little brothers and sisters giving him a rough time. No wonder he was able to pick out trouble before it even started.

"I wonder where she gets it from," Blythe smirked and threw a pointed look at the old man over her shoulder. *"He? Vurtigh i ne stenym or ch'eryt'ayna?"*

Niran only offered her a toothless, gummy smile that had her and the rest of the villagers cackling.

Before long, they had visited Medora and Rowan, two sisters who were tasked with taking care of the village children for this moon cycle. One would catch up with Blythe while the other would run after a giggling toddler. Then, they would switch, picking up where the other had left off without a hitch. Seamus looked after the goats, donkeys, pigs, and such. He had stopped his introduction to yell at a bunch of groaning and grunting camels, only to then have to dodge the wad of spit hurled at him. The incident had Blythe in stitches from laughing so hard. Elio was as tall as Rafe and wore her hair in a large bun with braids that crisscrossed over it. She was a woman of many trades and few words. She made lotions, cheese, soap, and butter. All from goat milk. Caius, a loud and boisterous man, sold rustic instruments that his family crafted. He wouldn't let Thea and Rafe leave until they tried the drum-type contraptions, much to the amusement of their entourage. Juno, a sweet older woman with graying hair piled ornately on top of her head, sold rugs of varying material. Some were woven from bark while others were the rough texture of wool-like hair. All were dyed in geometric patterns.

Finally, Thea recognized Chaska standing in one of the stalls selling silky, vibrantly colored shawls, scarves, and other clothing. An older couple was hovering nearby, and Thea assumed the two were Chaska's parents, for she looked identical to the woman behind her. She smiled excitedly as Thea, Rafe, Blythe, and the rest of the village crowded around. Then she was urging Thea closer and spoke. *"Henik' ead mika,"* she said, pointing to the lilac scarf she had given Thea earlier.

Trying not to rely on Blythe and Leslie too much, Thea took off the scarf and gestured with it. "This?"

Chaska may not have understood her, but she was nodding regardless and leaned over to take the scarf back. She quickly peered over her shoulder at the couple, and the two nodded with reassuring smiles. Chaska beamed and whipped around to grab a dark blue scarf. The woman held it up briefly, looking between it and Thea before nodding again and handing it over.

"Se evilo tighon i. Ean hemepetesk henym i dzir ech'k'iron."

Thea, confused, looked to Blythe. The sorceress was admiring the scarf and nodding in agreement. "She said this is more fitting since it matches your eyes."

"Wha—I—wait," she floundered for a moment. "Is she giving it to me?"

Blythe was giggling again. "Yes. It is, ah..." her brow scrunched as she tried to find the word she was looking for. "A...memento, to remember us all by."

They each graciously received one. A sea-green one was given to Rafe that made the color of his eyes stand out more than Thea thought was possible. Leslie was given a dark brown one that he proudly tied around his chin, gaining laughter from the villagers. Thea had wanted to face palm.

She turned to Chaska and gave a light bow. "Thank you for your generosity."

Blythe was quick to interpret her words, but she was cut off when Chaska took a large, sheer, sunflower yellow shawl and whipped the folded material out. It fluttered in the air as it took shape, catching the sunlight with its dazzling ebony patterns and sewn-in jewels. It was a magnificent piece, and Chaska handed it to Blythe with an equally magnificent smile.

"Virts'ry se, aiv shytuv virederdzor miz tisnily."

Again, Blythe's eyes began to mist as she hesitantly took the fabric. *"Hemuzvets ais?"*

Chaska nodded, her eyes a little watery too.

The last person they visited before dinner preparations were called was Atlas, the village-appointed guide for all nomadic trips. He had welcomed Blythe with a soft smile, open arms, and a fatherly hug that lasted for long moments. Everyone that had come across the sorceress had embraced her with joyous smiles and happy tears, but not one of them had been introduced as Blythe's parents. Thea didn't think Atlas was her father, but it was clear the two were close in that regard.

The exchange between the two was brief but private after that, and when Blythe rejoined Thea and Rafe amongst the other villagers, Thea's curiosity got the better of her.

"Who was that?" she asked quietly.

She saw the emotions trapped in Blythe's dark irises, and the woman sighed. It was clear she understood Thea wasn't asking about who he was to the village—that had already been explained—but who he was to her. "He is not my father," she went on to explain, smiling briefly at Leslie cracking jokes with the villagers at poor Rafe's expense. She tucked loose strands of hair behind her ear as the desert wind blew through the canyon. "He..." she paused, bit her lip, and her eyes danced around the ground as words once again failed her, but not because of the barrier of differing languages. "I believe he feels obligated to look after me after..." she sighed again, and Thea stepped in with a worried frown.

"You don't have to tell me, Blythe. I don't have to know. I'm sorry I asked."

Blythe gave her a wan smile. "It is all right. I just have not talked about this to anyone outside of Cressida. My parents were lost out in the desert after a sandstorm swept them away from the group." A faraway look settled on her face, and she took another deep breath. "They were never found. Atlas was leading the group, so he felt responsible." The ghostly glaze in her eyes fractured as a warmer smile slid over her once despondent expression. "I did not travel the desert alone when I came to Tolvade. He escorted me despite the risks he would face once he made his way back. I could not change his mind."

Thea nodded, gaze set ahead and aimed at Rafe and Leslie's tomfoolery but not actually paying attention to them. She didn't dare look at Blythe with pity. Blythe was too strong for that, and Thea knew what it was like to have pity aimed at her. Even though it had never been anyone's intentions, it was the one look that made her feel weak.

"Is...Is that why you left your village?" she questioned, referring to the disappearances of her parents.

She saw Blythe nod out of the corner of her eye. "I waited many weeks hoping for their return, but they knew this desert as well as Atlas did. They would have come back within days if they were alive. After so long, I could not stay contained in this village when everything reminded me of them. I wanted to be somewhere where people looked at me because I was strange, not because I was stricken by my parents' deaths." She giggled the last bit. "I came to Tolvade and fell in love with magic. I called the library home for a long time before I spoke your language well enough to hold conversations, and then I found Srbeveara."

Thea marveled at Blythe's tenacity, but before she could say anything else, the sorceress's eyes were lighting up. "Madam Odine is here."

Thea whipped back around. "Where?" she asked, but her question was answered soon enough when the crowd around Thea and Leslie started parting.

A lone woman in dark, sparkling navy robes drifted forward as graceful as smoke, carrying a matching parasol over her head. Her eyes were as dark as the bottom of lakes, and her hair was a mass of thick, ebon locks bundled up on her head like a beehive. Her skin though, was what set her apart from the rest. Everyone in the village had tanned, even skin, ranging from cool-toned sepia to rich and warm sienna. Madame Odine's though was swarthy in large patches but pale—as pale as Thea—in other, smaller patches. Her cheeks, over the bridge of her nose, and up to the center of her forehead were pale streaks of pink, rosy skin speckled with freckles around the edges. What was visible of her arms was much the same. Around her fingers were spots of skin that were several, dramatic shades lighter than the rest of her. She was the most unique looking being Thea had ever come across.

"It has been a long time since we have had visitors from so far away. Will you please join me, honored guests?"

Chapter Eighteen

Madame Dragon Whisperer

Thea's jaw dropped. "You speak…?" She looked Blythe's way, but the sorceress's gaze was also full of surprise. Her dainty hands had flown to her mouth in her shock.

Madame Odine hummed a hearty laugh, her wide mouth splitting in a display of teeth while her dark eyes danced with mischief and mirth. "Oh, I know many languages, my dear. The other civilizations in this vast desert all speak differently than we do. I used to have no use for your Eastern city language, but when our dear *Blathi* went off to explore the world, I decided I would give it a try."

"So, I was dragged out here fa nothin'," Leslie complained loudly from the side.

Thea shot him a look. "We still need you when we encounter the Draconians."

Leslie gulped.

When Thea looked back to Madame Odine, the woman's expression was curious, but there was something else swimming in the depths of her onyx eyes. She offered the Coven members another polite smile and waved a hand for them to follow. "This way, please," she said, turning around and walking back through the crowd. "My home is nothing grand, but it is out of the sun."

"I am going to catch up with you two later," Blythe informed from beside Thea and Rafe when they began to follow the matriarch through the throng of people. "I do not know when I will get the chance to see my home or friends again."

Thea glanced behind the sorceress to see the villagers watching them, eyes sparkling in excitement and a few bouncing on the balls of their feet. Silas had his eyes were zeroed in on the sorceress, so earnest hopeful it would have been a crime to keep the two separated. "Oh, okay. Yeah, sure." Though she was a little hesitant to let Blythe go, and only because she had sort of become their guide and cultural ambassador, she smiled and waved the woman off.

Let her have these fond moments.

She needed to enjoy these small moments of reprieve herself. This time tomorrow, she could be finding herself staring up at a living legend. Trying to coherence it into giving her its blood, no less. Would they even make it out of that encounter alive? There were so many things she had pushed aside in her head while she'd been on the tour of Blythe's home. They still had to cross the desert if they survived the meeting with the wyvern, fight their way through Banshee Bog all over again, and pray to the goddess there weren't more possessed people lurking around Herbon. And if they didn't get that blood? If they failed their mission, what was Winona going to do to them? She'd burned their file, but it wouldn't be surprising if she suddenly had a backup on—

Rafe jerked her hand in his grasp. "Stop tensing your shoulders," he whispered quietly beside her, just low enough that Madame Odine couldn't hear from the few paces she had on them. "We're only going to be here for one night. What's the worst that—"

"*Don't* ask that question," she all but hissed, but a half-smile revealed her amusement. Rafe matched her smirk with one of his own.

"Whe'es ya claws, Honey Badger?" Leslie teased with a nudge of his grubby elbow into Thea's knee. "Don' be such'ah worry wa't."

She rolled her eyes. "I'm not worried. I'm *not,*" she emphasized when Rafe aimed her a pointed look. "I'm just…anxious, I guess. We're *here,* in the Golden Sea Desert, and the sand wyverns could be right outside these canyon walls. I've got Winona breathing down our necks about finding the cure, the High One knows about Asmo, and there are still demons running around Aeristria while I'm out here on what feels like a vacation." She huffed out a breath of air and looked the Summoner's way, finding both his eyebrows were raised. When she swiveled her head in Leslie's direction, the imp looked equally as shocked. "Sorry… There's just a lot going through my mind right now."

Not to mention knowing about Cressida's impending demise and how Asmo spilled the magic beans. Thank the goddess Blythe hadn't believed him.

"Sounds like you need a nice drink to go along with your vacation," Madame Odine said with a smile tucked inside her voice, having stopped ahead of them before a set of carved stairs.

Thea looked to the ground and chewed on the corner of her lip. Guess she'd gotten a little loud during that last bit.

"Oh, I don't think a beverage would be very helpful, Madame Odine. You see, Thea has a problem drinking things as of l—*oof!*"

Thea jammed her elbow into Rafe's abdomen and glared while heat engulfed her face.

Madame Odine laughed heartily, hand over her heart as her eyes crinkled, and she shook her head. "Ah, you two. Come on up. We will see if there is anything I got that you can keep down."

Madame Odine's home was carved into the canyon just like every other home they'd passed by, and everything from the shelves to the doorways to the drawers were built into the open layout. There was no furniture per se, but there was round, padded seating on the floor atop a braided carpet made of soft, rainbow material. Stationed in front of the cushions was a suspended metal cauldron of sorts, covered by a mesh lid. It hung lazily in the air over a dug-out part of the floor where black coals were gathered. Behind it, Thea noticed a latch bolted into the stone. It was a very modest abode and, surprisingly above all, very cool.

The windows were covered by thick mats to keep the heat out, but it also blocked most of the light out as well. Thea felt that if she had to choose her house always being dim or always hot…her eyes would learn to adjust. She sat down on one of the cushioned seats and felt the need to keep her spine straight in the presence of the village's leader. Rafe mirrored her position, choosing the spot beside her, but Leslie had contented himself with sprawling out along the dirt floor and sighing obnoxiously.

"Let me see what I have in stock," Madame Odine said once she hooked her parasol onto the sculpted hall tree, though it looked less like a tree and more like nubby antlers morphing out of the wall. She sauntered over to the recessed floor hatch and lifted the door, reaching her whole arm in and grabbing three long-necked bottles. When she handed them to Thea and the others, the Spellweaver's eyes widened at the cold, dewy glass.

"How are you able to keep this so cold without..." she hesitated. Would it be rude to ask about their inability to perform magic? Or their lack of electricity?

Madame Odine chuckled, the sound deep, mature, as she settled on the cushion Leslie had chosen to forego. "It is fine...oh, *Blathi* never mentioned your names."

"Sorry about that," Rafe chimed in, extending his hand in greeting but hesitated when Madame only looked at it curiously. "It's, um, a handshake. We do this during introductions or when we come to agreements sometimes." He shrugged his one shoulder, arm still hanging suspended.

Madame Odine appeared enlightened, and a smile graced her lips. She extended her hand and lightly grasped Rafe's. "It is a pleasure to be acquainted with you."

Rafe grinned and took his hand back. "Likewise. My name is Rafe MacBain."

"Thea," the Spellweaver offered and gave a brief handshake of her own. "And that cretin is Leslie."

The imp sat up and offered his stubby hand to the woman. "Leslie Templeton, most handsome cretin you'll eva meet."

Madame Odine laughed good-naturedly again. "I say. I have met my fair share of creatures out in the desert, but none that have come up from the underworld." She took his hand and shook it before meeting Thea's gaze again. "Now back to your previous question. I understand you and others in the city use magic, but out here we utilize what we're given by the elements we live with." She gestured to the hatch and then around the room. "Things that are underground and out of the sun stay cool. Misting the walls and floor with a bit of water every once in a while keep things cooler as well. This," she tapped the hatch with her fingers, "is actually just a covering. Inside is a large clay pot lined with wet sand. Inside that is another clay pot that's been glazed to prevent water damage and is where my food and drinks are kept. When the wet sand evaporates, it draws out heat from the inner pot."

"That's ingenious," Thea marveled. She took a sip of water and, sure enough, the liquid that trickled down her throat was pleasantly chilled.

"Are you sure there isn't magic involved?" Rafe questioned, expression serious. "Because Thea has not choked o—"

"I swear to the goddess, Rafe," she seethed, sending him a vicious glare that only narrowed further when he began laughing.

"I did want to ask..." Madame Odine began with a wide smile, dark eyes alight with humor. "You mentioned something about the sand wyverns?"

The atmosphere grew somber as Thea and Rafe clammed up. Madame Odine paused and peered at the two of them questioningly.

"You are correct," Rafe started, hoping to keep the conversation flowing. "You see, there is someone very…important to Blythe who has fallen ill. This illness cannot be cured by magic or medicine, but Blythe believes that a cure can be found with the Draconians."

The village matriarch hummed in understanding. "And you are referring to the sand wyverns, specifically?"

Rafe's brow pinched in confusion. "Wha...uh, yes?"

"Smooth," Thea muttered.

Madame Odine broke into a chuckle again. "All the dragon-kind are of the Draconian race. The *Evez Voshepnir*—sand wyverns—are only found in this desert."

Thea leaned closer. "Only?"

"Only," she confirmed with a slow nod. "I spoke to one when I was a little girl." Her gaze began to drift to someplace far away.

Thea lurched forward, eyes wide in astonishment. "What do you mean you talked with one?"

"Yeah, wha'da ya mean?" Leslie piped up from the ground, having ignored the conversation until now. "You mean I came all this way fa nothin'?"

Madame Odine waved a hand in the air. "Forgive me. I misspoke. I talked to the sand wyvern, but it did not speak back to me…not with words, anyway. I was separated from my mother when a sandstorm came out of nowhere. I found myself half-buried beneath the sand, and when I sat up, eyes as big as myself and the color of my mother's favorite clay pot were staring at me." Her gaze floated down from out of the clouds and found Thea and Rafe's bewildered expressions. She huffed a laugh. "I thought I was done for, but as I waited for the killing blow or for the wyvern to swallow me whole...I realized his eyes were not predatory like our faithful *keresela* having spotted a scampering jackalope. No, these eyes were watchful, curious almost. Eventually, I started asking questions. The beast was able to understand me but I..." she sighed. "I wish I could have understood him as well."

"Do you know if their blood has medical properties?" Thea asked quietly as the silence stretched.

Madame Odine looked down at her arm and slowly traced the patches of her skin where the pigment was lighter. "I believe so. You see, I've had these marks ever since I was born. I was always treated special because of them. Everyone and yet no one wanted to be my friend. I had masses of people come to see me, thinking I had been touched by some greater being." The woman's expression twisted. "I wanted to be normal, like every other boy and girl in this village. I asked the wyvern if he could fix me. I remember it clearly: the sand shifted, and a large, golden, scaly hand blocked out the sun. Its claws were as big as this home. I believed I had offended it and was now about to be killed. But the claws only curled inward. So tightly that blood began to drip onto the ground below. I caught some in my hand and drank every drop." She laughed at the disgust that was easy to see in the Spellweaver's eyes. "Yes, it is gruesome to hear about. After I drank a few drops, I felt better than ever. My limbs that were sore from the day's walk were no longer tired. I felt energy flow through me as swift as sandstorms. My hair was glossy, and my curls were more springy than they ever had been before. However, when I looked down, my skin was the same. If wyvern blood could not cure it…well, then there must not be anything wrong." Her smile was wide, full of teeth with eyes crinkled in her silent laughter.

Thea swallowed around a lump that had suddenly formed in her throat. "That's amazing," she breathed out quietly. She wasn't exaggerating or placating the woman in the slightest. She knew what it meant to be different—not to this extent, but she could relate. This woman's existence hadn't been met with cruelty, but her circumstances mirrored Thea's own. She had wanted to be normal. She had not wanted the attention that came with the marks on her skin, but she learned to embrace it because there was nothing wrong with her.

I wish I had had your strength, she wanted to say. All she had done was run away from those that cast judgment on her, and while that was more commendable than letting her family continue to berate her, she had not come to accept the parts of her she didn't like. She still looked at herself some days and wished some things were different, that some things could be changed.

If she drank wyvern blood, would her height change? Would the muscle she gained after years of training her body go away? Would her wide shoulders shrink?

No, of course they wouldn't. Because there was nothing wrong with her.

"What's even more amazin' is the fact it didn' kill ya right then an' there."

And the moment was shattered.

"*Leslie,*" Thea reprimanded in a quiet hiss.

What? the imp mouthed back at her.

Madame Odine gave another warm chuckle. Nothing seemed to faze this woman, for she had been full of smiles since she welcomed them to her village. "I take no offense, Thea-*tokon.* I thought much the same when I walked away from that encounter."

The Spellweaver's brow pinched. "Thea-*tokon?*"

"It is an honorific used to address the person we are speaking to. That is the feminine one."

"And the male version?" Rafe was quick to ask.

Madame Odine grinned. "I would say Rafe-*perun.*"

"And tha imp version?" Leslie piped up.

The woman brought a hand to her chin in thought, expression pensive. "I will have to get back to you on that."

Thea nearly choked on her drink in her laughter.

Chapter Nineteen

What's For Dinner...or Rather, Who?

While Madame Odine's drinks were refreshing and cool and nothing out of the ordinary, when she lifted the lid to the hanging metal boiler and released a moist wall of heady spices into the air, Thea wanted to die on the spot. In the pot, amidst now bubbling, murky water was the head of a cow. Floating within were its hooves and...Thea could only guess its intestines.

"Oh, um," she tried to sound casual, "we ate on the way so…"

"Nonsense," the woman barked with a laugh. She set down a wicker-woven tray with their bowls and utensils beside them before she straightened up, turned in thought, and began rummaging around her drawers. "Your long travel must have made you half-starved. Eat as much as you like! You are honored guests, and this dish is one of our best delicacies. Now, where did my fan get off to..."

Hellfire. How was she supposed to say no now?

"Don't mind if I do!" Leslie exclaimed from his spot on the floor, grabbing one of the empty bowls. He greedily started spooning the slop before setting down his bowl, picking up the clawed utensils from the tray, and tearing into the meat of the head.

Rafe appeared apprehensive but prepared his food next. Thea was last and, for what it was worth, was able to steel her facial expression like a hardened veteran. Beside her, Leslie groaned long and with vigor, and Thea wondered which was grosser: the food or the noise he just made. "Ya gotta gib me tha recipe ta this," he said around a mouthful.

Carefully, Thea dipped the spoon into the broth and scooped out the contents within. She clenched her jaw to keep herself from cringing as an intestine hung like a limp noodle from the ladle. Into the bowl it sloshed, and Thea sat back with her meager portion. She fiddled with her spoon, eyes darting to Leslie—blasted imp was almost done with his food—and Rafe who appeared to be eating it with no apparent signs of disgust.

Just because you're not used to it doesn't mean it's disgusting. You wanted to explore and travel your country and that means trying its different customs and eating its food...even if it is unappealing to look at.

Pep talk motivating her, she took a quiet, deep breath and sipped some from her spoon. She hummed in sheer surprise. The broth was rich, thick, and had a savory flavor with hints of salt and garlic.

Then she bit into intestine.

No no no no no no no.

A mental barrage of images of cow organs still fresh and containing questionable things within had her gagging around her mouthful. She quickly gulped it down and gasped, swiped her drink off the floor, and chugged down its remains. When she looked up, Madame Odine had stopped rummaging around in her drawers and was giving her a concerned look.

"It was just...really hot, still," she managed to say after a second of internal panicking.

"Ah, I am sorry I did not warn you," the woman chuckled and began searching through another drawer for her mysterious fan.

"It's quite all right," she said as sweetly as she could.

She noticed Rafe trying to keep his laughter contained by biting down on his fist, but that didn't stop his large shoulders from shaking.

She could feel her cheeks flaming in embarrassment. "How can you stomach this stuff?" she asked in a voice as quiet as breathing so as not to let the chef hear her complaints.

Rafe's fist formed into a single finger over his lips as he eyed her with a still amused smirk. "I put a deliciousness spell over it."

Banish a banshee could she string him up by his toes right about now. "*Oh, I hate you,*" she seethed in a whisper, but this only seemed to make Rafe laugh harder. He was trying, and failing, to stay quiet as he cupped his mouth and held his stomach with his other hand.

She was about to punch his shoulder more out of embarrassment than actual anger (not that he wouldn't have found the action even more hilarious) but out of the corner of her eye, she noticed Leslie getting up to get more. With a quick glance Madame Odine's way and finding the woman still preoccupied, she snatched Leslie's bowl out of his hands and shoved her own toward him. He made a surprised sound that quickly melted into one of confusion. "Leslie," she chided just loud enough for the older woman to hear, "ask before getting seconds!"

Leslie gaped. "Wha—But I—You was—Ah, fa'get about it," he grumbled and sullenly sat back down with his second helping.

"Help yourself to however much you like!" Madame Odine called over her shoulder.

Thea jumped up and stretched with an over-the-top groan. "Well, I am just stuffed. I couldn't possibly eat any more. I think I'm going to go have a walk around." She edged closer to the door, looking back over her shoulder.

Madame Odine, too, stood back up from her hunched position and stretched her back with a grunt. "Stay in the shade if you can. Your pink skin will catch fire out here. Ask me how I know." She laughed again and waved the Spellweaver off.

Thea made eye contact with Rafe for a split second. He looked like he was having difficulty chewing something, but the possibilities of what he was chewing on nearly made her sick. "I'll be sure to do that." Then she turned and left.

The sun blinded her the moment she stepped out of the home. She braced herself up against the canyon wall as her eyes adjusted but hissed quietly as the baking rock sizzled under her palm. When she could open her eyes again, she could see the air warping from the heat coming off the ground, and yet the inhabitants of the desert village were working, playing, or relaxing as if the heat didn't even bother them.

She supposed it didn't.

As Thea carefully traversed down the narrow and steep stone steps, she quickly learned the intersections, where stairs met with other stairs, were fair game.

"Whoa!" she yelped when a couple of kids shoved past her as they raced each other up the stairs. She then had to flatten herself against the wall as a pregnant woman stepped off the adjacent stairway. Safely reaching the ground, she heaved a massive sigh. The dirt under her feet was hard, dry, and compact. Nothing like the shifting mounds of sand that had made even leisurely walking difficult. She made a face at the reminder that she'd have to be walking back through all those miles of sand again when they left, and they would need to leave soon. Hopefully, the villager's generosity would continue, and they could leave with some supplies and a full canteen.

She had begun ticking off items in a mental list when a sharp, zinging scent wafted into the air. Harsh spices accompanied the rich, heady odor, and it practically pulled Thea down the market. She followed the throng of people that seemed to have also fallen under the scent's spell. People began leaving their workstations unattended, and the children laughing and playing in the walkways bolted after one another in the direction of the smell. Soon she was packed in close with the others in a much wider part of the canyon where the smell was the strongest.

Standing on the balls of her feet, she was able to use her height to her advantage and see over most of those in front of her. In the center of the canyon was a large firepit the size of her master bedroom back at her duplex. Inside was a giant, naked bird that had been plucked of all its feathers. The head and feet were missing as well.

Maybe they're going to use them in another soup? Ugh, stop it, Thea, don't think like that.

While admonishing herself, she watched four to five people surrounding the huge grill. Two women were tossing jars' worth of seasoning onto the roasting flesh while the other men were using large, staff-sized sticks to stoke the coals in the pit. Now, that she looked closer, one of the women was Elio, the other Blythe, and Silas was standing beside them. They were talking, but Thea had no chance of hearing them from this distance.

"Excuse me," she said politely, hoping her tone alone would convey her actions. She was met with smiles and encouraging gestures to cut in front of them.

Everyone from the men and women to the children and elderly were dressed in vibrant, breezy outfits that covered their skin from the sun but allowed what little wind there was to pass through. It was like swimming through a rainbow. After several minutes of squeezing by what seemed like everyone in the whole village, many faces that were now familiar to her, Thea was able to get up front. She quickly spotted Blythe and jogged over. The sorceress looked up and aimed a grin Thea's way.

"We are almost done preparing the rok." She said with a happy little clap. "Are you hungry?"

"Starving."

Blythe peered back over to the large bird and flung more of the spices onto the meat, though she looked thoughtful. "I wonder why Madame Odine did not feed you. She used to always have something cooking."

Thea blanched just thinking about it. "Um, yeah...she did..."

Blythe, having caught the reaction, stopped seasoning the rok and brought her hand up to her face to cover her now o-shaped mouth. *"Ekh vuch', ne ch'o eril,"* she said under her breath. "She served you the cow head, didn't she?"

Thea's eyes widened. "How'd you guess?"

"It is our village's specialty. No doubt she wanted to share some with you. I hear it was prepared for Seamus's fiftieth birthday, but when he heard there was going to be rok for dinner..." She shrugged sheepishly. "I am sorry. I know it is not what you are used to. Why, you should have seen the first time I tried making it for..." she trailed off and swallowed. "For Cressi…" A faraway look glossed over her eyes for a moment. Then, clarity came back, and she scanned Thea over and asked abruptly, "Can I speak to you?"

Thea, taken aback by the change in demeanor, could only nod mutely. She watched Blythe hand over the jar of seasonings to Elio, say something softly to her, before turning, grabbing Thea's wrist, and gently tugging her through the sea of villagers. However gracious the people had been in letting Thea pass earlier, they were even more accommodating in allowing the women to exit. Less stomachs vying for the food.

Blythe kept walking until the dull roar of the crowd wasn't so loud. They stopped under the shade of a stall selling hand-carved beads in varying sizes, small jewels, and decorative strips of cloth. Thea couldn't exactly remember who specifically ran this stall now that they weren't there, but she was amazed the merchant had just up and left the shop to its own devices. Back in Tolvade, the goods would have all been pilfered by now.

She was brought back to attention when Blythe began fidgeting with her hands. There was a sense of worry now clinging to her that wasn't there a few moments before. "I wanted to ask you this earlier, right before the rok attacked... Is it true that the Blood Moon is tomorrow?"

Thea felt her blood run cold. Her eyes flicked to the side as she did the calculations in her head. The month, the day, where the moon had been placed in the sky the past couple of nights. Her eyes widened, and she looked up, catching Blythe's gaze. "Yes."

The sorceress looked seconds away from panicking. "We must leave tonight. We can travel faster while it is cooler. I must prepare some supplies, and we will need a map to get to the part of the desert where the sand wyverns are. It has been too long and I cann—"

Thea held up her hands and placed them gently on Blythe's small shoulders. "Hey, hey. Breathe." Though she was freaking out on the inside nearly just as much. If they did indeed decide to spend the night here, then they would be walking straight through the peak of the Blood Moon Festival. It was so dangerous that she had never been assigned patrol duty during the festival. Only seasoned Summoners and Second Chosens were strong enough to weather a fight with a crazed blood mage, let alone a hoard of them. It was how Riker got that nasty scar. It was how some Coven members wound up six feet under. The blood mages were powerful enough to level the city if not for the combined efforts of those in the Coven's higher ranks. They got more and more powerful each year on the night of the Blood Moon, but the rest of the year it was like grasping at ghosts trying to find and detain them.

"I'll go get Rafe and form a plan to get to the Draconians' location. You get us some supplies." She shrugged off her canteen and shoulder bag and handed them to the woman. "I'm talking water, food because I'm still hungry, a compass, and anything else you can think of. Maybe a vial or two for their blood. Meet us at Madame Odine's when you get everything."

Blythe nodded along with each instruction and woodenly turned to go fulfill her new duties. Her shoulders were still a bit tense as she drifted down the near-empty street, and Thea worried for her, but at the moment they had bigger issues at hand. She whirled around and raced back to the steps and took them two at a time. She didn't have to worry about anyone trying to get past her. She could smell the rok from all the way over here now, and its alluring scent had her mouthwatering. She hoped Blythe would pack some away for their trip.

At the top of the precarious stairs that led to Madame Odine's house, Thea could see down the canyon's alley for miles. She still needed to squint to make out those standing around the giant bird, but she found Blythe leading Silas away before they disappeared in the crowd. She could hear the celebratory whistles and jeers as those that had been patiently waiting could now help themselves to the meal.

She shook herself and pulled back the heavy mat blocking the entrance to the door. She immediately found Rafe hunched over a weathered piece of paper. Madame Odine was sitting beside him, murmuring and pointing to something, but Leslie was nowhere to be found. They both looked up at Thea's arrival.

She got straight to the point. "Rafe, we need to leave."

"What's the rush?" Madame Odine said with a look of surprise.

"We can't just leave, Thea," Rafe was quick to say.

"Rafe," she tried again, much more seriously. "If we don't leave now, we'll be walking right through the Blood Moon Festival on the way back through the city. I don't know about you, but I don't have any teleportation ingredients."

Rafe's posture grew rigid, and he cursed, swiping his hand through his short locks of hair. "We haven't even slept. We'll be running on fumes. That could be just as dangerous if we run into something in the desert."

"I'd rather take my chances catching my second wind than trying to make it through not only Banshee Bog at night but Borlimane on top of it during a Blood Moon."

Rafe wiped at his face, suddenly looking much older as he weighed their options. Thea came to sit in front of him and offered her quiet support by resting her hands in his open palm. He sighed heavily. She could see the weight resting on his shoulders. She could feel it as well. He was silent a moment longer. Then, he glanced up and caught her gaze. "We can rest for four hours and still make it back in time."

"Rafe—"

"We'll be going under the cover of darkness, which means we'll be moving faster. According to this map, the sand wyverns are only a few hours' walk from here. Madame Odine says they are aware as soon as someone steps foot in their territory, so we won't have to worry about trying to find one once we get there," he stated, gesturing to Madame Odine by his side. The woman nodded quietly in assurance. Thea glanced at both of them before looking down at the map. She reached over and drew it nearer. "We're here, and this is where we need to go." Rafe pointed at a specific spot on the map, and under his finger was a picture drawn of a canyon with a crude illustration of the guardian deities. He swept his finger over to a largely empty part of the desert. Across the map were more drawings with words written above in the Ernimoen language so she had no hope of knowing on her own what they were. She could only guess they were other villages inhabiting lesser-known races of people. One thing stood out to her through.

"What's this?" she asked, indicating a small drawing in the center of wyvern territory. Besides the small sketch, there was nothing else for miles.

Madame Odine leaned forward to study the map. Her mouth twisted into a grim line. "I have heard it is a forgotten temple, but no one has ever seen it in person. To do so would mean stepping foot in the sand wyverns' territory. All I know for certain, and all anyone knows for certain, is that it was there long before any of us or our parents were born."

"Don't get any ideas, Thea."

Thea glared at her partner, but it lacked any true heat. "Who said I was getting ideas?"

"That brain of yours."

"One of our brains has to do the thinking around here."

Rafe cracked a smile. It faded too quickly when he peered back down at the map. "If we weren't so pressed for time, I'd let you go explore some forgotten temple to your heart's content. As it stands—"

"Bet I could explore it in less than four hours."

Rafe sighed in exasperation. "We need some kind of sleep, Thea. You know how important that is."

Thea huffed a quiet sigh herself. Yes. She did know how vital sleep would be to them in wake of the oncoming night. Who knew what could come at them under the cover of darkness? Still, she was hard-pressed to try and convince Rafe to forego sleep and find out what was in the temple. They may never get another opportunity like this again.

She opened her mouth, but before she could say anything, she took in Rafe's haggard appearance. It was her fault they were here in the first place. It was her fault they had been backed into a corner by Winona. If she had just reported Cressida when she had the chance… If she had just had more faith in the Coven. The Celestial had been able to rid the world of Asmo...somehow, and everything they were going through now could have been avoided.

She slowly closed her mouth and nodded. "Okay." If something happened to Rafe because of lack of sleep, she'd never forgive herself. The man could sweep the Dark Market, patrol the worst of Herbon, and probably go up against a blood mage or two himself. But not on little to no sleep, and the desert wasn't familiar to him.

Better the devil you know rather than the devil you don't.

Rafe heaved a relieved sigh, and Thea offered a small smile. He rolled up the map and handed it back to Madame Odine, but she declined with a soft shake of her head, and a hand was held up to stop him. "Keep it for your travels. I can always get my hands on another just like it."

"Thank you, and thank you again for the meal," he said with an appreciative smile. He then caught Thea's gaze again. "Did you find Blythe while you were out?"

Thea nodded and checked over her shoulder at the door as if Blythe would come through at any moment. "Yeah. I told her to get some supplies together. She's actually the one that came to me and reminded me about the Blood Moon Festival."

Rafe's brow pinched before smoothing out as he seemed to think about something. "Well, she has lived in Vemeese for a while now, and no doubt Cressida knew about the festival."

Thea checked over her shoulder again and dropped her voice low. "Yeah, well, we both know how great Cressida is at keeping secrets."

"Yes, but I don't see her withholding something like that from Blythe. It wouldn't benefit her to keep it under wraps, and, besides that, the townspeople talk. It's not exactly like the Coven could hope to keep something like that from the beings of Tolvade."

Thea nodded in silent agreement. She looked around the room and sighed once more. "Okay, so… I guess we try and get some sleep?"

"That's the idea. It's a good thing it's pretty dim in here," he said with a wry grin. He stood up and stretched his legs and went to stand by the door, moving the mat out of the way and finding the sun's placement in the sky. "Madame Odine, would you mind waking us when the sun starts to set?"

Madame Odine was busy rummaging around in her drawers again, but this time she managed to find what she was looking for. She brought out two folded up bundles of cloth and two small pillows. "Of course. If *Blathi* has not packed up some food when she gets back, I will be sure to wrap you up something." She lay down and unfolded the thick bundles of cloth to create makeshift sleeping mats before dropping the pillows at the head of them.

Thea's lips thinned into a straight line, and she silently prayed that Blythe would handle the food preparations. She dropped down onto one of the mats and watched as Rafe did the same. The texture of the material was rough, and it held a musky, almost grassy smell. The batting inside was plush, though, and Thea's exhausted body settled into the bed easily enough even though her feet stuck out at the end. Rafe was much too tall to properly fit on the mat, but he was equally as tired and equally unable to care that much. He slid onto his stomach and propped the pillow up with his arms, almost out in seconds. Without thinking, Thea slid her hand out and placed it on his arm. She'd barely closed her eyes before she felt him shift, but she didn't need to open them to feel her hand being held in his. As weary as she was, and as anxious as she felt at what was to come, her body relaxed, and her mind cleared.

Chapter Twenty

An Ironic Sized Friendship

Thea slept so hard she didn't remember dreaming. When she was roused from her slumber, her eyes felt like weights were trying to pull them shut, her limbs were not cooperating with her, and she could tell her hair was a disheveled mess. Did she care? No.

She squinted angrily at Blythe's gentle face, but even as sleep deprived as she was, she couldn't stay mad at the sorceress. She huffed like a petulant child before standing, albeit not gracefully. Rafe was already gathering their things together, and Thea's sluggish brain immediately snapped into work-mode. She blinked away her remaining drowsiness and got to work packing up their things alongside her partner. Leslie, having apparently come back and fallen asleep next to them, was not quite so quick to adjust to being in the waking world, and he groaned his protests enough to make Thea wish she could knock him back out. She may now be alert and awake, but she was still grumpy.

When they were done, they turned to say their goodbyes to Madame Odine, but the woman yanked them both down around their necks into a bone-crushing hug. With her being shorter than both of them, it was quite an awkward affair.

"I wish you well on your journey. May Gitk' be with you until your return home."

Thea returned the hug as best she could. She would miss Madame Odine. When the older woman let them both go, poor ol' Leslie was next. Thea didn't know how she would describe the noise that came out of the imp when Madame Odine picked him up and squeezed him as well.

"Whaa—What a' ya doi—oh." Leslie went limp in the woman's arms and awkwardly patted her arm.

Then it was Blythe's turn, but the hug lasted far longer. Soft words were exchanged between the two, and Thea turned away to keep from staring at what felt like a private moment. She heard someone sniff, and more soft words were uttered followed by another sniff.

"Take care of each other," Madame Odine said once she let go of Blythe. "In the desert, we only have each other to rely on."

They each nodded. No more words needed to be spoken. Rafe was the first to leave through the door, then Thea, though she nearly ran into his back. She looked down where he was staring and gasped softly.

The village had come alive in the dark. Small fires flickered in the window of every home, and colorful paper lanterns filled the street below as they drifted on secured twine ropes. It was more than that, though. Everyone in the village had come to see them off.

As they made their way down the steps, the villagers smiled and waved but mainly stayed quiet. She recognized so many faces. Caius and his wife, Chaska and her parents, Juno with her motherly smile, Medora and Rowan each holding a toddler in their arms, Elio standing tall next to Jorah, Zemira supporting Niran with her arm under his, and so many others. Passing through the crowd, Thea was again jostled by friendly pats on the shoulder. Rafe earned a few soft slaps on the back, but Blythe was being stopped frequently with hugs from her people. When Thea looked over her shoulder, she could see how glassy the sorceress's eyes were even amongst the low light of the lanterns.

Reaching the entrance to the canyon took longer than it would have normally, but Thea felt a strange surge of energy she didn't have before. The encouraging smiles from everyone around her, the kind gestures, the sense of community within these rock walls was unlike anything Thea had ever felt before. To think a whole village could feel more like a family than a few people linked together by blood was...astonishing.

The guardian deities, Moje and Gitk', were just as colossal as Thea remembered. She felt it this time for sure; the sense of being watched, being protected. She didn't know if it came from the villagers sending them off, the goddess herself shining down on them, or if it really was from the giant stone statues standing alert in front of the canyon.

Rafe pulled out the compass and the map from his pouch pockets when a shout from behind them gained the party's attention. The villagers were crowded around the entrance of the canyon as well, but Silas had broken free to run up to Blythe. He stared at her for a moment without saying anything before he leaned in and embraced her. She wrapped her arms around him and held on tight.

When he pulled back, he brought out a small, cinched bag and placed it in her palm. *"Ais gotim, vur dziz onch'-vur ben i pitk' eastigh hirrets'nily hemer. Se dzurits' pleteknir i."*

Thea glanced down at Leslie to see if he understood what was being said.

The imp shrugged. "He's givin' her stuff so she can teleport back 'ere wheneva."

Thea felt her heart clench. Blythe must have told them she could perform magic now. She wanted to kick herself in that moment. Why hadn't she thought to tell Blythe that? So much had happened, but she should have remembered one of the most common spells.

Blythe clasped the bag to her chest and nodded. She was trying so hard to stay strong, but the emotions swimming in her eyes spoke for her. Neither said anything else to each other. They didn't have to. So much could be said without words. So much could be felt without hearing a thing.

Silas stepped back, but he never looked away. Someone in the village yelled something, and then the night sky bloomed in color as the hundreds of paper lanterns that had lined the street were released. Ambers, sapphires, scarlets, fuchsias, emeralds, violets, and every shade in between filled the gaps amongst the stars as the flickering flames within glowed just as brightly. The villagers finally released a loud, collective cheer.

And Blythe...Blythe let the emotions within her free as the tears she had been holding back finally fell.

The moon was almost completely full and already showing signs of the approaching festival. A crimson tint was beginning to form around the rim. Tomorrow, the entire white surface would bleed a horrifying red. A gaping wound in the endless black that would surround it. No star would shine amidst the stark vermillion.

As of right now, it was giving plenty of light for the lone travelers in a never-ending sea of sand. The golden hue had faded until the sand was now a bleached bone color. The billions of stars overhead were just as bright in their intensity, and the black and white scars in the sky were still crossed in a forever duel. In the far distance, miles away by now, Thea could still make out the lanterns floating above the canyon.

They had been trekking for nearly two hours. Leslie, without his allocamelus, had been demoted back down to commoner status and now had to walk just like the rest of them. He let them know just how unhappy he was about the fact every twenty minutes or so. Thea had perfected the act of ignoring him, and Rafe was too preoccupied with the map and the compass to really hear what was going on around him. Blythe had stayed quiet since the spectacular send-off from her village. There was no telling what was currently going through her mind at the moment.

Thea shrugged off her bag and groped around in its contents until she pulled out the food Blythe had packed for them earlier. It felt like her stomach was caving in on her. She'd lost her appetite earlier at seeing the woman's tears, but now…

Thank the goddess Blythe had saved her some rok. She bit into the juicy meat and had to stop the moan that threatened to leave her throat as flavor from the spices burst across her tongue. So much better than cow head soup.

She was still enjoying her meal when a fast wind blew past them out of nowhere, bringing with it the chill that had been missing during the day. Thea shivered and rubbed at her arms. A fire would be nice, but they had to keep moving. The wind picked up again, and Thea swore an air nymph was messing with them. Grains of sand from the surrounding dunes drifted in the air and pelted them when the wind suddenly changed direction, as fickle as a child.

"Is that normal?" Thea called over her shoulder to Blythe, mouth still somewhat full, and pointed at where the wind had condensed into a little whirling tornado before disappearing.

Blythe hummed, as if coming out of a trance and glanced over to where Thea had indicated, but the wind had already disappeared. "Is what normal?"

Thea squinted as she looked around, before spotting the wind doing the same thing a couple hundred paces away. "That!"

Blythe squinted as well before chuckling softly. "Yes. It is quite odd, almost like it is alive. But, yes, it is normal."

Rafe looked up from the map. "Is what normal?"

"Ugh," Thea groaned. "Pay attention."

Rafe flapped the map around noisily. "I'm trying to navigate us to the sand wyverns, so *excuse me*."

Thea snorted. "I think that is the sassiest thing I've ever heard you say."

Rafe grunted. "There's more where that came from."

"Never mind. *That's* the sassiest thing."

A loud rumble gurgled from beside her. Thea turned her wide eyes on Leslie, and even Rafe turned around with an impressed look. "Leslie, if you were that hungry you should have said something."

Leslie threw up his hands. "Now, wait ah minute. I knows whatcha thinkin', but that wasn' me makin' that noise. I ain't takin' responsibility fa that. No siree."

Thea stopped in her tracks, as did everyone else. "So..." she said carefully and licked her suddenly dry lips. "You're saying that...*wasn't* you?"

Leslie placed his stubby fists on his hips. "What's a matta, Honey Badger, ya got ya ears clogged?"

Blythe stepped forward, dark brown eyes wide. "Then, if that wasn't you, then what was it?"

Leslie faltered.

The sound came again, deeper and surrounding them on all sides. The sand beneath their feet shifted, and both Thea—having dropped her meal with a curse—and Rafe quickly unholstered their weapons. With a flick of his wrist, Rafe's staff extended to its full length, and his tri-bladed boomerang was clutched in his other hand. Thea hastily strapped the arrow launcher to her arm, cursing herself all the while. "We should have been better prepared for this!" she snapped, more toward herself than to anyone else. She ripped her sickle out from its holster and wrapped its long chain several times around her fist.

Again, a low vibration rattled the shifting sound. It was closer, so much so that Thea could feel the quivering sand shift under her feet. Blythe and Leslie huddled close, and Rafe's back rested against Thea's. Her eyes flicked everywhere in search of the threat, but it didn't prepare her in the end.

A blur of movement came from her peripheral, and the next second Rafe was ripped away from her backside. She let out a scream as claws tore through her arm. She dove away, rolling onto her side and righting herself before unleashing arrow after arrow at the creature.

It dwarfed Rafe's body with four, thick legs, a wide body plated in horns and tough scales. Yellow eyes with slitted pupils glared down at the Summoner as its jaw full of overlapping teeth clamped down on the staff he was holding up in defense with shaking arms. The magic in the arrows sunk deep into the creature, past the scales, and it let out a beastly growl that punched Thea in the chest with the sound. She clenched her jaw and aimed.

Several things happened at once. Rafe wretched his staff away from the beast and slammed the bladed end into the beast's jaw, Thea unloaded several arrows into its thickly scaled head, and Blythe flung a wave of glittering silver magic that crashed into the creature. The impact catapulted the giant lizard off of Rafe, but once it was back on the ground, its body slipped under the sand and disappeared.

Thea jumped up and sprinted the short distance over to her partner. "We gotta get out of here!" she yelled, grabbing him by the arm and yanking him up. Pain flared briefly at harsh movement, but it was masked in the wake of adrenalin flooding through her.

The sand under her feet shifted, and Thea's footing slipped out from under her. She yelped when she dropped to the ground and connected with rough hide, and her palms cut themselves on yellow spikes. She was flung back and sent crashing into a dune. She heard Blythe screaming for her and a vicious snarl that thundered around her like a storm.

An explosion of sand pelted her body. One after another, it was like lightning was raining down from the heavens. She hauled herself up from the sand and jumped up, only having seconds to react as the beast barreled itself right at her. She dove to the side, landed on her hands, and sprung herself into a backflip. Pain shot up her wrists when the sand shifted under her, and she collided with the ground again. Lightning struck the ground by her feet, and she scrambled back with a screech.

"Thea, get up!" Rafe shouted over the explosions.

She flipped over and clambered to her feet before bolting up the dune. Rafe was wielding his staff and shots of yellow electricity erupted from the head, striking the ground.

She grabbed him by the arm and jerked him back. "Come on, we have to run!"

"Go, I'll catch up!"

Thea hesitated only a moment before nodding and grabbing Blythe and taking off into the night, Leslie tucked under the sorceress's arms. The blood leaking hot from the wound in her shoulder cooled uncomfortably as they ran, but Thea couldn't think about it too much at the moment.

Rafe drew his arm back and used both hands to grasp his staff. "Barbarous foe standing tall, time winds down thy greatest fall. Return to which thou came, I banish you in Her name!" He raised it over his head and unleashed the wrath of a warrior. The staff glowed brightly, the bladed hoop at the end blazing a swirling crimson before light exploded out. Cracks of lightning shot down from the sky, igniting the night in a blaze of white fire. Glass shot up into the air from where the lightning slammed into the dunes, pelting the ground in fragmented daggers.

An enraged, inhuman, hiss-like scream filled the air and had Thea whirling around. She saw Rafe turning and taking off after them. The sand around him shifted as something large and angry moved under the surface. She dropped Blythe's hand and aimed her arrow launcher, shooting a continuous stream. The creature sprung out from the ground and launched itself at her, face and body half burnt from Rafe's earlier attacks.

She shoved Blythe as hard as she could away from her, hurled her good arm back, and slung her sickle through the air. She snapped the chain to the side and watched the weapon strike the beast's neck. It released another sharp hiss and gurgled up blood, crashing into the sand below them. She ripped her sickle out and slung the chain back, catching her weapon in the air.

"Don't wait to see if it's dead, just go! Go!" Thea yelled over her shoulder, pointing her weapons at the beast until Blythe and Leslie were running again. Rafe had caught up to them, and she darted off after them once he passed.

"I thought I had it!" Rafe growled as he ran. His eyes were flashing silver-blue in his anger.

Thea drew in ragged breaths as she managed to keep up. "It's okay, it's a resilient son of—"

"It is getting back up!" Blythe called frantically back to them, eyes wide in fear.

Thea whipped her head around and employed a much more profane curse. "Are you serious? What *is* that thing?"

"Not dead," Rafe griped, flinging his staff out and blasting more orbs of lethal energy toward the creature, but it kept dipping in and out of the sand as it chased them like a fish splashing through water. "We can't keep running!" he bellowed over the noise. "We're going to run out of stamina!"

"Like we won't lose stamina fighting it?" Thea yelled back, pointing her arrow launcher at the beast, rune glowing bright as she concentrated more of her power, and the arrows flew out of the weapon at rapid speed.

"You will not be able to kill it so easily!" Blythe called back to them as she too shot out sun flares from her glowing palm. "There is a reason my people do not come this far north!"

Thea snarled and skidded to a halt. "What are we supposed to do then?" She shoved her hand into her belt pouches and grabbed handfuls of white, blue, and silver dust and flung them over her sickle. She felt the electricity in the air as Rafe blasted energy orbs at the creature. She screwed her eyes shut and mumbled, "Imbue me with your strength, bless me with your agility, leave me at length, enhance my ability!" The weapon glowed brightly, pulsing a vibrant teal, and Thea dropped the sickle close to in the sand before slinging the chain out in front of her. The bladed end soared through the air, glinting in the moonlight, and sliced through a chunk of the creature's neck. Blood spurted out of the wound, and the beast once again came crashing back down.

Rafe aimed a shot of noxious, green magic at the laceration. The flesh bubbled and smoked, stained a muddled scarlet and verdant color. Without hesitation, Thea yanked her sickle back and slung it down again, and again, and again until the head rolled away from the scaly body. The sickle's sharp edge sunk into the sand, and the chain fell away from her hand and dropped down beside her. She gasped quietly and slumped to her knees. Rafe was beside her in an instant.

"It's sure dead now," she huffed with a smile before clearing her throat and rubbing at her neck. "Can you hand me the canteen?"

"Bit brutal there, T." Rafe grinned and handed her canteen over, taking a swig himself after she was done. Before she could swat his hands away, he'd prepared a healing spell and was running it over her arm and then moved to her previously injured leg. She wouldn't be completely healed, but she'd retain more use of the limbs.

Thea wiped her mouth and chuckled. "You're one to talk. You brought down the goddess's wrath back there. I've never seen that trick before."

"Yes, it was very impressive," Blythe said as she came up and sat beside the Spellweaver, dainty hand resting over her surely racing heart.

Leslie waddled over and slapped Rafe on the shoulder now that the Summoner was the same level as him. "Ya did good, big guy. You too, Honey Badger. Bit showy, but ya get points fa creativity."

Rafe's mouth twisted. "It barely did any damage. What was that thing?"

"It was a kumi lizard," Blythe informed, staring at the dead creature. "Their territory spans a small distance, but they will go looking for food if they're desperate. It was probably attracted by the smell of the roasted rok."

Rafe offered the canteen to the sorceress, and she gladly took it. "Is it the most dangerous thing out here?"

Blythe took a few sips and hummed. "Hmm? Oh, no, not by a long shot," she giggled.

Thea groaned and got to her feet, dusting off the sand from her clothes and running her fingers through her hair. "Then what is the worst thing out here?"

Sand erupted around them as a monstrous pair of jaws shot out from the ground and clamped down around the kumi lizard. Thea and others froze, unable to fathom what just happened. A large, amber eyeball rolled in its socket to lock onto them, slitted pupil dilating.

"Th-That is," Blythe whispered hoarsely. "A wyvern."

A blast of sand ejected out of the ground as the wyvern clawed its way to the surface, kicking up tremendous clouds of dust in its wake. The group scrambled back to put as much distance as they could between themselves and the Draconian. Blythe dove her hand into the backpack she'd been carrying and shoved scarves at everyone to wrap their face with.

Thea was already hacking from the lack of air and quickly pulled the scarf up to her mouth and nose. She could barely make out the creature because of the swirling dust clouds, but its silhouette allowed her to take in the sheer size of the beast. It was larger than HQ, bigger than the guardian statues, and more gigantic in size the canyon itself. Its massive head rose above the dust, and Thea watched with eyes wide as it tossed the kumi lizard in the air and gulped it down like it was a snack.

It peered down at the group, and unparalleled terror filled her entire body. She felt her heart beating wildly against her chest, yet her limbs were frozen in fear. The skin along her arms, down her spine, and all the way down to her toes prickled like thousands of needles stinging her all at once. She swallowed, but her throat had closed up shop and refused to work.

Large nostrils flared, and a strong exhale blew out to clear the remaining dust clinging to the air. When the dust was gone, Thea was able to take in the beast in its entirety. From head to the tip of its long, serpentine tail, the wyvern was longer than the canyon. Its head could fit in the widest part, but there was no hope for its immense body. Sleek scales the exact color of the golden sand under them covered the top of the Draconian while smooth, paler skin covered its belly and throat. Its arms were as thick and as long as Moje and Gitk' and were connected to paper-thin wings, unlike depictions of the red dragons in the mountains where the creatures' wings were completely separate from its limbs.

It stared down at them, assessing the ones that had been foolish enough to wander into its domain. The only movement came from its tail that slithered in the sand. The heavy back and forth *draaaaag* was loud in the stillness of the night.

"Go on, Leslie," Thea bit out without moving her lips.

The imp jerked at the sound of his name and eyed Thea out of the corner of his all-black eye. "What?" he whispered, mimicking the lack of movement of his mouth.

"Go *on*. Speak to it before it decides we're next on the menu!" she hissed. "You're the only one who *can*."

It was like the words had broken the spell that kept Leslie's body stiff. "Uh, yeah, right. I knew that!" He stepped forward confidently only to freeze up again when the wyvern turned its head and locked eyes on the tiny creature in front of it.

There was a moment of silence that stretched.

"*Leslie*," Thea all but growled.

Leslie glared over his shoulder and tapped his temple with his finger. "I'm talkin' to 'im, I'm talkin' to 'im."

The Spellweaver faltered. "What?"

"Like telepathically?" Blythe whispered in awe.

Leslie puffed out his chest. "Yeah. You humans can't do it, but thas how wyverns communicate wit' one another. Don't ya even know that much?"

Thea rolled her eyes and relaxed her posture. "What's he saying?"

Leslie craned his head back to look up at the enormous creature for a moment before humming. "He's sa'prised I'm able ta understand 'im. Says he hasn' spoken wit' anyone outside his kind in hundreds of years."

A massive sound rumbled out of the wyvern, and it reared its long neck back and jerked its head about. Thea jumped back, as did Blythe and Rafe. Leslie was the only one unfazed, and he turned his head to look back at them in confusion.

"What's wit' you guys. He's happy! Can't ya tell?"

Thea pointed at the Draconian, expression incredulous. "That's happy?"

The imp merely shrugged. "Well, yeah. Wouldn't you be if afta hundreds of years ya finally gotta talk to someone that wasn' that one annoyin' aunt or ya weirdo cousin?"

Rafe whistled. "Wow. I think I'd go insane if I had to listen to only my family for centuries on end."

"I think we all would," Thea agreed with a grimace. "Anyway, now that you're all buddy-buddy with each other, ask him if we can have some of his blood."

Leslie's expression fell to deadpan. "Ya don't have a lot of friends, do ya?"

Rafe crossed his arms and sighed. "Thea, you can't just walk up to a stranger and start demanding things."

"Oh, *I'm sorry,* I just assumed since we're on a time crunch—"

The Draconian rumbled out another bone-rattling noise, silencing everyone. Leslie peered back up, and the two continued their private conversation. Thea could only wait with bated breath and hope Leslie of all beings managed to seal the deal in getting some wyvern blood. Then they could high tail it out of here and make it back into town before the sun set tomorrow.

Leslie snapped his fingers and finger-gunned at the wyvern with a grin. "We'll do it."

Thea shared an equally confused look with Rafe before asking, "We'll do what?"

Leslie looked as if he just remembered the others were there. "Huh? Oh, big guy wants us ta do somethin' fa' 'im 'fore he hands ova tha goods."

Now, Thea was even more confused. "He wants us to do something for him? Leslie, we don't have time for games!"

She could tell Leslie was rolling his eyes. "*Relax*. Ya want the blood or don't ya? 'Sides, he's offerin' us a ride."

Blythe gasped, fingers flying to her mouth as excitement sparkled in her gaze. "He wants us to climb on top of him?"

Rafe stepped forward, shrugging his bag higher on his shoulder. "Where is he planning on taking us? And to do what exactly?"

Leslie looked back up to the wyvern for a moment before nodding along with whatever the creature must have been saying. "Ehh, somethin' 'bout lost magic. Gotta right the wrongs an' all that."

Thea sighed. This was not clearing anything up. "Okay, so if we...what, get some lost artifact or something, he'll give us his blood?"

Leslie finger gunned again. "You got it."

"Don't do that." Then it clicked, and Thea gasped. "The temple!"

"Temple?" Rafe parroted, only for realization to surface. "The one you wanted to go to."

"Are you talking about the forgotten temple deep in wyvern territory?" Blythe queried, but by the excited look in her eyes, she already knew the answer to her question.

Rafe whipped out the map from his pouch and unfolded the piece of paper, flicking his wrists to keep the material taut. He then pointed to the small drawing placed in the center of the northernmost part of the desert. "I don't see anything else around, so that has to be where he's taking us."

Thea grinned. "I guess I'll be checking it out after all."

"On the back of a wyvern, no less," Rafe said around a dubious chuckle as he put the map away.

Blythe cheered and tossed her arms about in excitement. "*Yrre*, this is amazing! We will get there so much faster, and then we can leave much quicker too." She spun around, loose clothing whirling around her, and bowed low to the Draconian with her hands together out in front of her. "I give my thanks to you, legendary wyvern."

Then Thea witnessed something amazing. The wyvern ducked his large head in a bow. Hastily, Thea and Rafe copied Blythe's form to also show their appreciation.

"All right, let's get this show on tha road, you three," Leslie said from above them.

Thea jerked up to find the owner of the voice already sitting atop the Draconian's back. Leslie was waving them on, so with one last final look at one another, they picked up their supplies and weapons off the ground and holstered them, climbed up the wyvern's large, bent forearm, and hauled themselves onto its spine. Thea tried to grab onto the parts of the wing that were not paper-thin and fragile. The somewhat transparent membrane quivered under her touch, and she wondered if the beast could feel the pressure they placed upon its body as they climbed up, or if the scales numbed some of the sensation.

The bony plates covering its vertebrae were bumpier, rougher, and aided them in holding on. When everyone was situated, there was a short pause where Leslie was undoubtedly telling the creature they were ready, and then they shot forward into the night.

Chapter Twenty-One

A Sea of Sand and Serpents and Secrets

Thea felt her stomach drop out from under her, left behind in the dust as the wyvern zipped through the sand like a serpent in water. Half its body had sunk below the surface, leaving only its back and the upper half of its winged arms above ground. Its wings acted like fish fins, propelling the beast forward while at the same time pushing the sand out of its way like it weighed nothing. Its long neck slithered like a snake, and its body followed. The desert parted for the Draconian as if in the presence of the goddess herself. They weaved through the dunes at an incredible speed, and the wind whipped against them in a brutal onslaught.

Leslie had secured the first spot for himself, and he was having a grand time with no one in front of him to block his view. Blythe was taking it all in as well from behind Leslie, though she was twice as tall as the imp and could see the miles and miles of desert horizon stretched out before her. Thea sat squished between her and Rafe, though they blanketed her from the sharp winds slicing through them all.

She turned and watched as they passed by dune after dune from large to mountain-sized, but when they passed a particularly huge one, Thea gasped. Another wyvern appeared from behind the dune, racing across the sand alongside them.

"Look!" she shouted, pointing at the beast blazing parallel to them. Blythe squealed in excitement, and Thea felt more than heard

Rafe's sharp inhale. The wyvern beside them then dipped its entire body into the sand and disappeared.

Sand exploded like a volcano from the other side as another wyvern sprung out from the ground. Suddenly, they were surrounded on all sides by wyverns. Great cries echoed throughout the night as they called to one another, jumping out of the sand like splashing fish before disappearing amongst the dunes once more. As they sped through the desert, they witnessed more and more of the creatures. Some were lounging along the dunes, some were rolling around in the cool sand, and a few were kicking up dust as they wrestled with one another.

"He says we're almost there!" Leslie hollered over the playful screeches and deep rumblings of the clustered Draconians.

Blythe sighed, turning to and fro in her seat as she tried to take everything in at once. "This is so...magical."

Thea had to agree. She gazed around and dedicated the sight before her to memory. She would always recall this night where she raced across the Golden Sea with the legendary sand wyverns.

It wasn't long before she could see some structure of some kind up ahead. Partially hidden by a rather large hill, they happened upon it quicker than they expected. The wyvern slowed down until it stopped on top of the giant dune, though it was still a good walk a ways from the building. As big as a small house, it could easily be crushed under the foot of a massive wyvern. Thea was curious as to why that hadn't actually happened yet. Being so close to the wyverns' most popular hangout, it was odd an accident hadn't occurred. Unless the Draconians were consciously aware of it for some reason.

The structure was made entirely out of tawny-colored stone, and each detail was meticulously carved into it. Four pillars rose above the roof, more so for decoration than for any specific purpose. There were no windows, but there was a large, rounded door for them to enter through. Guarded by half-scorpion, half-humanoid creatures, of course.

Thea eyed over the guards in disdain. "We have to fight our way in? Or is your new best friend going to scare them off?"

Leslie scoffed. "You gotta earn what ya want, Honey Badger! You gotta put in tha work! Ya already got a free ride ova 'ere. 'Sides, those two ain't nothin' in comparison to that lizard lug you guys took down."

Thea felt Rafe shrug from behind her. "He's right. We'll probably have them knocked out in a few minutes or less." He placed one of his hands on Thea's hips as he began alighting off the wyvern, and she had to hold herself stock still to keep herself from jerking as the searing pads of his fingers brushed the skin where her shirt rode up.

She cleared her throat and managed to keep her voice steady as she asked, "What is it we're even supposed to be looking for once we're inside?"

Leslie hummed in thought, going quiet once again. Thea busied herself by dismounting while she waited for a (hopefully) concise answer this time. Rafe was waiting for her at the bottom and held his arms up to help her descend. She slid down the scales of the wyvern's forearm the rest of the way, grasping at Rafe's outstretched hands so she wouldn't tumble into the sand.

"He says it's some tablet," Leslie called down to them while both Thea and Rafe helped Blythe descend.

"A tablet. What are we supposed to do with a tablet?" Thea grumbled.

"He said ya gotta connect all four or somethin'. S'pposed ta help with some big, powerful spell," Leslie informed with a shout as he was still on top of the Draconian.

Thea blinked up at him.

The imp pointed at his overly large ears. "You think these a' just fa show?"

"You're saying there's more than just one?" Rafe intercepted, brow pinched in either exasperation or confusion. Thea couldn't tell, but she related with both.

Leslie climbed awkwardly down, though he tripped and flopped down into the sand most inelegantly. He stood on wobbly legs and spit out the dust coating his tongue and slapped away the sand sticking to his body. "Gee, thanks fa all you guys' help. And yeah, 'course there's more than one. Be too easy otha'wise, am I right?"

Thea sighed. "For once, you are right. Where are the others? In temples like this?"

Leslie was bent to the side, whacking the top of his head to dislodge the sand in his ear, but straightened and shook himself like a wet dog. "I resent that. But anyways, they ain't here. Sa'pposedly, there's three more in tha jungle, the Black Forest, and tha mountains. Our business just lies wit' tha one in this temple. He says there's s'pposed ta be bein's inside that'll shed some light on tha situation."

Thea shared a look with Rafe. "This is starting to sound way above our paygrade."

Rafe's mouth was a firm line. "Yours maybe. Not like that's ever stopped you before, though."

"Ha. Let's go kick some scorpion butt and talk to the beings who will 'supposedly shed light on the situation,'" she said while checking the straps on her arrow launcher. She unholstered her sickle, and her touch brought to life the spell she'd imbued it with earlier. Not that she thought she'd need it going up against scorpion men, but the spell would activate under her touch two or three more times depending on how much she used it. She'd have to be careful not to overdo it this time. She wasn't trying to kill the guards for simply protecting what they were assigned to protect.

When she looked back at Rafe, he had his staff prepared, but his boomerang was still holstered. "Ready?" he asked.

"Ready."

Blythe fidgeted with her hands and gave a rueful smile. "I am sure I will just be in the way, so I will stay up here."

"Don't worry, we'll be done in no time at all," Rafe assured as he warmed up his staff with his magic. The bladed end pulsed with glowing light, signaling it was ready.

Their walk down the large sand dune was slow going. If possible, they were going to wait until the scorpion men went on the offensive. As they neared, the half-humanoid creatures snapped to attention. From their torso up their bodies were tan, chiseled, and very male. However, instead of two arms each, both guards sported four. The closer Thea got, the more she was able to recognize all the other differences, like how they had six eyes apiece. Their dark brown hair fell past their broad shoulders, and they carried long spears, crossing the two to bar entrance from the temple when Thea and Rafe neared.

Their lower bodies resembled that of a giant scorpion. The wicked-looking tail behind them flexed in warning, and their thin, plated legs scuttled in fidgety movements as if the guards were holding themselves back from striking.

"Mytk' ch'ke!" they hissed in unison.

"They're probably spelled to keep people out, and the only ones around here are the Ernimoens. It would make sense for them to at least know that one phrase," she whispered to the side.

"Madame Odine said there were more languages out here besides Ernimoen though," Rafe said with a contemplative frown.

"Fair enough. Shall we?"

Rafe grinned. "We shall." He pulled his staff out in front of him and aimed it at the guards. A powerful, yet slightly less terrifying, orb of energy blasted out from the bladed end. It slammed into one of the guards and thrust him back into the wall of the building hard enough to crack the stone. The creature dropped to the ground in a heap as the other charged them, snarling its anger.

Thea swung her sickle, aiming to tangle the scorpion legs with her chain, but the creature deflected her weapon with its spear right before impact. Rafe directed his staff at the scorpion man and blasted him with a ball of razing energy. The creature dodged each attempt, and his multiple arachnid legs had him upon the Summoner in no time.

He slashed at Rafe with his spear while his other set of arms pulled out twin daggers from the belt slung over his human hips. Thea launched herself at the creature and slammed her full weight into the being's side, knocking him off of Rafe and sending them both to the ground. She caught her weight right before impact, momentarily struck by the pain from the wound in her arm, but spun her legs out just in time, kicking the scorpion man in the jaw with the heel of her left boot.

She didn't anticipate the creature's other set of arms grabbing her around her ankle and yanking her away. She was sent rolling through the sand, coming face to face with the guard as he landed on top of her. His tail struck down, aiming at her face and missing by a hair after she jerked her head to the side. She snarled and pulled her knees up and kicked upward, knocking the creature up and off of her. She shot to her feet just as a blast of energy blew past her, nearly frying the ends of her hair, and connected with the guard. He was flung backward and landed unconscious in the sand.

Thea spun around, eyes ablaze, ready to tell Rafe off about being more mindful of where he's aiming, but she collided right into the man. He grabbed her by the upper arm, causing her to grunt in discomfort from the still sensitive skin of her wound, and dragged her closer, leaned down, and crashed his lips into hers. She gasped into the kiss, felt herself tensing up and melting all at once. It was over too quickly, leaving her dazed as she stared into flashing, ice-blue eyes illuminated by the moon's glow.

"Be more careful next time," he demanded. "He nearly stabbed you in the face."

Thea blinked. "But he didn't," she said, reaching up and brushing her hands over the sharp planes of his cheekbones. "I'm okay. Now, come on, before they wake up."

Rafe's eyes narrowed, but he released a deep breath of air and dropped his hand. He then realized where he had grabbed her, and his expression turned aghast. "Banish a banshee, Thea, are you—?"

"I'm fine," she deflected. Yes, it throbbed something fierce, but it hadn't affected her fighting that much. It was probably just red from all the sweat and sand getting into it.

Rafe went to reach for his dust pouches, yanking Thea back by the wrist when she went to move toward the temple. "At least let me heal—"

One of the scorpion men groaned. Thea twisted out of Rafe's hold and grabbed his forearm, shouting up to the others, "Blythe, Leslie! Hurry up!" before racing for the temple doors.

She hit the doors with the brunt of her shoulder and barged through, dragging the Summoner in with her. Right afterward, Blythe and Leslie came crashing through.

Thea dropped Rafe's arm in favor of hoisting up and readying her sickle. It glowed once again in her grasp, though faintly, but it gave off enough light to see in the dimly lit area. There was no one but them in the temple. It was completely empty.

The inside was large, open, with a mysterious breeze that drifted in from somewhere. The inside of the temple was multilevel with the higher level wrapping around all four walls with four, short sets of stairs leading down to a small pit. Lush, green fern plants in clay pots decorated the walls and sat on either side of the stairs. A large, round, and shallow mantle sat in the middle of the pit with a small fire flickering inside. The ceiling's border was decorated in pale blue and red square paintings carved into the stone. Pillars were used to support the tray ceiling's outer perimeter.

The only thing that interrupted the flow of the design was on the opposite side of the temple. On a stone altar designed to replicate the many pillars in the room was a stone tablet floating in the air. Thea squinted in the dim light, but she couldn't detect any sort of magic holding the artifact up. It was just...floating. Without magic. Above it, carved into the ceiling and disrupting the artful border was a plain slab with a single, circular swirl. She'd never seen a symbol like that in any textbook before.

She looked down at Leslie and nudged the imp with her knee. "I thought you said there would be someone in here."

Leslie, jostled from admiring the temple's interior, turned to slap away Thea's offensive prodding. "Yeah, yeah, I don' know what ta tell ya, toots. Din' seem like," a weird, guttural sound escaped him, "would lie about somethin' like that."

Thea stared down at the imp. Blythe and Rafe were also looking at Leslie with equally surprised expressions. "Like what?" she asked after a beat of silence.

Leslie, unperturbed by their strange looks, began picking at the gunk in his ears and inspecting what was found in there. "Ya know," and made the same noise again. "Our new buddy out there."

"Is that..." Blythe trailed off, brow quirking in confusion, "Is that the sand wyvern's name?"

Leslie flicked the questionable substance off one of his claws. "Yeah, what else would it be?"

"I don't know. I thought he kind of looked like a Harrold." Rafe piped up with a flat look.

Thea sent an amused look Rafe's way before turning back to the altar. "So all we have to do is grab the tablet and get out of here, right?"

Leslie shrugged. "Tha's what he said."

"Mm, just like he said there would be someone here," she said with a sneer, stepping down onto the steps.

The temple was eerily quiet aside from the soft crackling of the fire and the heels of her shoes on the stone. The hairs on the back of her neck rose, and when she stepped down into the lower leveled pit, the fire went out completely and the air snapped to an icy chill.

Thea was plunged into darkness, and her weapon was raised in an instant, but nothing jumped out at her. A burst of wind whirled past her, and it felt as if fingers had danced across her shoulders as it swept by. Another burst of air came from in front of her, silent, soundless, and grazing her body in searing cold before disappearing. She spun around and around, trying to catch a glimpse of something, but she was blind without any light.

Giggles filled the temple, and the hairs on her arms now rose to attention as well. A flash out of the corner of her eye had her spinning around, weapon ready, but it was only Rafe crowding close to her with his own weapon glowing in the dark. Blythe and Leslie were right there with him, fear easy to read on even the small demon's face. Rafe closed his eyes briefly, and the light of his weapon blazed. The darkness ebbed away, but seeing, Thea came to realize, was so much worse.

Surrounding them, on all sides, were a thousand ghosts.

Chapter Twenty-Two

Time: A Forgotten Concept

Thea gasped sharply and backed up further into Rafe. She dropped her sickle, and her hands flew to her dust pouches. Weapons were useless against ghosts—or whatever these things were—but magic was not. At least, most magic.

"We have visitors," hundreds of voices whispered, carrying the words in a ripple through the mass of bodies. The glow of Rafe's staff cast dramatic shadows over the beings, bringing more depth to their transparent figures.

"Yes, it has been too long," hundreds more whispered back.

Thea paused, fingers hesitating on the buckles of her pouches. They didn't seem malevolent, and they weren't attacking her. They hadn't exactly attacked her earlier either, just spooked the goddess's faith right out of her.

"What are they here for?"

"What are you here for?"

The hushed voices overlapped as the mass of bodies undulated closer. Thea pushed herself back further, wishing she could disappear right into Rafe. She'd rather go up against another hellhound or soul eater or, hellfire, Asmo at this point. Ghosts creeped her *out*. Intangible and impervious to weapons, and even some magic was useless on them.

"We-We're just here to get the tablet," she stuttered out, though in hindsight that might not have been the best thing to say.

Hey, I'm here to steal something from your temple. Hope you don't mind! Goddess above, you're so stupid, Thea!

"They are here to get the tablet."

"We will be set free."

"We can go home."

"Home, home, home, home."

The voices became a hushed roar, the bodies moving about as their excitement grew. A cold brush of fingers skittered up her arm, and Thea flinched as one of the beings floated around from behind them. Suspended in its airy grasp was the stone tablet. The being stopped just in front of her and let the tablet float over to the Spellweaver.

"You must right the wrongs," it said in its quiet voice.

"Right the wrongs, right the wrongs," the others echoed.

Thea stood frozen before slowly straightening up. She wavered only another moment before holding out her hands for the tablet. "What wrongs do we have to right?" she asked carefully.

"She does not know."

"We must tell her."

"Tell her."

Thea felt Leslie huddle behind one of her legs and, for once, she envied the imp. Being the size of a child would be really handy right now. She would happily hide behind the "big, strong man" at her back and let him take the lead, her pride the last thing on her mind.

"We are air elementals," the one who handed her the tablet said over the voices, though the words carried as softly as wind blowing over a valley.

Air elementals? She racked her brain for a moment before locking eyes with the being's ghostly, transparent, soulless gaze. "You're sylphs?"

The sylph nodded. *"All elementals were tasked with guarding the four tablets after the Great Divide. We are air."* It pointed at the ground, and Thea looked down. An invisible hand etched the same circular swirl into the floor. *"We guard the western temple, salamanders guard the northern temple,"* a circle with a dot in the center was drawn next to the first symbol, *"undines guard the eastern temple,"* connected together were three, swirling circles, *"and gnomes guard the southern temple."* The being appeared upset as it drew a square box. *"The gnomes were the first elementals ordered by the Light Elf King to guard one of the tablets, but he summoned malign gnomes by mistake, and the jungle has suffered ever since."* The box was harshly filled in.

Thea's head was swimming with so much information absorbed all at once. Great Divide? Light Elf King?

Rafe moved at her back, his arms brushing up against hers, and Thea had to bite back a wince as pain tingled hotly along her skin. When she looked over her shoulder, a less wary expression was gracing his features. "Did you say the Light Elf King?"

Incomprehensible murmurs threaded through the mass of ghostly bodies. Thea couldn't clearly make out what they were saying, but unease gripped her as the air in the temple surged with tension.

The sylph's ghostly face twisted in anger. *"The elves do not refer to him as such, but yes. They treat him like a god, yet he is nothing in comparison to the true High Elves. He has kept us here for hundreds of years while he hides away in his utopia."*

Blythe was visibly upset, coming forward with pity in her dark irises. "You have been trapped here for centuries?"

"Yes," a thousand bodies whispered all at once.

Chills raced up Thea's spine, and she swallowed around the lump in her throat.

"We tried to reach out," echoed some of the voices.

"After so many years trapped here," murmured the rest.

"May the light be with you—"

"Be brave, daughter of Saellah."

"The power—"

"—is in you."

"Defeat the darkness— "

"Defeat the darkness!"

"—push back the evil!"

The voices were getting louder and louder, cresting as the energy in the cave became crushing.

Then, silence.

The air elemental in front of her sighed out softly, *"We do not know if we were ever heard. We do not even know if our pleas have yet to be reached or if they were heard too soon, too long ago."*

Thea's brow quirked in confusion. "Well...we hear you now."

"We'll set you free somehow," Rafe promised from her side.

"We will remain here until you do."

Thea wanted to turn and leave now, but she had one question nagging at her, and she was going to get an answer regardless of her fear. "You said...You said that the gnomes were in the southern temple? In the jungle?"

The sylph before her nodded. *"They destroyed the temple, and the tablet's magic has affected the jungle and its inhabitants beyond repair."*

Rafe stiffened behind her, and she could hear his grip tightening around his staff. "What do you mean?" he asked softly.

The elemental gestured around the temple, and wisps of air trailed off its cloudy fingers. *"The tablet holds great power. All the magic that users cast is collected throughout the year and held within. Because the tablets have not been used in over two hundred years…"* the spirit trailed off.

Thea's eyes widened as she looked down at the tablet in her hands. "You're saying that two hundred years' worth of magic is collected in this thing?"

The sylph nodded. *"And as such, time in the temples is warped. That is why when the southern temple was destroyed by the malicious gnomes, the magic from the tablet leaked out into the jungle."*

Thea was left speechless. She'd spent what felt like hours in the jungle, and a whole week had passed. It had all been because of gnomes, who were usually gentle and shy creatures. When benign. Malign gnomes were as bad as low-level feral demons.

She heard Rafe curse behind her, bringing her out of her thoughts.

Double-dip a candlestick! There was no telling how much time had passed since they entered the temple!

"We have to leave!" Blythe frantically cried out beside them.

"Wait," every sylph pleaded, and the voices echoed throughout the temple.

Blythe looked ready to flee the building at any moment. Her eyes were wide, panic swirling in the dark irises, but she stopped and waited for the beings to continue.

"You need all four tablets to right the wrongdoings," the air spirit continued. *"All four tablets together form the tool that you must use to complete The Wild Hunt spell every year."*

"But we *do* complete The Wild Hunt spell every year," Thea rushed to say.

The one sylph gave the Spellweaver a forlorn look. *"Then you have been doing it wrong, and I pray for the world if all four tablets are not found soon."*

Chapter Twenty-Three

Flying on the Wings of Freedom and Arriving at the Gates of Hell

The doors to the temple slammed open, and Thea and Rafe were the first to exit, weapons raised and at the ready. The scorpion men were standing by the entrance doors waiting, and they attacked as soon as they saw the Coven members. Rafe lunged back to miss a strike from their spears, and Thea was there to block the attack with her sickle. She fought back a pained growl and kicked out, sending her boot into the gut of one of the humanoid creatures. The other made to grab her, daggers aiming for her blind spot. A blast of energy careened into the beast's jaw, sending him flying back into the sand with a chittering scream.

"Go!" Thea shouted behind her, and Blythe and Leslie raced out of the temple and toward the still waiting wyvern. Dusk was upon them now. They had spent nearly a whole day in the temple when it had only felt like minutes. The moon was barely visible in the sky, but its red hue was as obvious as it was ominous.

Thea blocked another of the scorpion man's attacks, jumping out of the way just before Rafe slammed his staff into the being's chest. Blood sprayed out from the wound, and the creature howled in pain, rendered immobile for the barest of seconds. That was all it took for Thea to slam down the blunt end of her sickle into the back of its head, knocking it unconscious.

They spared each other a quick glance before they were running for the Draconian. The beast had half buried itself in the sand but was now shaking itself off.

Blythe was panicking by the imp's side, knees in the sand and on his level with her hands clasped together as she implored Leslie to hurry up and get the wyvern's blood. "Did you tell him we got the tablet? Did you?"

Leslie had his eyes closed with a look of concentration that appeared to be breaking under the sorceress's frantic inquiries.

Rafe, with his longer legs, was the first one to make it up the sand dune, but Thea was right behind him in seconds. Immediately, she asked, "Is he going to give us his blood?" They had held up their end of the bargain, after all. The tablet had been safely secured in Blythe's bag since it was obvious Thea and Rafe were going to be having their hands full fending off the scorpion men.

Leslie growled and whirled on all of them. "Do yous guys know how rude it is ta keep intarupting me when I'm tryin' ta have a convasation? Yeah, he said we can get 'is blood. Get tha vile out, Yippy," he directed at Blythe. "Now if yous guys don' mind, I'm tryin' ta get us a ride home so's we ain't gotta walk. Is that all right wit' you?"

"Who knew so much sass could be contained in such a little body," Rafe murmured into Thea's ear, and the Spellweaver had to suppress a huff. This was no time for jokes, and she reminded the man in as much as she could by swatting him away. Rafe ducked back with a smirk, but his smirk fell when he noticed how angry-looking Thea's wound had become. He went to brush his fingers against it, but Thea grabbed his hand and laced their fingers together.

"I'm fine," she assured. "Another quick healing spell and it'll be gone. It doesn't even hurt that bad."

Rafe didn't look convinced. "Let me try and heal you again."

"Worry about it later," Thea huffed with a small smile. She'd had worse. A little scratch was nothing.

"Okay, but as soon as we get back to HQ, go see Dr. Snow."

Thea scoffed. "For something like this? I'm not running up a bill."

"Then suffer the humiliation as I heal you in front of everyone," Rafe said with a wicked grin.

Thea's face flamed. "Yeah, right. Like I'd let people catch you babying me in the middle of the Coven. I have a reputation, you know."

"Better make sure it gets healed up right then." Rafe chuckled and laid his arm around her shoulders, pulling her close.

Thea huffed again. "Fine."

Blythe had not caught their quiet exchange, too busy digging around in her bag for the two vials she brought along. She finally pulled the glass containers free and handed them to Leslie when he reached his weathered hand out.

Thea's brow rose. "You brought two?"

Blythe glanced up with a small smile. One is for Cressida, but I knew your doctors would like to be able to study the DNA structure and possibly replicate it."

"Always thinking ahead," Rafe commended.

Thea peered over his arm still draped over her shoulder and cursed when she saw one of the scorpion men twitching with the beginning stages of consciousness. "Don't mean to be a killjoy, but we need to hurry this up, guys," she said in warning.

A large shadow blocked out what little light remained in the day, and Thea looked up to find the sand wyvern's large, clawed hand raised high in the air. Its connecting wing spread out in a fan of thin flesh. It lowered its arm to just above the vial Leslie held out, and its claws curled inward, and, just like Madame Odine had witnessed, blood began to drip down from its scaly palm.

What little drops of blood did not fill the container sizzled as they touched the ground before turning into tiny hills of sand. The vial filled up quickly, dribbling over some when Leslie capped the lid, but that blood too turned to sand and drifted away in the breeze. The next vial filled up just as quickly.

Thea heard the scorpion men groan behind her.

"Okay, time to go," Rafe said instantly, and grabbed Thea around the waist and hoisted her up onto the beast's arm before she had time to complain. She climbed with haste, keeping her indignant comments to herself all the while, and turned back to give Blythe a hand when she made it onto the Draconian's spine. Rafe had grabbed Leslie next, picking the imp up with one arm despite the heavy protests coming from the small demon, and carted him along as he climbed up the wyvern.

Leslie was tossed the rest of the way up when Rafe was a few feet away, and the imp gave a girlish squeal at being airborne. He landed at an awkward angle and righted himself with a glare. "What's a matta wit ya, huh?" he snapped when he regained his dignity (what little he had to begin with) and settled in front of Blythe, out of Rafe's reach.

"Let's get a move on," was Rafe's response as he got situated behind Thea. She could hear the imp grumble some snippy comeback and snickered.

A moment of silence was all they were allotted before the sand wyvern shot off toward Tolvade. The beast slithered back and forth like a snake at a breakneck pace while its forearms and wings pushed aside the sand, and Thea was struck by the incredible way the creature had adapted to life amongst the endless dunes.

The wind whipping them in the face caught some of the sand the wyvern had kicked up, sending the debris flying onto the group huddled on its back. Thea hacked at the dust sucked into her lungs, but when she pulled back her hand, she froze.

Droplets of blood, small and sticky red, now rested in her palm. Under the cover of the falling sun, she was able to wipe away the evidence without Rafe seeing. If she was coughing up blood, then a simple healing spell wouldn't help her. It went far deeper than that. She glanced at her wound, and, even in the dim light, she could tell it was getting worse. She looked up and found the moon, now deep crimson in color and glowing like a beacon of Hell. It was already bleeding into the night and tainting the darkening sky, snuffing out the appearance of the first stars in its wake.

She could only hope they made it through Herbon without trouble and got to HQ. If Dr. Snow couldn't heal her… well, they had some of the best medicine in the world with them. She'd be fine.

She had to be.

The sun was long gone now, and the sand had soaked up the red tint from the moon. Their eyes had long adjusted to the night, but the moon's glow was so bright in its intensity that it had hardly been done with effort. They could clearly see the dark mass of trees just up ahead, marking the end of the desert. They were going to have to fight their way through Banshee Bog, and if they didn't die fending off the bog's most terrifying and lethal nocturnal inhabitants, they'd be walking through the worst of Aeristria's districts weary, exhausted, and sapped of their magic. During the Blood Moon Festival, no less.

They hadn't made it in time. It was too dangerous. They would have to camp out the rest of the night on the Golden Sea's border, and if Blythe put up a fight… Thea would have to tell her the truth. She knew Blythe. Being so close to Cressida and carrying what she believed would fix all the woman's ailments, there was no doubt she'd go charging off into Banshee Bog by herself if she had to. Thea couldn't let her do that, even if it meant telling her Cressida was going to die. Regardless if she received the wyvern blood.

Thea would also have to come clean about her injury as well and administer a drop of blood to the wound. She didn't want to waste such precious medicine on herself over what should have been just a simple scratch, but they couldn't make it to Dr. Snow quick enough.

She was going to have to deal with Rafe's frantic concern and, what was maybe worse than that, his disappointment that she hadn't confided in him. She was going to have to deal with Blythe…and how the woman reacted, she honestly couldn't say. Would she be angry and lash out? Would she break down and cry? Would she become a lifeless doll, intent to give up on life altogether?

Thea took a long, deep breath and released a shuddering sigh. Despite how close she'd like to believe they became during their time in the desert, Blythe would most likely never speak to her again. And she would be...okay with that. She was used to not having friends in her life. She had Rafe and Mokana. She had Namara. She had her job to keep her busy.

So why did her heart feel so heavy?

The sand wyvern began to slow, lifting its half-sunken body out of the sand, and Thea took another deep breath to prepare herself for the descent and the fight that would inevitably ensue. But she didn't get the chance. Right as the beast fully emerged from the sand, it began to run on all four of its monstrous legs.

"What's it doing?" Thea shrieked over the sudden burst of speed, wind picking back up and slicing through their clothes once more.

Leslie shouted back and pointed up to the sky, "We're goin' up! Betta hang on!"

"We're going wh—!" The wind cut off Thea's scream as the wyvern sprung up off the ground and took flight. The beast's arms spread, and the wings underneath caught the breeze and fanned out. Rafe's arms wrapped around her waist, and she gripped them hard, knew her fingers were biting into the skin, but she couldn't make her hands let go. Her heart was slamming into her chest even as the rest of her was frozen stiff. She'd never been in the air before. Was this what flying was like for those with wings? She could see everything for miles. She could see the city of Herbon, dark even under the moon's brilliance, HQ in the far distance, and all the tops of the Banshee Bog's trees. Only the trees were getting closer, and closer, and closer.

"Why are we going down?" Thea yelled, voice muffled by the wind.

"He can't really fly too good. His wings ain't built fa air travel!" Leslie called back over his shoulder. "He says he can get us over Banshee Bog no problem, but thas the end of the line!"

Thea went to say something else, but another coughing fit took hold of her. She could feel how raw her throat was becoming, could feel the blood collect in her hand, and she wiped it off on her pants without looking. She didn't want to know how dire her situation was right now, but more so she didn't want to give Rafe the opportunity to peek over her shoulder and accidentally see.

The sand wyvern's feet began to scrape along the tops of the trees, but they were close enough now to the high stone wall that separated the bog from Borlimane. It landed with surprising grace along the barrier. All four of its gigantic, clawed feet were perched atop it like a cat trying to balance on a fence post. The only sound that was made was when parts of the wall crumbled under the strain, but other than that it was mostly a quiet landing. The beast's neck lowered until its head rested on the empty cobblestone street, signaling it was time to get off.

As soon as they had climbed down the wyvern's neck, the beast turned and slipped into Banshee Bog's forest. Its long, serpentine body curved and bent around the vegetation as if it were made of fabric rather than flesh and bone, and it towered over the trees until, at last, it was out of sight. Three of the four of them were left standing in awe, but Thea was panicking internally (and also probably bleeding, but she elected to ignore that thought). Though they managed to skip over the deadly, man-eating-tree- and banshee-infested swamp, they were standing in the middle of a soon-to-be warzone.

As if sensing her panic, Blythe spoke up. "I know of a smaller sanctuary around here. It is more of a halfway house for hurt creatures. They have a secret passageway underground, and it can lead to all the other sanctuaries in Aeristria."

Rafe placed a hand on Thea's shoulder. "I know where you're talking about. I passed it once in my early Summoner days while patrolling Herbon, back before I got promoted to Dark Market raiding."

"Excellent," Blythe sighed in relief. "I knew its general location, but I was not sure exactly where it was. We can be sanctioned there and take the underground passage to Srbeveara. You may stay the night there if you wish and rest up."

Goal in mind, Thea's heart began to slow its erratic pacing. She could tell them she'd need medical attention when they got to the sanctuary. For right now, she just wanted to get out of the streets before the Blood Moon Festival kicked off.

"Welp." Leslie cleared his throat, gaining everyone's attention. "This is where I leave yous guys."

Thea eyed the imp incredulously. "You're leaving?"

He only scoffed at her remark and shoved his stubby hands in his pockets. "Course I am. I live not too far off from 'ere, as ya well know. Plus, I got plenty of hideouts 'round this joint if I need 'em."

Rafe crossed his arms over his chest and stared the imp down. "Are you sure you'll be all right?"

Blythe also looked hesitant to let Leslie walk away. "You could come with us."

"Look, guys, I been gettin' on jus' fine in my line'a work. You Coven membas are tha only ones able ta get ya grubby hands on me. Everyone else," Leslie shrugged with a deviant smirk, "I slip through their fingas like wata." He turned and began walking away, raising a hand into the air and waving a final goodbye. The shadows of Herbon swallowed him up in no time.

Thea tugged on Rafe's shirt. "He'll be fine. He's too resilient to get caught and too much of a pain in our rear ends to die out here. We, however, need to get going *now*."

"Right." Without another word, the Summoner led them down the street, and they, too, soon blended into the night.

But not before the chanting started.

Chapter Twenty-Four

Chains Break Before Bonds

The three of them stopped where they stood, time seemingly halting as their horrified surprise rendered them immobile, and the short, sharp, bizarre chorus of the blood mages resonating throughout the streets chilled them to their core. Rafe grabbed Thea by the wrist and started hauling her down the back alleys, Blythe hot on their heels. The chanting grew louder, faded when they rounded a street corner, but it was growing in volume with each passing second. The blood mages were taking to the streets, filling the town with their hollowed chants, the notes taken straight out of a demon's lullaby. They would encircle all of Herbon before long, moving down certain alleys until they created an ancient and archaic symbol that could only be witnessed in its entirety from the heavens.

The strike of a sudden drum met the tempo of Thea's racing heart, and she could see just up ahead a blood-red glow from the candles carried in each of the blood mages' hands. Rafe cursed under his breath and skidded to a stop, backpedaling and shoving both Thea and Blythe into the closest alley. The glow of the blood mages illuminated the streets, setting the shadows to fire, tainting the air with their song.

"They're closing in on us," Thea whispered between frantic breaths. She pried her wrist out from Rafe's hold and started digging in her pouches. Her magic had had some time to replenish itself, and even though she was nowhere near complete health, they had no other option. The same spell she applied to her sickle back in the desert was reapplied.

She wasn't going to be stuck relying on a weapon with hardly any juice left in it. She uttered the spell, though the words were hard for her ears to even pick up as the chanting got louder.

Her sickle glowed the same disturbing red as the candles edging closer and closer to them. When she looked up, she could feel the blood drain from her face. Their small alley was completely surrounded by the candles' flaring flames. The chanting was so loud now she could hardly hear herself think. Distant screaming was cut short, followed by mad cackles catching on a breeze and rising into the air like embers of a bonfire.

Rafe pushed her back into the wall as if that would protect her from hundreds of blood mages. He would be ripped to shreds in seconds, and Thea would rather die than let that happen. "We're surrounded," he said, and his voice held so much fear it didn't even sound like him anymore.

Thea pushed him off of her and turned around to face the wall. "We can't fight our way through them. I'm going to make a door, and we can hide in whatever shop or hovel this is." Her fingers were trembling as she pulled out what little gold dust she had left. This was a highly classified spell, it would take the rest of her magic to pull off, and if not given some of the wyvern blood right after, she could possibly die. But she was definitely going to die if they just stood there and did nothing.

Rafe pulled her away from the wall and spun her around. "There's no time for that!"

"Do you have a better idea!" she hissed and yanked her arm back. The action pulled something in her chest, and she was brought down to her knees by the cough that suddenly took over her. Blood filled her mouth and splattered all over the stone floor. There was no point in hiding her condition now. Rafe was crouching by her side before she could pull herself to her feet, but it would have been useless. Another coughing fit took hold of her, and more blood painted the ground.

Breathing ragged, she let Rafe steady her. She couldn't look at him, couldn't handle the fear she knew she'd see there, not for their impending demise, but for hers. She felt the warmth of his fingers laced with hers and took a moment to remember the feeling. It might be her last opportunity.

"I'm going to distract them. They'll follow me, and I need you to get her out of here."

Thea's head snapped up in disbelief. She did not just hear what she thought she just heard.

"I cannot do that," Blythe was crying, tears straining her voice.

Thea's hands flew to Rafe's shirt and pulled him close. "And I won't let you," she growled.

Rafe barely budged under her actions. His lips were thinned in a stern line, his eyes flickering in the approaching red glow. "There is no other choice, Thea."

"No! I can't lose you," she whispered fiercely, and she saw it, there in the depths of his endless blue-green gaze, the cages starting to form. The cages she saw in flat brown glamoured eyes in the Dark Market. The cages that would always linger after coming back from a raid.

He placed his palms over her hands fisting in his shirt, threatening to rip the material apart in her desperation. "I've gone up against them before," he said, but faltered, looked over his shoulder as the group of blood mages descended closer around them. The hesitation was there, and she pounced on it mercilessly.

"Not alone. You would never survive battling them alone."

He looked down at her, eyes hard, icing over like glaciers. "I can do this—"

"You can't!"

"I'm stronger!" he finally yelled. Warm hands grabbed her face and yanked her close. Eye to eye, she saw everything. Everything. The fear. The uncertainty. He knew he wasn't going to survive this. "I'm stronger. I'm stronger than you. I always have been because I've always had a reason to be. You're my reason, Thea. Now, get that tablet and that blood to the Coven."

Tears were blurring her vision, and she shook her head as much as she could in his iron grip. "I won't leave you! I can't lose you! You're all—" she hiccupped, coughed on the lump forming in her throat, and she could feel blood dripping down her chin, but she didn't care. Years of memories crashed her into her like a speeding ox cart. Every side glance they had shared, every battle, every drink at Tasgall's, every laugh, every line in the sand that became more and more blurred as time passed, every hope, every single night that kept her awake and every morning waking up to the smell of coffee coming from the kitchen they now shared, every image of the future together, every dream she dared to dream, slammed into her again and again. "You're all I have, Rafe! I can't lose you! I won't lose you!" she roared, shoving at him with every word. "If you go out there, then I'm going out there by your side! If you die, then I die with you because I refuse to live life without you!"

Rafe's fingers bit into the sides of her face. "Thea, listen to me—"

"No!" she sobbed, her own fingers gripping his shirt even harder. "I won't let you go out there alone." She coughed again, gasped, eyes searching his as she whispered, "I won't lose the man I love."

The cages snapped into place.

"Thea," he whispered, bringing his lips closer to her ear. "I have always loved you, and I always will...but you don't have a choice." He leaned back, hands suddenly glowing white. "*Confine.*"

Thea felt her body lock into place. Rafe crashed into her and sealed his lips against her own. She tasted everything: regret, longing, terror. She tasted goodbye.

Then he was gone.

"Blythe, you have to unbind me!" Thea pleaded though she couldn't even move her head in the woman's direction. She could already hear the angry shrieks of the blood mages, the beginnings of chaos ensuing around them. Blythe dropped down in front of her, and Thea could see how torn she was. Her hands hesitated in the air, expression lost. Thea didn't care about the emotions she'd rip out of the woman as the words poured out of her mouth. "Think of Cressida! If she was out there fighting these mages by herself and you could do something, would you just sit back and let her fend for herself?"

She could see the words slice through the sorceress, and fresh tears began to drip down the woman's flushed cheeks. A blast of energy careened into the building beside them, and they both flinched. She screwed her eyes shut, took a deep breath, and finally nodded.

Thea licked her dry lips and tasted the awful tang of copper. "Grab the white dust out of my pouch and grab my face like Rafe did. He used a simple binding spell we use on criminals who resist. To undo it you have to grab whatever part of the body was grabbed when confined."

Blythe's placed her shaking fingers, dusted in white powder, around Thea's face.

"Good. Now, say *'Release.'*"

"Release."

Thea felt her body go lax, and she immediately stood to her feet and dragged Blythe close to her so she could look the sorceress in the eyes. "Take the tablet and the blood to the Coven. Don't look back. Run as fast as you can. The Coven will protect you, and they'll come save us." She turned, ready to jump into the fray but stopped, spun back around, and found Blythe's dark, watery eyes. She slammed the sorceress in for a hug, arms gripping the woman in a harsh embrace. This could be the last time she ever saw her, and their friendship had been brief, but Thea had been thankful for it all the same. "Thank you, and I'm sorry," she said, and the words, so simple, held so much. Thank you for everything. I'm sorry for everything.

She let go, turned to face the battleground the center of Herbon had become, and jumped into the fray. The spells she had cast over herself had never dissipated, and now they burned along her skin as she felt her speed increase, her strength grow, and the weapons in her grasp lighten as if made of air.

Rounding a destroyed stone house, she ran into a blood mage and sank her sickle into the woman's neck before she had time to scream. Her mind was clear. Her soul had grown cold. All her power came flooding to the surface. The rune on her weapon glowed bright.

She found him. In the center of it all, dodging the blood arcane magic slung at him. His staff was held high in the air, blasting orbs of stinging light at everything surrounding him. He brought the weapon down and sliced a mage in two. His eyes were the color of ice, his magic wrapping around him in a tangible blanket of fire and azure.

She ran to his side, and the rest was a blur. She dodged a blast that took out buildings seconds after where she had been standing. Herbon was infested with mages, skittering about like a sea of cockroaches. They were swarming the air on whizzing broomsticks and channeling the strength of the blood moon to warp the liquid running through their protruding veins. She pointed her arrow launcher up in the air and began shooting. She couldn't afford to aim for legs or arms. No. This was not a mission. This was not the time to save those corrupted by the dark arts. This was not the time to show mercy.

This was the time to kill.

She shot an arrow into the head of another mage, ducked just as a blast of dark red magic blazed through the air, and whirled around to send her sickle into the neck of a mage who had come up behind her. She ripped her sickle out of the torn flesh and stomped the being out of her way, arrow launcher immediately going up to shoot another one down.

She turned, stormed through a small group that had surrounded her and jumped, twisted in the air, and shot multiple arrows into their backs.

She landed with a roll, used the momentum to sweep a mage off their feet and put an arrow through their skull. Blood had splattered her entire body, and she felt the dulled pain of the wound on her arm coupled with the scrapes along her body that were now bleeding. Scrapes that could now be used against her.

She brought her sickle up and deflected a shot of arcane magic before raising her other arm and shooting down the mage riding the chilled breeze. She grabbed her amulet and let the purple magic dome slam down around her and then dove a bloodied hand into her pouch and threw the dust over herself. Her entire body glowed teal as the healing spell took effect. Angry red scars formed over the open wounds.

She then grabbed three more dusts and tossed them over herself and sharply inhaled the dust wafting around her. The amplifying powder sliced its way down her throat and felt like hundreds of knives were stabbing her lungs. She grabbed the dagger at her side and carved a shallow X at the base of her throat. The spell was highly illegal because the repercussions were so deadly.

Her throat was on fire, but she rasped the words that brought life to the spell. "Cast myself before my foe; death awaits my soul; pardon my sins 'fore I go."

The bubble of the amulet spell popped, but she would be fine without it. The healing spell would keep going, repairing any damage that she succumbed immediately. It would drain her of all her magic as she used it continuously, but she was prepared for that. If she was to die from this battle, then all these blood mages would go down with her.

One launched themselves at her just as two blasted her with more arcane magic. She shot the first dead center in the chest, grabbed the body as it landed lifelessly on her, and used it as a shield as the two bolts blasted and charred through the layers of clothes worn right down to the flesh. She dumped it at her feet and threw the sickle out from her grasp, chain wrapped around her arm. She swung, and the blade ripped through the other two, coming back to her with a flick of her wrist. She brought up her arrow launcher and shot down two more mages that were crowding Rafe.

Rafe.

He was bleeding from the side of his face, and his arms had grown stiff. Several blood mages were screaming in glee, chanting as they waved their arms up in fluid motions.

Rage consumed her, bringing her cold body to an incontrollable heat as emotion warred with instincts. She screamed and flung out her sickle once more. The blade connected with the first mage, blasting right through the body and into the next.

Claws descended around her neck, scratching at her flesh, and she cried out in anguish and lost control of her sickle. Her arms snapped to the side as if pulled back by strings. She whirled around, still somewhat able to use her legs, and her boot shot out to connect with the ribcage of the mage manipulating her. Her arms became hers once again, the wound now healed crudely, but before she could dispose of the mage that had attacked her, pain sliced down her back. She screamed and fell to her knees.

Without thinking, she rolled to her side and jumped up, yanking the sickle's chain and whipping it around her to drive the blade into the throat of another mage. Rafe's pained roar ripped through the night, one she echoed as agony sliced through her once again. She couldn't go to him. Couldn't look. Her arms were being forced back by blood magic. She had one last chance, and it would push her strength past its limits.

She grabbed the bone handle of her sickle so tightly she was sure lacerations were forming on her palm. She yanked away from the spell that had gripped her body as soon as the injury healed, spun on the balls of her feet, and cut down the blood mage behind her. All around her were more and more occultists, circling her from all angles. She dodged a blast of an arcane spell, deflected a shot of magic, and cried out when something stabbed through her leg.

She growled, dodged another blast of a spell, and let the words of an incantation flow from her mouth. "Forfeit my life to the cause; bleed for me with the last of my rage; possess my soul and fall beneath my blade!"

Her body began to glow a crimson red, just like her sickle, just like the moon above them. She let the sickle in her hand drop to the ground and wrapped the chain around her upper arm. She slung the blade out into the crowd and twisted, screamed as the bite from the chain gripped her bicep, and spun. Screeches erupted into the air, but they were like music to her ears. She yanked the sickle through the crowd, turning with the momentum of the blade and throwing her body weight into keeping it moving. She roared, throwing everything she had into the swing of the weapon, and one after another, the mages that encircled her went down.

The glow around her body dissipated all too soon, and like starving wolves after their next meal, the blood mages pounced. She didn't have the power to fight them off anymore. Her arms were ripped behind her body by unseen fingers, and she dropped to her knees as the last bit of strength left her. She wasn't given a reprieve, though. Her body was forced back up into a standing position, and the arm with the arrow launcher was dragged in front of her. It bent, and the weapon was placed under her chin. She closed her eyes. She was to die here. So be it. Rafe might still be alive. Help had to be on the way. After everything that the mages had blown up while trying to kill them, it was probably the biggest racket the town had ever suffered. The Coven would have to come for them. Blythe had to have reached them already.

"Let her go!"

Thea's eyes snapped open. Rafe was walking toward her, struggling the entire way with eyes wild and near silver in their intensity. He suddenly dropped to his knees, and Thea's arm unbent itself.

No. No, no, no, no, no, no.

She fought herself, her mouth opening on a scream as she thrashed in her invisible shackles. Her arm visibly shook from the effort, but now every blood mage had surrounded them and were pulling the strings, arms moving in weird, fluid motions that forced her to aim her weapon at Rafe.

Rafe's eyes were wide as they settled on the arrow launcher set to shoot him right between his eyes.

"No!" she shrieked, her whole body convulsing as she tried desperately to pull the weapon up, away, to the side, anywhere that wasn't pointed at Rafe. Not Rafe. She yanked and yanked and yanked while tears poured down her face. "No!"

"Thea," Rafe said, voice strangely calm. Resigned. She looked at him through watery eyes, his image blurred, but she could see the small smile he had for her. For her only. "It's okay."

"It's not!" she wailed, throwing back her head and bellowing her frustration at the sky. "Don't make me do it! Don't!"

"Thea," Rafe tried again. She looked back, watched him lick his lips, eyes never leaving hers. "Say it again. Let me hear it one more time."

He didn't have to clarify.

"I love you," she cried. "I love you, I love you, I—" She felt her finger tighten on the trigger.

"STOP!" A voice exploded from the darkness, and Thea's eyes snapped to the side in time to see Blythe holding the tablet above her head, the stone glowing bright enough to engulf the sorceress in radiant light and rival the luminosity of the moon itself. Power that could have rivaled the Celestial's shot out from the stone tablet, slamming into the Blood Moon Festival like a tidal wave of vengeance.

It hit Thea right as her finger pulled the trigger.

Chapter Twenty-Five

Are There Ever Only Two Choices?

Blythe raced as fast as her legs could carry her through the confusing cobblestone streets of Herbon. Her sandals had been kicked off along the way, allowing her to race down alleys and side streets without hindrance. She only ducked behind a dilapidated building when she heard the pounding footwork of mass people approaching. She peered from around the crumbling stone structure with a hand cupped over her mouth to keep her gasping breaths from reaching the blood mages' ears. She watched as more and more cloaked figures flooded the street, destination clear as they moved toward the center of the borough. When they were out of sight, she took off in the direction of the capital. More specifically, Coven HQ.

You have the cure. You could be saving Cressida right now.

Her heart throbbed, and tears threatened to blur her vision. "I will! But first I have to save my friends!"

An image of Cressida smiling danced through her mind, drew its arms around her heart, and squeezed. It whispered memories in her ear of Cressida's bright, infectious smile, a time when her eyes were alight with affection. Blythe felt the familiar pang of longing unfurl in her chest. She saw Cressida laughing, carefree and without the presence of ghosts in her vision, without the weight of exhaustion tugging at her shoulders, dragging at her eyelids, holding back her movements. Image after image of her smiling, laughing, crying, flinging something across the room in shock as Blythe snuck up behind her, smirking as she wrapped her arms around her, all of them hammering into her like the final nails in a coffin.

She was so *close*.

She was brought to an abrupt halt when she reached the edge of town. Wiping at the tears that clouded her sight, she took deep breaths to calm herself down. Left would take her the shortest route to the sanctuary but going right would take her to HQ.

They're Coven members. They've been trained to deal with this alone.

Blythe took one step in the left direction but faltered.

They are your friends.

A whine tore itself from her throat, and she pivoted, about to start running toward the Coven.

Cressida is dying.

She stopped moving altogether. She didn't know what to do, and it was tearing her apart. She pulled the bag off her shoulders and opened it, revealing the vials of wyvern blood within. This was the key to her oath bound's recovery. She had found it. She had truly found it.

She remembered Thea coughing up blood all over the alley floor. She remembered Rafe plunging into the fray to buy them some time, how Thea pleaded with her to let her fight by her lover's side.

An anguished cry rose above the pandemonium, echoed by a similar howl of pain. Blythe whipped her head toward the source of the noise, then glanced back down at the bag in her grasp. Next to the vials of blood was the tablet...with over two hundred years' worth of pent up magic. Without a second thought, she tossed the bag back over her shoulders and took off back the way she came. The Coven was too far away still, and Cressida…

Cressida could be gone by the time you save them.

Blythe clenched her jaw and picked up her pace.

Cressida is stronger than that.

Blythe lowered the tablet and stared, dark eyes impossibly wide, at the now still battleground before her. Her feet ghosted over the ash around her, desperately clinging to her soles like shadows as she skirted past faces frozen on howls, stiff arms locked in place, flesh charred and smoking and filling the air with a fragrance so sharp, so pungent it could only be described as death. Her eyes wandered over the bodies laid in heaps at her feet, their limbs positioned unnaturally, their identities unrecognizable. They were no better off than the crumbling buildings that horseshoed around the clearing, awashed in crimson so deep Blythe couldn't see what was blood and what was puddles of standing water. The moon was unrelenting, pouring its light onto those who had worshiped it. It remained unaffected even after their passing.

Her gaze landed on equally still bodies, seemingly untouched by the tablet's powers. She rushed over to Thea first, dropping the shoulder bag down by the woman's side and inspecting the angry-looking claw marks nearly pulsing along her shoulder. Fresh blood was dripping down her chin and the side of her face, and her breathing was slow and heavily labored. The noise that left her chest with each breath was a quiet rattle.

Her clothing was torn in many places, but the skin under did not reveal any fresh scars or bruising. Beside her, her sickle lay splattered with red, dribbling liquid. On her other side, her arrow launcher was busted in two places. The rune that kept it powered was shattered.

Blythe blindly grasped for one of the vials of blood and uncapped the lid. She pulled Thea closer and propped her head up in her lap. For a moment, it was Cressida in her lap. For a moment, she was hunching over disheveled ginger hair on the floor of the basement chamber, listening to the echoing laughter of a demon. She shook the thoughts away, yet they remained in the recess of her mind, taunting her with prickles of fear, apprehension. Her brows furrowed, pushed the images back further, cupped Thea's jaw, and pried her mouth open and hovered the vial of blood in the air.

Steady. *Steady*.

One drop fell, then two. She pulled back and recapped the vial.

The change was instant. The glaring claw marks along her shoulder vanished, her color returned to a healthy complexion, and she gasped a large breath of air as if she'd been holding her head underwater for too long. Her eyes still refused to open.

"Thea? Thea?" she tried, shaking the Coven member gently. The woman continued to breathe in slow, reassuring breaths, but she wasn't gaining consciousness.

A hard groan alerted her of someone *else* gaining consciousness. She peered over the rubble and collapsed bodies to find Rafe struggling to sit up. She pulled Thea off of her lap and grabbed her bags, rushing over to his side before plopping down. Her fingers were adept, agile, glancing over his torso, arms, face even.

"How are you feeling?" she was quick to ask, fingers inspecting a cut on his cheekbone and then the deep gash on the side of his head. She pulled the cork off the second bottle but stopped when Rafe raised a hand to ward her off.

"Don't," he sighed and washed a hand down his face. "I was using a healing sp—" His eyes widened, and he was struggling to his knees before he could finish, scanning the area until he landed his sights on Thea. She'd been blown further back in the blast, and now he scrambled to his feet and staggered over to her. Blythe grasped him by the upper arm just before he pitched forward and held onto him until he dropped down beside Thea and gathered her in his arms. The images lashed out from the back of her mind as she watched on.

Cressida in the dungeon. Her glazed eyes. Soft smile. Her confusion. Asmo's laugh ringing like a thousand bourdon bells.

She took a quiet breath at the sharp sensation punching through her chest. "She will be all right now," she managed to say. "I have already administered a few drops of the wyvern blood. She is in better shape than you are right now. She just needs rest."

Rafe didn't respond, but she knew he heard her from the way his shoulders relaxed. He had Thea pulled up into his lap with his arms wrapped tightly around her. His eyes were shut tightly, forehead resting against hers. It looked as if at any moment he could break, so Blythe stood and quietly placed the bag with the tablet and the vial of blood within beside him.

"I have to go now," she whispered.

Rafe nodded and pulled away from the Spellweaver in his arms. He stood as well and hoisted the woman up and over his shoulder, staggering when his legs refused to steady themselves. Blythe's hands went to hold up his weight, but he managed on his own. He looked up and found her worried gaze. His voice was gruff, words weighted by exhaustion as he said, "I'll go slow. Don't worry about us. Just go."

Blythe hesitated, but she couldn't deny the tugging on her soul any longer. She grabbed the second bottle of wyvern blood and turned, but before she could take off running, she was stopped by Rafe.

His hand rested on her shoulder. Warmth seeped through the cloth, pouring over her in a wave of reassurance more than any she'd felt before. She met his soft blue eyes. "Thank you," he said before letting his hand drop. The hot prickle of tears in her eyes forced her to nod and look away before he could see them fall.

Then she was running.

Chapter Twenty-Six

Come Cure, Come Peace

She hadn't stopped to grab her shoes. The chipped, cobblestone roads were unforgiving under her flying feet, and they were not any less forgiving when she cut through the main market. The air was so cold still, yet it burned in her lungs. She couldn't feel any of it. Numb to everything but the thoughts in her head, she pushed herself faster until roads were not paved with rock but woven from the breaks in trees.

The doors to Srbeveara had never felt so light under her fingertips, and into the walls they slammed. She was home. Because this was where her heart rested, upstairs, where her feet carried her past a worried Ma, up the planks that squeaked their greetings, and down a hall narrow enough to offer sheltered comfort. The warmth of the sanctuary brought feeling back to her toes, but a chill had entered her chest at seeing the shell her lover had become. For a moment, she could only stand there and catch what little breath her body would allow into her lungs.

"Cressida," she called softly, but the words barely left her throat. The woman on the bed stirred, but beautiful, gem-like irises did not open. A stunning smile did not stretch lips thin. A graceful body did not rise, and strong arms did not wrap themselves around her and envelop her in the soft scent of honey soap and black tea.

For how could they, when none of those things existed anymore?

Time slowed with each step she took toward the bed, even as she berated herself to hurry, hurry, *hurry*. Her hand rose, and with it fingers that shook and trembled, to card through locks of hair. Gently, so, so gently before sliding down to cup a once strong jaw. Her thumb traced the cracks in Cressida's lips, felt every ridge and bump, as fingers fell into the hollows of her cheeks. Her mouth fell open with ease, no strength left to keep it shut, and Blythe's other hand, having held the bottle of wyvern blood the entire time, uncorked the vial. The soft *pop!* echoed around their bedroom. She hovered it over Cressida's lips only a second before she tipped it and let the liquid within freefall. Somewhere, in the back of her mind, she heard a voice to save most of it for the creatures at the sanctuary. It sounded like Cressida.

If it had been her own voice, she wouldn't have listened, but she pulled back. More than half remained.

She waited with her breath held captive in her lungs, refusing to move, to blink, to breathe until something happened. It felt as if forever was suspended in the span of a moment, and when it was over Blythe felt the tears start to fall.

Cressida breathed in a soft exhale, and another, and another, and they were no longer burdened by wheezes or whines. With each breath she took, her skin's grayish hue receded until it nearly glowed. Another breath and the dark marks under her closed eyes faded completely. Another breath and her cheeks filled, as did her arms, as did her stomach.

Another breath and she opened her eyes.

"*Cressi*," Blythe sobbed, fat tears rolling down flushed cheeks and nearly blinding her. She wiped at her face furiously, but her sobs would not relent. Tender, warm hands cupped her face, and she desperately grasped at those hands, but it wasn't enough. She collected her weakening strength and dove onto the bed. Strong arms caught her, and a soft voice shushed her cries.

A blurred vision of the most important person in her life looked up at her, and through her tears, Blythe could see a faint smile. "I thought," she choked out, but the lump in her throat strangled her voice. Nails scraped softly at her scalp, and she tried again. "I thought you were going to die. Asmo said the cure would not fix you, but you are better. You're not going to die." Her tears fell, dropping onto Cressida's cheeks and mingling with her own.

"The cure fixed me," Cressida said softly, and Blythe felt the weight of the three worlds lift from her shoulders, and fresh tears gathered in her eyes. "But I'm still going to die."

Blythe wiped her eyes and sat up straight. Her gaze found Cressida's. A lone tear was trailing down her pale cheek, but otherwise, she appeared content. At peace.

Blythe's voice was hoarse. "W-What?"

Cressida pulled the sorceress down until they were a hair's breadth away. It was only then Blythe saw the slight tremor on her lips. "I love you. I wish I could have given you everything that you deserve. I don't have much longer, so...I will leave you with this." She pulled Blythe forward so their foreheads touched, and it was like electricity shot through Blythe. She screamed, but her voice did not reach her own ears. She saw everything. Everything.

A great fire. Black smoke clotting a darkening sky until the embers outmatched the stars. Thousands of books with millions of words, millions of spells, stored under a ceiling of watery nebulas. A woman with ginger hair and lifeless eyes holding out a hand gripped by a screaming child. A man of unknown origin smiling. A moon holding up the sky as howls of mourning reached the heavens. A beautiful woman with dark skin and bright eyes and a full heart and a door shutting in her face. One that would open to let her in, eventually accompanied by a smile. A hug. A kiss. With words of affection. With actions of something deeper.

Blythe saw herself through the eyes of the one she loved, and tears poured down her face and cries tore from her throat as the hand at the back of her head gradually lost its strength.

"No, no, no, vuch, vuch, vuch," she was yelling, reaching up to grab at Cressida's falling arm. "I cured you! I cured you!"

"Yes," Cressida breathed. "And I am forever grateful. I will always love you, Blythe. I love you…"

Her eyes slipped closed.

She's too far gone. It will kill her!

Blythe grabbed Cressida's face in her hands and shook the woman. "No! No, he was lying! Asmo was lying! He was lying!"

I would not lie about this.

"Yes, you would! You would! You want her for yourself!"

Of course! If you think that makes what I said any less true—

Blythe shook her head violently and pulled away from Cressida's limp body. A shaking hand shoved away shiny, ginger tresses as her confessions fell from trembling lips. "I love you, do you hear me? Do you—" her voice broke. "Do you hear me? You cannot die! You cannot die! I love you, so..." she sobbed and buried her face in Cressida's shoulder. "So, stay with me. Please, Cressida, please, *om keresela.*"

But Cressida didn't answer her. Blythe reared back and grabbed her by her shoulders and shook her again, screaming, "Wake up! Wake up, wake up, wake up!"

I just...I just wanted to tell you that I…I love you, and it's okay if you don't say it back right away.

A wail ripped out from her chest and tears blinded her vision.

You are so beautiful, you know that, right?

"Don't go. You cannot go yet, Cressi."

Blythe, what are you wearing? I love it. No, don't you dare go change.

"Cressi! Wake up!"

Can I braid your hair? Why not? I can braid!

"Please."

Can we go see your village one day? You keep talking about the stars.

"We...We were supposed to go see the stars." She gripped Cressida's chemise, tears streaming down her face and falling to land on her hands. "You were supposed to live with me here forever!"

I don't have any family. You're my family. The sanctuary is my family.

"How am I supposed to be a family without you!"

Srbeveara? What does it mean? 'Where one's heart heals'?

"Please, wake up."

You know I will do anything for you, right?

"Wake up. *Cressida.*"

I love you.

Everything's fine.

I'm okay.

I didn't want you to find out!

Do you not love me? If you love me, let me do this!

I just want to live! I just want to live life with you!

I love you. I wish I could have given you everything you deserve.

"Wake up!" Blythe sobbed. "You can still give me everything I deserve if you just—" she was losing her voice, "if you just *wake up!*" She grabbed Cressida and pulled her up, wrapping her arms under the ex-sorceress's and hugging her close. Cressida's arms dangled by her side.

Pounding feet thundered and fists beat down on her door. Shrill voices full of panic shot through the symphony of sobs.

"My room isn't working!"

"Help! Why are the rooms vanishing?"

"Cresssssssida! Help ussssss!"

Blythe looked down at the woman in her arms. Dark ginger lashes fell across full cheeks where tracks of saltwater were already drying. A look of peace had settled over her features, and Blythe's heart broke into a thousand pieces.

I don't know who I'll entrust the sanctuary to. Blythe, don't look at me like that. I know you wish you had magic. We'll find someone. I won't ever leave these beings without a safe place.

Her voice thick with tears, she cried out, "How? How do I fix this?" Her body shook with tremors, and she shuffled down to rest her head on Cressida's breast. "What am I supposed to do? What do I do?"

Her eyes screwed shut, and she shoved the world away. She stopped listening to the wails. She stopped hearing the banging of inhuman hands, the rattling of wood under a straining frame.

She listened for a heartbeat that was not there, but she would find it. Ear pressed to an empty chest, she cleared her mind. It was there. It had to be there.

She pushed the images of life lived with Cressida and swam through murky waters of darkness until the edge of the world fell away, and she was suddenly suspended in gray fog.

"Cressida!" she called, whirling around in circles, but she wasn't in the sanctuary anymore. She was wading through thick, opaque air, mist curling around her feet and fingertips. Her voice echoed all around her until the fog swallowed it.

Where was she?

"Cressida!" she tried again, turning about. She felt her heart kickstart in her chest, and she squealed when her feet sank into the ground. She looked down and gaped at the gray sand covering her toes. It was cool to the touch.

She glanced around her, but the world had become nothing more than fog. She took a step forward, but she was only met with more of the bleak haze. She spun around, stopping with a hitched breath as vivid green eyes gazed back at her. She took a step back, only to pause when those eyes blinked. Eyes that were so...familiar.

"Cressida?" she whispered and gasped when a *keresela* as large as a horse emerged from the fog. Those familiar green eyes bore into her, and she felt something click in her soul. Her knees gave out, and she fell into the sand. Soft fur brushed up against her forehead.

You cannot be here in the spirit world, soremerg grofin.

Fresh tears beaded reddened eyes, and Blythe brought her hands up to cup whiskered jaws. "Come back with me then. You are my familiar. There is no other room in my soul for anyone else."

I will always be with you, but I cannot live among you in this form. Please, do not ask that of me.

"What does it matter!" she cried. "I cannot love another, and I will not love anyone after you!" Emerald eyes blinked at her, so human despite the face framing them. Every emotion flickered through them all at once.

We do not have much time left before you are trapped here forever. When you get back, imbue your life essence into the sanctuary's amplifiers. Without it, Srbeveara will stop working.

Blythe was shaking her head, fingers digging into fur as if that was all it would take to keep her in that one spot forever. "Let me just stay here with you."

I cannot do that, either. I love you. Remember the amplifiers.

The giant cat spirit vanished from under her fingertips, and Blythe cried out in anguish. She jumped to her feet and whirled around, but Cressida had disappeared among the clouds.

Suddenly, the world cleared around her, the sky bloomed in midnight blues, spackled by thousands of stars, and the crossed swords of lovers long past speared the heavens.

So, this is what they look like.

She looked back and saw Cressida's human form standing before her, transparent like a ghost. It reached out, cupped her face softly, and, just as Blythe thought it would close in for a kiss, it shoved her backward.

I will forever love you. Goodbye.

Blythe jolted and fell back on the bed. Her heart was racing, but there was no air in her lungs. The world came back to her quickly; the smell of rose incense wafted about in the air, the soft light of scattered halite crystals and candles glowed in the room, the distressed noises from the hall were reaching catastrophic levels of chaos.

And Cressida was cold to the touch.

The cries from out in the hall had faded into nothing more than background noise, so it was jarring when the sounds abruptly stopped.

Blythe sniffed. Her nose was stuffed, her head felt like it weighed a ton, and her eyes were swollen and vision bleary. She sucked in an uneven breath against the pain that throbbed in her chest and stumbled off the bed. Her legs were numb and caused her to trip over her own feet as she slowly made her way to the door. Her fingers trembled upon gripping the handle, and when she pulled the door open, nothing but empty space greeted her.

Empty except for Ma.

The imp held out her arms, a look only a mother could give open on her gnarled face. "I already took care of it," she said. "Now c'mere, baby."

Blythe felt her strength leave her, and she fell to her knees and into Ma's embrace. Her arms weren't strong. She didn't smell like honey soap and black tea. She wouldn't give her a stunning smile when she pulled back. She wouldn't look at her with vivid green eyes. She wouldn't say 'I love you.'

She wasn't Cressida.

Remember the amplifiers.

The voice she loved most tore through her heart all over again, but its message wasn't lost in the warring emotions within her. Blythe took a deep breath and sat back. She wiped her eyes and straightened her shoulders.

Cressida may be gone, but this sanctuary was still their home.

She took another deep breath, looked Ma in the eyes, and said, "Show me the amplifiers."

The End. For now.

www.ingramcontent.com/pod-product-compliance
Lightning Source LLC
Chambersburg PA
CBHW030355310726
48979CB00001B/319
9781955222969